Judgement Day

The Intern Diaries Series- Book 5

D. C. Gomez

GOMEZ EXPEDITIONS

Cover design by Christine Gerardi Designs

Edited by Cassandra Fear

Proofread by Michelle Hoffman

ISBN: 978-1-7333160-4-0 for Paperback Editions

ISBN: 979-8-9857369-2-2 for Hardcover Editions

Published by Gomez Expeditions

Request to publish work from this book should be sent to: author@dcgomez-author.com

For every reader who believed in a dream,
This book is for you.
Thank you for making the Intern Diaries a Reality!

Chapter One

"Isis, RUN!" Like I really needed Shorty to be yelling the obvious at me.

"What do you think I'm doing here?" I shouted in between ragged breaths.

"That pig is going to spear you to death," Shorty continued with his less than helpful commentary.

"Pig? That thing is a miniature bear." I leaped over a fallen tree stump while the wild boar rammed right through it.

Being chased by ghouls, zombies, vampires, and even demons was a normal part of my everyday job as Death's Intern in North America. A wild boar trying to kill me was a new one. That miniature demolishing truck had a one-track mind. Right now, those three-hundred pounds of solid muscle were fixed on turning little, old me into an Isis kabob.

"Isis, climb a tree!" Bob shouted more useless instructions.

"I'm carrying thirty pounds of gear. I'm not climbing anything." I took a quick left turn around a tree hoping to lose the wild freight train, but he followed right behind me. "One of you, please shoot this infernal beast."

"We don't carry elephant guns with us," Shorty yelled, and thoughts of choking him crossed my mind.

"Run back this way!" Bob shouted. "I have an idea."

I grabbed the closest tree limb, using it to help me spin around. Bob and Shorty stood in the bed of Shorty's new truck, a Ford F-150. If vehicles exploded in my vicinity, Shorty had a way of destroying transmissions at a faster pace. My legs burned from all the quick sprints in the middle of these woods, but I pushed harder. Bob and Shorty had rifles pointed at me. God, please make sure Shorty is wearing his contacts today.

"Isis, drop!" Bob did not have to tell me twice.

I slid down as Bob and Shorty opened fire on the deranged swine. Unfortunately, our new friend was not going down without a fight and kept on charging at me. Shorty unloaded another round, finally knocking the beast out. Too bad he fell on top of me, squeezing the life out of me.

"Help." I squirmed left and right, but the boar had me pinned.

"Honestly, how many tranquilizer darts does it take to knock down a boar?" Shorty asked as he made his way towards me.

"How many did you fire?" Bob wiped the sweat off his sandy blond hair.

From my angle flat on the ground, Bob looked like a giant. He was a little taller than six feet, but next to Shorty, who was only five feet four, the height difference was overwhelming.

"At least fifteen," Shorty replied.

"Plus my seven. Then roughly about twenty-two," Bob confirmed.

"I'm glad that has been clarified," I mumbled from underneath the beast. "But can you two please get this thing off me? It's drooling all over me."

I had no idea how I always managed to get covered in disgusting fluids during every mission. This was supposed to be a simple job: find a tree nymph and to talk to her.

Granted, we did break into the Army Depot using fake government IDs courtesy of Katrina.

Katrina was War's Intern and had access to every military facility, technology, and ID in the world. Minus the small breaking and entering, this was supposed to be easy. Instead, I was being pinned down by a wild boar in the middle of the woods.

"Boss Lady, you are going to have to jimmy out because we won't be able to pull this monster off you," Shorty announced, trying to pick up the boar by himself.

"Shorty, this thing weighs more than you," I told him as I focused on slowing my breaths so I didn't think about the comatose pig on me. "Your hundred and twenty pounds is not moving our little friend here."

"Give me a hand, Shorty," said Bob, squeezing a log underneath one side of the boar. "On the count of three, pull Isis out. Ready?"

Shorty marched around the pig and grabbed both of my hands. Bob angled the log over a rock while Shorty and I waited for the signal.

"One, two, three." Bob pushed as hard as he could, which gave me just a few inches to wiggle out of the beast with the help of Shorty.

"Got her," Shorty exclaimed as Bob dropped the boar back down.

"Thank you so much," I told the guys as I took a deep breath, the air filling my lungs like a refreshing cup of lemonade on a hot day. "I think I'm safer with the supernatural community than with nature."

"That is saying a lot considering we spend the majority of our time breaking up domestic disputes." Shorty pulled me to my feet as he spoke, and at five feet nine inches, I looked like an Amazon woman next to him.

Bob brushed the back of my shirt and clumps of dirt fell off. I ran my hands through my hair, picking out twigs and leaves. My normal silky black hair was matted with mud and all sorts of debris.

"Where is she?" Bob scanned the woods that were suddenly a little too quiet.

"Natalie," I said, moving slowly away from the boar. "Please come out, we are from Reapers."

We glanced around the woods waiting patiently. When dealing with supernatural beings, patience was essential.

"Maybe she left," said Shorty, stepping over the pig.

"She couldn't. That's the whole reason we are here," Bob explained, eyeing the treetops.

"I'm here," a soft, child-like voice answered.

We looked around the clearing but couldn't see anyone. Bob wandered over to the right and I went left. Shorty climbed on the bed of the truck to search.

"Where are you?" I asked, walking in circles.

"Here." The voice came from a tall oak tree in front of me.

Shadows extended from the oak, taking shape in front of me. I jumped back a few feet as the shadows formed into a girl. She was the same material as the oak, but her face was soft with green eyes the color of the leaves.

"Wow." Shorty whistled from the truck.

"A true dryad. Impressive." Bob was our resident expert on supernatural creatures and knew all their official names.

Bob was a man of many talents, and probably the only one that read every book Constantine gave him. Constantine was the guardian of all the Death's Intern, a five-thousand-year-old talking cat. He was also an evil dictator who was still mad at me for losing my Intern manual and never actually reading it.

"Hi," I told the shaking, little nymph. "I'm Isis, and this is Bob and Shorty."

"I know," she replied, her eyes not on us.

"We have been shouting for the last twenty minutes, so I'm sure the dead know our names by now," Shorty added from the truck.

"Thanks, Shorty." He really was full of wisdom today. "We got your message and here we are."

Being one of Death's Interns came with many responsibilities. One of the major ones that nobody explained was, if I ever decided to settle down in one location for more than six months that location would become a haven for every supernatural being in my continent. At first, it didn't sound too bad. Not until I was informed that I was responsible for the welfare of those residents. So, when a shifter stopped by our doors at Reapers two days ago carrying a message from a mysterious girl in the depot's woods needing assistance, it didn't seem all that strange.

The shifter worked at the depot. What he never explained was the reason he was out in these woods doing installations on a Sunday. The industrial facilities where the civilians work were located at least twenty minutes away, closer to the Interstate Thirty.

"Trees are being cut down and the animals are going wild." Natalie glanced around with big, green tears rolling down her cheeks.

"I think some of this area is marked for harvesting." We had passed several areas with trees chopped down on our way here. "I'm not sure how we can help."

"Make them stop." Natalie sobbed uncontrollably.

"What?" Shorty looked around the area. "How?"

"Natalie, sweetie." I moved slowly towards the dryad. "This is outside our jurisdiction. We have no control here."

"We are going to die." Natalie's tears changed from green to brown.

I held her shoulders, and it was like holding a tree trunk. There was nothing soft about her.

"We? Who else is here with you?" I asked her in a gentle voice.

"My whole family." Natalie turned to face the trees behind her and six other nymphs appeared

"Okay." That was impressive, but too bad my vocabulary failed me at that moment.

Natalie's relatives were all over six feet tall and were technically called nymphs. True dryads were spirits from Oak trees. Two of them looked like young trees while three were almost ancient. A young female was the only one that resembled Natalie.

"Why are you here?" Bob asked Natalie, keeping an eye on her family.

"We were transplanted here," Natalie answered, keeping her gaze locked on us.

"Can you leave?" As exciting as it was being back at an Army post, we were in the middle of the woods. Did it really make a difference what woods they were staying in?

"We can only go so far." Natalie kicked a few rocks with her feet.

"We can help," Bob jumped in. "If we transport you somewhere else, would you be willing to move?"

Natalie peered back at her family, and they all glanced at each other before one of the ancient trees nodded to us.

"Great." Bob smiled widely.

"Natalie, excuse us for one minute." I dragged Bob towards the truck. "Exactly how are we moving tree spirits out of these woods, and where are we taking them?"

"Bringle Lake Park," Bob answered a little too quickly for me. "It's a growing area and nobody is going to be harvesting those trees anytime soon."

"You know that Lake has crocodiles," Shorty added from the truck.

I crossed my arms and angled my chin towards my chest as I waited to hear Bob's solution for that little problem.

"One, maybe two," Bob offered. "Besides, it's better than wild boars."

"Let's say the lake is a feasible location, how are we transplanting them there?" I looked over my shoulder at the seven nymphs.

"Same way you would move a tree. In a container." Bob gave us a movie-star smile.

"Are you making this up?" I had no way of confirming his theory.

"It's easy. We got this," Bob announced.

"Fine. What are we going to use to move them?" Easy was not a word I would use in this situation.

"I got buckets," said Shorty.

"Do you normally carry buckets in your truck?" This time, I turned my glare on Shorty.

"You never know when you'll have to move trees around." Shorty imitated Bob's million-dollar grin. I threw my hands in the air and stepped away from their madness.

"Natalie, we think we have a plan," I announced to the little dryad.

"Here you go, Boss Lady." Shorty handed me seven five-gallon buckets, all white.

"But we might need your help," I told Natalie, my eyes falling to the buckets before landing on her family again. "I have no idea how we can get you moved in these."

"That's simple. We can magically shrink the trees we are bonded to and then we are joined with them for the move," Natalie told us, and her family all nodded in confirmation. "But we must hurry. We only have a few hours after we do. If we are not rooted quickly in our new location, we will perish as the trees expand in the small containers."

"'Easy,'" I repeated.

There was never anything easy in my job. I rubbed my temples to make sure this insane plan had a happy ending.

"Shorty, get some men over to Bringle Lake and have them find us a location to plant seven nymphs," I ordered. "Just make sure they don't hurt any of the current trees there. We need the hole dug out by the time we arrive."

"Yes, Boss Lady." Shorty pulled out his phone and made the call.

I had no experience running a city, but at least I wasn't alone. Shorty was the leader of the Underground, which was originally made up of transient and street people. Now they were informants, employees, and the backbone of Reapers. Under the training of Bob, the Underground was a force to be reckoned with. If anyone could pull off strange missions in a short period of time, they could.

"Shorty, please tell me you carry shovels in the truck as well?" I really didn't want to dig these poor trees up by hand.

"Underneath the back seat," Shorty replied.

Bob rushed to the passenger side of the truck and grabbed the shovels.

"Natalie, we have never done this before, so you will need to walk us through it," I said.

"We can do that," Natalie complied. "First thing, prep all the buckets with enough dirt before we move the trees. Then we can start the transplant."

Goosebumps ran down my back. The idea of transplanting actual living beings was a bit terrifying. I looked over at Bob, who was rolling his sleeves up in preparation. At least one of us was excited.

"Boss Lady, holes will be ready in forty-five minutes," Shorty announced.

"Perfect. It will probably take us that long to get over there from here," I told Shorty, taking off my jacket. "Grab a bucket Shorty, we need to hurry."

Natalie was an incredible teacher and transplanting was not nearly as scary as I imagined. It took us roughly thirty minutes to get all the nymphs back inside their trees, and in small enough sizes to fit in the buckets. Once all the saplings were secure, we had to arrange them neatly in the bed of the truck to make the trip to town. I was covered in dirt from head-to-toe. We were ready to head out, trying to find a way to maneuver around our friendly swine monster who was still passed out.

"Freeze," a man shouted.

"Not good," whispered Shorty.

"Thank you, Captain Obvious," I told him.

Shorty, Bob, and I turned around slowly to face a young military police officer holding a gun in front of us. He looked too young to be an officer, but I had soldiers in my unit younger than him. Age was not a qualifier for talent. The officer looked competent, and his hands were steady.

"Hi, officer," I said with my hands in the air.

"I need back up," the officer said over a radio. "I have trespassers and they are armed."

"We can explain," I said softly, not making any sudden moves.

"Isis, we need to go." Natalie picked the worst time to appear out of her tree.

"HOLY. JESUS. CHRIST!" screamed the poor officer.

"Sorry, dude." Bob shot the poor kid and he dropped like a sack of potatoes.

It was a blessing the only bullets we used were tranquilizers or we would have a lot of injuries in this town.

"Should we go?" Shorty asked still holding his hands up.

"Can you handle a high-speed chase through an Army installation carrying seven tree spirits?" I asked Shorty, pointing at our precious cargo.

Shorty drove like a bat out of hell on a regular basis. A high-speed chase would not be a problem for him. Keeping the poor nymphs in the back would be almost impossible, though.

"I wouldn't recommend it; you won't make it out of here alive." Two officers sauntered from the same direction as the now-fallen officer. "Lieutenant, please take the newbie back to the car."

"Not a problem, Captain," the Lieutenant replied, picking up the officer with ease.

"Captain?" Bob asked.

"Yes, I'm the Captain for the police officers here, and you are?" The Captain rested his hand on his gun, letting us know he was ready to use it. I was sure his bullets would kill us.

"We are from Reapers," I replied.

"It's about time." The Captain strolled over to us and extended his hand. "Captain Johnson in Texarkana told me about you. I figured you would be stopping by a lot sooner."

"You are outside of our jurisdiction," I answered.

Four months ago, in the middle of our Spring Equinox fiasco, we made a partnership with the Texarkana police chief. Relations have improved, and we have been providing covert training to many of his officers.

"That hasn't stopped the madness from reaching us here," the Captain stated. "The name is Welch."

"Isis, Bob, and Shorty," I told the Captain. "You are the second Welch I met."

"I'm sure he wasn't nearly as charming." The Captain had a contagious smile.

"That's a tough one," I replied.

"Boss Lady, we got to go," Shorty reminded me.

"Yes, unfortunately we are short on time," I said, pointing at the back of the truck. "We have clients to transport."

"Is that going to stop the wailing and crying in the woods?" Captain Welch looked over at the small saplings.

"Maybe," I answered, not wanting to give him false hope.

"In that case, you'd better hurry, but I do expect a visit." Captain Welch grabbed his radio. "I need the South Gate opened. I have a white F-150 that needs access ASAP."

"Ten-four Captain," a female replied.

"When you reach the main fence, turn left. The South Gate will be less than thirty feet from there," Captain Welch told us.

"Good call, Cap," Shorty said running to the driver side.

"We can stop by Monday if that works for you?" I asked him.

"That would be perfect. I don't need to be completely traumatized heading into the holidays," the Captain informed us.

"You will be traumatized, but at least you will enjoy the Fourth of July," Bob told him and headed towards the truck.

"Thank you again, and sorry about your officer." I had forgotten to apologize for the young man.

"How long is he going to be out?" Captain Welch asked.

"At least eight to ten hours since he's such a small fellow." Those bullets were meant to take out full-grown shifters, not small humans.

"Great. This is going to be hard to explain." Captain Welch picked up the radio the officer had dropped and left the clearing.

I ran to the truck and jumped in the bed with the saplings. I was not planning to lose any of them after all the trouble we went through to get them.

"Shorty, hurry, but try not to kill me back here!" I shouted from the back.

Hurrying and not killing someone were two things Shorty was not able to pull off at the same time. I made myself comfortable in the bed and placed the saplings as close to me as possible. Maximum concentration was needed for this part of our mission.

Chapter Two

Bringle Lake Park was on the North side of Pleasant Grove near the new campus for Texas A&M University. It was a beautiful location with a lot of visibility and new walking trails were being created all the time. Constantine had coordinated with Trish, our resident gnome, to secure a suitable spot for the new residents of Haven. It appeared having a relationship with the police chief was paying off for us. The Triplets—three men named John that Shorty had renamed—had managed to get the cops to block the area for our transplant.

With the help of the Triplets and Trish, the planting took less than ten minutes. Moving the nymphs to their new homes was a lot easier than getting them out of the depot. We waited patiently, which translated to me pacing back and forth, to see if the transplant had worked.

"It takes some time for the roots to take hold of the new terrain," Trish reassured me.

"What if we did it wrong?" I asked, my voice soft.

"You would know," Trish answered. "The trees themselves would wail for the death of the nymphs. The spirits are powerful, and the woods feel their essence."

"Wailing trees is something I would like to avoid." I glanced around the area with a new appreciation.

It took twenty minutes for the first sapling to move. Once it started, it took the tree less than three minutes to bloom to their original height. The rest of them quickly followed. While they were barren in the woods of the depot, they were covered in leaves here.

"Look, one is a magnolia tree." Trish ran over to the tree.

White magnolia flowers covered the beautiful tree. Trish made circles around them. Watching Trish with her ten-inch body covered in flowers and limbs while she danced around the larger tree was mesmerizing.

"Thank you, Isis," Natalie's sweet voice broke my spell.

"I'm glad we could assist," I told her. "Trish, do you mind helping them get situated here?"

"Yessss," squealed our little gnome.

"Natalie, this is Trish, Haven's head botanist," I told Natalie. "If you need anything, Trish knows how to get ahold of us."

Trish beamed with joy as Natalie sat on the ground next to her.

"Bye, Trish," I said, heading back to the truck.

"Bye, Isis." Trish waved before resuming her conversation with Natalie.

"Not a bad day in paradise," I told the boys.

"Not bad at all," replied Bob. "Are you heading back to the station with us?"

"No. Do you guys mind dropping me off at Reapers?" I looked at my watch. "It's almost two and I really want to be in Salem before eight today. I'm supposed to have dinner with Godmother."

"In that case, you'd better hurry," Bob said, eyeing me up and down.

"Why do I always end up dirty at the end of every job?" I asked him, rubbing more filth from my hair.

"You take your job very seriously," he answered, jumping in the truck.

"Thanks." I hopped in the back seat and buckled up.

Reapers was in the Nash Industrial Park, less than fifteen minutes from Bringle Lake. But anything could happen in fifteen minutes, especially with Shorty behind the wheel. The last thing I needed was to crash through the windshield out of carelessness.

Shorty dropped me off at the pedestrian door of Reapers. While Union Station in downtown Texarkana served as the headquarters for the Underground—as well as our court and jail—Reapers was the Interns' headquarters. It was an incredible facility that housed a shooting range that doubled as a lab, a gym, a garage for our multiple vehicles, and our living quarters. Originally, Reapers only had the Loft on the second floor for living quarters. Later, Constantine added Bob's apartments on the first floor across from the shooting range and next to the pedestrian's entrance. As we became friends with the other horsemen's Interns, a second loft on top of Bob's apartments was added. We had plenty of space for a small company of troops now.

After the careful inspection by the security system, which I found out is easily triggered by unidentified people, I made it in. I ran past the cars, Death's yellowish Mustang —the Deathmobile—Constantine's yellow Camaro— formerly known as Bumblebee—and my midnight-blue Mini Cooper—Ladybug. We didn't splurge much, but cars were our thing. Bartholomew had a dirt bike, something totally illegal for a thirteen-year-old. Unfortunately for the cops, he was now five feet ten inches, and a genius. If anyone could make a fake ID, it was him. Bartholomew was also Death's ward and my pseudo brother.

"Constantine, do you mind if I take the jet?" I asked as I entered the Loft.

Constantine was lounging at the far end of the Loft in the computer area. The front of the Loft was divided into sections primarily by the furniture. On the far side, we had the command station, Bartholomew's computer area, and enough monitors to spy on the world. Facing the monitors was the most comfortable couch ever made, followed by the dining area and the kitchen.

"Where are you going again?" Constantine asked, pressing buttons on the keyboard.

"To Salem for the fourth of July," I answered as I advanced to the fridge.

"Don't you find it weird that the headquarters for the Order of the Witches is located in the same place that burned their comrades to death?" Constantine asked, not turning towards me.

"Do you want me to ask Godmother about it tonight?" Constantine and my Godmother had a love/hate relationship. They both loved to hate each other.

"You should. It has been bothering me for years," replied the goofy cat. "What does the high priestess of the land have planned for you?"

That was something I was still not used to. My Godmother had been my guardian since the death of my parents when I was a child. I had no idea until a mission last year that she was a witch, and even more, she was the head priestess. That image was hard to grasp.

"Hopefully nothing involving dancing or rituals," I replied.

After the equinox, I would pass on the Order's rituals. All I wanted was a quiet holiday for once. With nothing extravagant or out of this world taking place.

"Isis, are you coming to the meeting?" Eric asked busting through the door.

"Hi, Eric, how are you? How have you been?" I replied as sarcastically as possible.

"Don't bother. He is in work mode," Constantine chimed.

"Sorry about that," Eric said, and his cheeks changed to a slightly pink color.

That was a surprise because Eric never blushed. He was a complicated being, a witch who worked for the humans as a cop. He took his job extremely seriously and now was serving as the liaison between his chief and us. Eric was also Reapers' martial-arts trainer. If his sessions were not murderous, spending time with him would not be so bad. He was pure eye-candy, over six feet tall, muscular with soft, brown hair, and just drop-dead gorgeous. Too bad his taste in women only ranged in the 'hot blondes' category and I had long, black hair.

"Now, from the beginning and slowly, what are you talking about?" I grabbed a bowl of grapes from the fridge and popped one in my mouth.

"Our community meeting is tonight, and the chief wants to know if you will be attending." Eric leaned against the counter.

"That's tonight?" I pulled out my phone to check my calendar.

"Last Tuesday of every month," Eric replied.

"Sorry, Eric." I closed my eyes tight. "I'm heading to Salem today."

"You are actually taking another vacation?" Eric asked, glancing at Constantine when he asked.

"Why are you so surprised?" I crossed my arms over my chest.

"You have tendencies to wait until you are ready to kill people before taking a break," Eric told me. "I'm impressed."

"That is not a compliment," I replied.

"Don't worry, I will get Bob to come," Eric told me, giving me the million-dollar smile he rarely used. "Have fun and I will see you next week."

Eric left the Loft before I could reply. I turned back to Constantine, who was busy with the teleconferencing remote control.

"Is it me or is Eric in a much better mood?" I asked.

"He is dating again," Constantine replied.

"That explains it." I walked over to see what Constantine was doing. "Do you need help?"

"No, I'm supposed to be setting up the bridge for my monthly conference call with the Interns," Constantine answered me.

"Do you know how to do that?" I glanced at the lists of numbers in Bartholomew's handwriting that Constantine was following.

"Unfortunately, yes. I do this all the time," Constantine pressed buttons. "I usually have the numbers memorized, but Bartholomew changed the dial-up for security reasons."

"How come I'm not included in these calls?" I was the only Intern that never attended the conference calls.

"I see you every day, Isis." Constantine stopped to look at me. "It makes no sense to take time to yell at you during calls when I can do it anytime."

"You are one evil dictator," I told Constantine.

"You should not be surprised," he replied. "Go shower. You stink."

His overly-developed sense of smell never failed to pick up all my horrible scents.

"I'm blaming the wild boar that tried to eat me today." I marched back to the kitchen area and grabbed my grapes.

"Something is always trying to eat you or kill you," Constantine added. "I'll have George get the jet ready to fly at three. You'd better hurry."

"Thank you, Constantine." I saluted my guardian and headed towards the back of the Loft where the bedrooms were located.

Constantine had more money than God. A private jet was one of the many toys he owned. I used to love to fly first class, but I was getting really used to having a plane available at any time.

I opened the door to my room and turned the light switch on. Jazz filled the room. Thanks to my genius brother, everything was connected. Best part, the room was soundproof to avoid disturbing any of the other residents.

A long bath would be amazing, but I didn't have a lot of time. I still needed to pack, so a quick shower would do the trick.

Ring.

"Yes, Bart," I said when I answered the phone.

"I need your help," Bartholomew replied.

"What's going on?" I asked, going into full sister-panic mode.

"I'm buying fireworks for Constantine for the fourth but I'm on my bike," Bartholomew replied, and I breathed slowly.

"How much are you buying?" I asked, trying to hold back a smile. I needed to be serious here.

"Enough to make Sparks in the Park look like a children's birthday party," Bartholomew answered.

Sparks in the Park was Texarkana's celebration of the Fourth of July that took place the Saturday before the event. It was a nice event, but this meant Bartholomew was buying way too many fireworks.

"Where are you at?" I asked, no need to argue at this point.

"I'm at the stand closest to Walmart on Eighty-Two," Bartholomew said.

"I still need to shower and do some quick packing, so can you give me twenty?" I started throwing clothes in my bag as I spoke.

"That's perfect. It gives me time to look at everything he has," said Bartholomew.

"See you in a bit," I said before he had a chance to hang up on me.

Constantine's evil habit of hanging up on people after he was done was contagious.

If Bartholomew was planning to buy that many fireworks, we were going to need help. I texted Bob to meet us with Shorty and a truck. It appeared trunk space was essential for this mission. On the bright side, with Bob and Shorty's help I was guaranteed to make it to the airport on time. I did not want to keep George waiting.

Chapter Three

I would like to brag about my skills of being able to sneak out of the Loft without Constantine noticing me, but it would be a complete lie. That demented cat was too busy shouting orders at all the other Interns on the things they were doing wrong to even notice me. I did not feel bad for them. I was normally the subject of his tirades. It was nice to share the torture with my peers. They needed Constantine's love at least once a month.

The fireworks stand was less than seven minutes from Reapers. The owner set up a small trailer on an empty lot on New Boston Road—or Highway Eighty-Two as some called it. The only customer in front of the little trailer was Bartholomew. It was not a huge surprise the place was empty considering it was a Tuesday afternoon and most people were working. Bartholomew had boxes stacked next to him and the poor little vendor was bringing more around. I parked Ladybug on the far side of the parking lot to give the truck room to pull up. We were definitely going to need a truck for all those boxes.

"Are you buying the whole place up?" I asked Bartholomew as I approached.

"I thought about it, but I figured I don't need any noise makers or wands," Bartholomew explained.

"True, if your goal is to rival Sparks in the Park." I leaned against the counter and watched the vendor pack more crates. "Why didn't you order this?"

"Constantine has been monitoring all the deliveries coming in." Bartholomew pointed at a row of fireworks for the vendor. "He is convinced someone is watching us, so I couldn't take any chances of him finding this."

"Is someone watching us?" I asked, inspecting the area.

"I don't know." Bartholomew stopped to look at me. "I have checked all my systems, every line I have, and found nothing. Constantine says it's a feeling."

"Let's hope his feeling is wrong," I told him.

"I agree," Bartholomew replied.

I played with his curly, brown hair as he read over at his list, remembering when he was shorter than me. He looked so grown, but that mischief every kid possessed remained intact. Bob pulled up in Killer, his Land Rover Discovery. After several trucks were blown up on missions, Bob had switched to something different.

"Are you good here?" I asked Bartholomew.

"Are you leaving?" Bartholomew turned to face me.

"Not yet, just going to check on Bob. I thought he was bringing a truck," I replied.

"We might need a truck." Bartholomew inspected his boxes that continued to pile up.

"You think?" I chuckled at him and stepped over to Bob, who sat comfortably in Killer.

"Is that all going to Reapers?" Bob asked, sticking his head out the window.

"Actually, it's all going to the station," I corrected him. "He wants to surprise Constantine on Saturday."

"He is going to surprise the whole city with that many fireworks," said Bob.

"I thought you didn't believe in overkill?" I teased him.

"No such thing," Bob replied. "But you were right, we will need a truck. Shorty should be here any minute."

"With Shorty driving, it won't take that long," I told Bob and headed back to Bartholomew.

The next sound I heard was unmistakable. A high-pitched whistle pierced the sky. After serving in Iraq, I knew the sound of incoming mortar like a long-lost melody. The problem was, by the time you heard it, the impact was not that far behind.

"Isis!" Bob's words were lost in the explosion.

I flew a few feet in the air and landed disoriented on my back. Ladybug had exploded. The flames were escalating, and I needed to get to Bartholomew. If the fire reached the stand, that thing would light up like a match. I struggled to roll over.

"Isis!" Bartholomew screamed.

My mind whirled as I tried to comprehend what I was seeing. Three men were dragging Bartholomew away to a creepy serial-killer van without windows. I pushed past the dizziness and reached for my gun. I was unarmed. My guns were in Ladybug, and she was now roasting like a marshmallow. The only thing I had was my scythe. Getting up was a struggle but I managed. I shuffled towards the van, which had Bartholomew inside and was taking him away, but I stumbled to the ground as my eyes caught a second van barreling towards me.

"Isis, stay down!" Bob shouted, maneuvering Killer behind me. Once he was in position, he opened fire on the incoming vehicle.

Bob parked Killer next to me and I pulled myself inside the passenger side before the men from the second van could climb out.

"Bob, what is going on?" I asked as I slammed the door shut.

"I have no idea, but hold on tight." Bob hit the accelerator and we went flying out of the parking lot.

Bob was chasing the first van that housed Bartholomew. I barely had my seatbelt on when we were hit in the side by a third van.

Did the Chevy's dealership have a sale on vans and nobody told us?

We rolled down the side of the road and landed sideways. My head was spinning, and I was dangling at an odd angle. Bob had blood running down his face. Considering our windshields were bulletproof, he probably hit his head against the glass. We were sitting ducks and the vans were closing in.

"Isis, can you reach my gun?" Bob asked.

"I can't even move." I pulled on the stupid seatbelt that had me pinned.

"We are not going down like this." Bob ripped at his own seatbelt as we watched the men coming closer.

The firing of a 50Cal machine gun stopped the men and had them running back towards their van. Shorty's F-150 sped past Killer towards the men. As the men ran away, Shorty used his door to help one of them on his way, sending the guy flying face-first to the ground.

"Big Bob. Boss Lady. Are you guys okay?" Triplet number one shouted.

The Triplets positioned their truck in front of us to give us coverage.

"Yes. Get us out!" Bob shot back.

The Triplets used the jaws-of-life to get us out of Killer. Bob was bruised but no major injuries. Besides my heart breaking, I was perfectly okay. I sat on the ground next to Killer trying to replay the events but nothing made sense.

"Boss Lady, it's the fur man." Shorty handed me his phone.

"Constantine, they took Bartholomew," I screamed into the phone.

"Are you okay?" Constantine asked me instead.

"Who cares about me? They took Bartholomew." Tears were rolling down my cheeks, my throat hurt, and I was nauseous.

"Isis, listen to me," Constantine said very slowly and quietly. "We are under attack. Every Intern has been taken besides you and Antarctica Bob. I need you to get to cover and focus."

"What?" I stopped breathing.

"Isis. Isis!" Constantine screamed. "Sergeant Black, do you hear me?"

That snapped me out of my mental chaos. We were at war. I was a Non-Commissioned Officer in the United States Army, and this was war.

"Yes, Constantine. What do you need me to do?" I swallowed my tears, my fears, and every feeling I could. I had no time for emotions in war.

"Get out of the street and head to Reapers if you can," Constantine ordered.

I hung up the phone and handed it to Shorty.

"Isis, what is going on?" Bob asked, helping me up.

"We were attacked. Every Intern has been taken," I relayed Constantine's message. "Antarctica Bob and I are the only ones left. We need to head back."

"Triplets, we need a crew to clean this mess up," Bob told them.

"We might have a problem, Big Bob," Triplet Number Two said.

"Now what?" Shorty jumped in.

"The station was just hit by mortar rounds," number two told us.

"What's the casualty count?" I asked moving closer to him.

"None," number two announced with a smile. "The fur man's new reinforcement held, and the building is intact. But the lock-down procedures are in place. Nobody goes in or out for the next twenty-four hours."

"Shorty, we need to get all of our people underground now," Bob ordered.

"Way ahead of you man." Shorty was texting faster than Bartholomew.

My heart hurt just thinking of him, but I couldn't fall apart now.

"I'll text Eric and see what he can do on his side about this," Bob told me, not leaving my side.

"Boss Lady, it's the fur man again," Shorty said, walking towards me again.

"Put it on speaker," I told him.

We didn't have time to be relaying messages back and forth.

"Yes, Constantine?" I said.

"Pestilence and Famine's labs have both been hit as well," Constantine announced.

"What? How?" Bob asked putting his phone away.

"How? Every damn chicken plant in this country has been blown the hell up," Constantine yelled. "Bad news for KFC and Chicken Express."

"What about Eugene, Junior, and all the other Interns?" Interns being kidnapped was hard enough, but dead Interns was something my brain would not be able to process.

"I can't get a hold of anyone." Something crashed on Constantine's side. "I can't find Katrina either."

"We are being hunted down," I muttered.

"Whatever this is, we are a lot harder to kill," Constantine hissed.

"Have you tried Eugene's burner phone?" Triplet number three asked.

"Eugene has a burner phone?" I asked, gaping over my shoulder at the third Triplet.

"Yeah, for his special deliveries," he answered, busying himself calling Eugene.

"Hey, my man, what's the deal?" Eugene's cheerful voice came through the speaker.

"Oh thank God, where are you?" I shouted at the phone.

"At the cemetery with Ninth," Eugene said, a little less perky. "What is going on?"

"Are you armed?" Bob asked.

"After hanging out with you guys, of course I am," Eugene replied.

"Eugene, listen to me very carefully. We are under attack," I said as calmly as I could. "I need you to text us your directions. We are coming for you. Whatever you do, don't trust anyone!"

"Isis, you're scaring me," Eugene said after a long minute.

"Be scared, Eugene. Just stay alive," I replied back.

"Constantine, you got all that?" I turned to Shorty.

"Got it," Constantine replied. "Send me a copy of his location. I will keep searching for Junior and Katrina."

"Please let us know as soon as you do," I told him.

"I will," said Constantine. "Bob?"

"Yes, boss," Bob answered.

"Keep her safe," Constantine ordered him.

"Always," Bob answered.

Rubbing my face, I took a few deep breaths. I wanted to scream, to kick, or to just do something but I had no idea what. Instead, Bob hugged me. Not the fatherly hugs he normally gave me, but the type of hugs soldiers give each other when everything was going wrong.

"I can't break down. Not now," I whispered.

"I know," Bob murmured. "We will get them back and make those who did this pay." He kissed my forehead and looked me in the eyes. The same raw pain I was feeling was mirrored in him—that haunted look every soldier had when losing someone. It was a lot like when the mission had to go on, no matter how big the sacrifice or how much of your soul would cry because of it. Bob understood all of it, so no words were necessary.

"Triplets, let's strip Killer down." Bob marched over to the back of the Land Rover. "We are going to need every bit of fire power we can find. Isis, please program the directions in Shorty's truck. Eugene is going to need us."

Shorty handed me his phone and I headed to his truck. The Triplets were busy with Bob, tearing Killer apart. Guns, rifles, machetes, and grenades were being pulled from the vehicle. Thank you, Lord, for not having anyone fire on us. With that amount of ammunition, we would have burned to a crisp.

"Boss Lady, we are going to get them back," Shorty told me.

"You sound pretty sure, Shorty." I worked the navigation system on his truck as quickly as I could. "Whoever these people are, they are coordinated with lots of resources."

"I don't know who these people are, but I know you." Shorty tapped my shoulder and I looked up at him. "Do you know why we follow you?"

"Because we pay really well," I tried to joke.

"Yes, you do," Shorty agreed, a small smile forming on his lips. "We were all homeless, remember, so any money is good money. Besides the money, though, what is the real reason is why we follow you?"

I stopped pressing buttons and faced Shorty. "I don't know, Shorty. I guess I never thought about it."

"If you were willing to go to purgatory to save Big Bob, and you hardly knew him, we know you would tear the earth apart for any one of us." Tears sparked in Shorty's eyes. "We all know you will never leave one of us behind. You would go down making sure we got out. So, we will get them all back, and whoever did this will pay."

Shorty left to help Bob and the Triplets load the weapons in both trucks. I closed my eyes and centered myself. My pity party could come later. Right now, I needed cold steel running through my veins. I needed to lock everything away and focus on now.

Shorty was right, we would get them back or I would die trying.

Chapter Four

Cedar Grove Cemetery in Fouke, Arkansas was our destination. According to the navigation system, we were twenty-four minutes away from Eugene. Even with Shorty driving, it felt too slow.

"Shorty, please hurry," I begged from the back.

"Boss Lady, you know traffic laws are not my thing," Shorty answered. "But we will kill ourselves on these little country roads if we go any faster. Then we will be of no use to anyone."

"Why is Eugene at a cemetery, anyway?" I asked as I punched the empty seat next to me.

"I'm not complaining. At least he wasn't at the lab," Bob said softly.

"Good point," I agreed.

Shorty took a sharp left onto County Road Two Hundred and Sixty-Six. It was a dirt road with very few houses on it. He drove as fast as he could while trying to avoid the potholes, but flames were visible not far down the road.

"Hold on tight, everyone!" Shorty shouted as he hit the gas.

I bounced several inches off my seat but I didn't care. We couldn't lose Eugene and Ninth, too. The sound of gunfire reached us as Bob opened the sunroof. I grabbed one of the rifles and loaded it. A small church stood next to the cemetery, and in front of it the hearse was parked, which was Eugene's company car. The scene was macabre with the hearse covered in flames.

"Not the hearse!" shouted Shorty. "I loved that car."

"Shorty, focus," said Bob. "I got combatants around the church."

"Can you see Eugene?" I asked.

"They must be in the church," Bob replied. "He is holding his own from the looks of it because they aren't getting close."

"Then let's give him a hand," I told Bob.

Bob didn't need my approval when he opened fired around the church with the semi-automatic he was holding. I lowered the window and sent several rounds in the direction of our enemy. The Triplets had the 50Cal out and were nailing our friendly neighborhood kidnappers with rounds. One of those stupid vans exploded, while the tires in the second were punctured.

"That's payback for the hearse, you bastards!" Shorty shouted.

With both the Triplets and Bob sending shots in towards them, the men took off. Only one van remained, which they all piled inside of. Their tires peeled as they sped away. The Triplets shot a few more round in their direction for good measure, then Shorty parked next to the church. I jumped out.

"Eugene? Ninth?" I shouted as I ran towards the church.

Eugene opened what was left of the door and rushed out. He was still wearing his lab coat but it was dirty, sporting many scorches and rips. Eugene was handsome and had that young Will Smith look to him. Today, he looked so much older and way more dangerous. We hugged each other, neither one of us letting go of the weapon we were carrying.

"Please tell me you are okay?" I asked, searching him for marks.

"I'm fine," Eugene replied, inspecting me as well. "Ninth was hit."

"It was only a flesh wound, child. No need to panic." Ninth strolled out of the church carrying the biggest revolver I had ever seen.

Unlike Death, who had one Intern per continent, Pestilence had ten at all times and they were always in the same place. Pestilence was demented, but crazy about her Interns. Once in the service of Pestilence, her Interns all took numbers based on their length of service. Eugene was called Rookie by his peers as the newest Intern. Ninth was the oldest at over a hundred years old. It was incredible how well he moved for his age, but I was sure Pestilence's powers had something to do with it. Pestilence was not one of my favorite horsemen because she made her Interns call her Mistress. Now that I thought about it, none of the horsemen were my favorite, besides Death.

"What is going on? Who were those men?" Eugene asked as Bob started working on Ninth with his first aid kit.

"Those men? We have no idea," I answered. "What is going on is even more confusing. We are under attack."

"When you say 'we,' what do you mean?" Eugene asked, looking around the group.

"I mean us. All the Interns, all the horsemen, the people that work with us." I pointed at him, Bob, the Triplets, Ninth, and myself.

"Oh Lord, the lab." Eugene covered his mouth.

"It was bombed," Shorty told him.

"Can incoming fire hit the lab?" I asked both Ninth and Eugene.

"It wouldn't matter if the lab was hit or not," Ninth explained. "If the air vents were compromised or nobody was able to get out, we have three days before protocol has to be followed."

"What is the protocol?" Bob asked the centennial man. "You guys have the most drastic protocols of anyone we know."

"This one is not any different," Eugene said, sitting on the ground.

"In three days, if no sign of escape or help is available, the lab is to be destroyed and each Intern will enter their own cryogenic chamber and wait for the apocalypse," Ninth told us as calmly as if he was predicting the weather.

"Your protocol in case of attack is to freeze yourselves to death?" I looked at Eugene and then at Ninth, who both just nodded. "Your protocols are not drastic, they are deranged."

"Have you heard from anyone?" Eugene asked, pushing dirt with the butt of his gun.

"Oh, hell no," I shouted at him as I grabbed both of his shoulders. "You are not giving up on me. Do you hear me?" I was in his face and didn't care what anyone thought.

"Isis, you don't understand," Eugene pleaded.

"I don't have to." I was only inches from his face. "They took Bartholomew and most of Death's Interns. Junior and Katrina are both missing, and the only ones left to do something about it is us. We don't have time to feel sorry for ourselves, not now." Tears were fighting to come out, but I willed them away.

Eugene nodded and Ninth laughed as Bob cleaned his wound.

"I knew I liked her for a reason," Ninth announced.

"What do we need to do?" Eugene asked, swallowing hard.

"Shorty, call Constantine. Tell him we have Eugene and Ninth." I watched Shorty dial and place the call on speaker.

"Tell me you found them," Constantine said.

"We are here Constantine," Eugene answered.

"That's what I'm talking about!" Constantine cheered.

"Do you have any news for us?" I asked, hoping for something good.

"Sort of," Constantine answered.

"That's not very encouraging, fur man," Shorty told him.

"I picked up the signal of a car crash. The vehicle that was hit was Junior's," Constantine explained.

"Do you have any information on what happened?" I braced myself for the worst.

"Sort of. The good news, whoever hit the car did it in front of a State Trooper," said Constantine.

"How is that good?" Bob asked, this time watching me. I just shrugged.

"Because they were not able to finish the job or take him away," Constantine clarified. "The accident was severe, and Junior was transported to the Mount Pleasant Regional Hospital. I recommend you guys get there before that group tries again."

Constantine disconnected the call and we all just stood in silence.

"Basically, we are going to have to break Junior out of a hospital." Shorty translated Constantine's orders for us.

"Last time we tried that, it ended really badly," I told the group, remembering our attempts at getting our elven princess Ginny out of Wadley Hospital.

"I have an idea," Eugene told us. "We just need to stop by a uniform store before we get there. And I need a suit."

"Sounds random but I'm in." I raised my hand.

"Let's do it," Shorty jumped in, raising his arm as well.

"We can do this," Ninth said, but Bob lowered his hand.

"You, my friend, are heading to Reapers," Bob told him. "Triplets, please drop Ninth off with Constantine and then join us at the hospital."

"That's no fun," Ninth complained.

"At the rate we are going, we will have plenty of occasions for fun," I told Ninth, hopping to my feet.

The Triplets escorted Ninth to their truck and helped him inside. Shorty, Bob, Eugene, and I marched over to Shorty's truck.

"Nice job back there," Bob told Eugene, slapping his back.

"I took those lessons you gave me seriously. Handling a gun is the least of my worries," Eugene said, putting his 9mm back in his holster. "I'm out of bullets, tranquilizers, everything."

"We have ammo in the truck. Make sure to grab plenty," Bob told him. "It's an hour and a half from here to Mount Pleasant. I recommend everyone start cleaning your weapons. We are going to need them."

"Thank you for coming," Eugene told me as we climbed in the back of the truck.

"We wouldn't leave you here alone," I said.

"I know, but I'm still grateful." Eugene closed the door behind him.

"Eugene, we have a couple of stores between here and Mount Pleasant. Do you have a preference?" Bob asked, pressing a button on the navigation system.

"The closest will do," Eugene replied.

I hoped Eugene's plan was simple. If not, I was ready to march in the hospital guns blazing. This was war, and whoever was after us would not hesitate to do the same. Bob handed Eugene and I each a cleaning kit and I started taking one of the rifles apart. I needed the distraction before my mind and the guilt swirling through it took over.

Chapter Five

It was only five pm by the time we reached the hospital in Mount Pleasant. The long summer days were working in our favor and giving us plenty of sunlight. That was the only thing working with us today, though. Eugene had a simple but brilliant plan. As one of the leading members for the CDC—yes the Center for Disease Control and Prevention—he had a lot of power. We were going to the hospital and Eugene was going to quarantine the place while we got Junior out. What could possibly go wrong with this plan? Everything.

Shorty pulled up behind an ambulance in front of the Emergency Room. Bob, Shorty, and I were all wearing hazmat suits. Eugene had a black three-piece suit that looked incredible on him. Shorty stayed in the truck while Bob and I followed closely behind Eugene.

"Attention everyone, this facility is quarantined by orders of the CDC," Eugene announced, marching towards the registration desk. "You brought in an Ebola patient early this afternoon. The man had been in a car accident. We need to take him now."

"Wh-what?" the poor receptionist stuttered.

"You heard me. Lock down this hospital," Eugene repeated to the young lady.

"This is not a drill. Initiating lockdown procedures, I repeat, initiating lockdown procedures now," the young lady announced over a loudspeaker.

"Where is the patient?" Eugene asked.

"Down the hall, in room Nine C," the young lady checked one of her clipboards.

"Good. We will evacuate the potential threat," Eugene informed her. "My team will be here in twenty-eight minutes. Have everyone readied for testing. You two with me."

Eugene signaled for Bob and me to follow. I kept my face down to avoid making eye contact with any of the staff who were running like wild ants in the hospital.

"Twenty-eight minutes, are you serious?" I asked Eugene, trying to keep my voice from sounding like Darth Vader.

"Trust me. We are good," Eugene told me.

"Did you actually call this in?" Bob asked, his hazmat suit making swishing noises.

"I had to or everyone in this hospital would be searching for us for kidnapping a patient." Eugene stopped as three men in scrubs ran in our direction. "Get him out. I got this."

Bob and I moved quickly down the hall as Eugene stepped in front of the men.

"Did you not hear the announcement? What exactly are you doing?" Eugene was chastising the men.

Bob and I did not wait around long enough to hear the reply. We found room Nine C. Bob stood watch as I slowly opened the door and entered the room, only to be knocked against the wall.

"What the—?" I started, screaming as a pair of strong hands shoved me to the ground.

"What do you want?" Junior demanded.

"Junior?" I asked instead.

"Isis?" Junior pulled my hazmat hood off as he sat on me. "Oh, thank God."

"What are you doing?" I asked as he dropped a syringe to the ground.

"Trying not to die here." Junior wiped the sweat off his forehead with his hands.

"Nice job, but could you get off me now?" I asked, trying to wiggle out from under him.

Junior was a little taller than Shorty, but not by much at only five feet five inches. In his early twenties, he was of Latino decent, but I had never asked his nationality. Junior was Famine's first official Intern and a brilliant CEO. As the face for the diet industry that Famine ran, Junior had been making huge moves on the scene. At the moment, he wasn't looking like a CEO, but a very desperate hospital patient. Junior wore one of those weird gowns with no back.

"Sorry." Junior rolled off me and sat on the floor to face me. "What is going on here?"

"Is everything okay in there?" Bob asked, peering through the door.

"I found Junior," I told him as I pointed at him.

"Good. Can we leave now? The clock is ticking," Bob reminded me.

"Yes, we need a gurney," I told Bob as I climbed to my feet.

"A gurney for what?" Junior asked as Bob closed the door.

"You are technically an Ebola patient and we are transporting you out of here," I explained, walking over to the wall of medical equipment.

"I'm hoping you are kidding, right?" Junior asked following me around.

"Where are your clothes?" I stepped around the small room but couldn't find anything.

"That's a great question." Junior had stopped in the middle of the room to tap his foot. "I came in wearing a Brioni's suit, and now I'm wearing this backless, cotton gown. What happened to my clothes and where are my underwear?"

"You are not wearing underwear?" It was tempting not to peek behind him, but I contained myself due to the nature of our rescue mission.

"Do you know how much a Brioni's suit cost?" Junior ignored my question and kept rambling on.

"A lot. I saw the price tag." I was very familiar with the price tag of most designer suits thanks to my obsession with Death's clothes. "Can we focus now?"

"Fine." Junior threw his arms in the air and sat on the bed. "Isis, it was a car accident. They happen all the time. Why do I have people trying to knock me out and planning to kill me in a hospital? I've been hiding most of the day."

"Junior, your crash was no accident." I sat next to him on the bed. "Someone is targeting all of us. They are probably coming back to finish the job."

"Why?" Junior's black eyes were wide with worry.

"We have no idea, but we need to get you out." Bob pushed a small bed through the door as I finished.

"Your ride is ready, sir. Climb on board." Bob patted the bed for Junior.

Junior hopped on it, and I rushed to get him a blanket. Bob grabbed an air mask from his pocket and placed it on Junior's face.

"We need to make this look real," Bob told him, and Junior nodded.

"Here." I handed him a gun I pulled from inside my hazmat suit. "If anything happens, use it. It's loaded with tranquilizers, so don't hesitate."

"That won't be a problem," Junior replied as he placed the gun under the blanket with him.

"Ready?" Bob asked, and both Junior and I nodded.

I secured my hazmat mask and helped Bob push Junior out of the room as quickly as possible. The hospital staff was on full alert. Nurses and doctors were running from room to room carrying clipboards and laptops with them. Bob and I avoided conversations and pointed at Junior anytime anyone got near. That was enough to have the staff rushing away from us. As we made the last turn towards the exit, we heard footsteps behind us. Two men in scrubs were coming towards us, and they were carrying guns.

"I don't think those are PA," Bob told me.

"Not the ones I'm used to, that's for sure," I replied.

Before either one of us could react, Junior shot them both. The two evil PAs dropped flat on their backs. The boy had incredible aim.

"Wow," I told him.

"You said to use it, right?" Junior asked as he glanced over his shoulder.

"Absolutely. Nice shot," Bob told him.

"Can we go now? I'm sure more will be coming," Junior pointed out.

"Moving," I replied as I pushed the gurney out of the hallway.

"It's about time you two showed up!" Eugene yelled at us. "Were you taking a scenic tour of the hospital? Never mind. Get that man in that ambulance now because we are running out of time."

Bob and I pushed Junior as fast as we could out of the emergency room. Eugene was right behind us, giving last minute orders to the passing staff. When Bob opened the back of the ambulance, I stopped him.

"You remember what happened last time," I told him. "We should secure the driver seat first."

We lost Princess Ginny after we loaded her in an ambulance. I was not taking that risk again. Explaining that horrible mistake to Constantine had been a nightmare.

"Way ahead of you, Boss Lady," Shorty shouted from the front.

"Would you two get in now?" Eugene commanded as he climbed in the passenger seat.

Bob and I pushed the gurney in the ambulance and jumped after it. Shorty was out of the driveway before we finished locking the doors.

"Shorty, where is the truck?" Bob asked.

"The Triplets have it, and they are meeting us outside the city limits," Shorty replied as he blared the sirens.

"Do we really need all that?" I asked, removing my hazmat suit.

Bob did the same, dropping his heavy contraption in the corner of the ambulance.

"What's the point of stealing an ambulance if we can't play with the toys?" Shorty was driving the poor thing like a sports car.

"Please try not to kill me. I already experienced one car crash today," Junior told him, taking a seat on the bed.

"We got you, my man," Shorty told him.

"Hi, I'm Eugene. We haven't met." Eugene waved from the front seat.

"You are Pestilence's Rookie," Junior replied. "Junior, new rookie for Famine."

"Does Famine plan to get more Interns?" I asked.

"After this mess, I doubt the Boss will keep me." Junior rubbed his dark hair, making it a giant mess. "Can you please explain what is going on now?"

"Someone attacked all the horsemen's headquarters today," I told him. "Your lab, as well as Pestilence's, were hit. Most of my peers and Bartholomew have been kidnapped. We are still trying to find Katrina."

"Isis, I'm so sorry." Junior squeezed my hand.

"Me, too." I clasped his back. "Junior, does Famine have any crazy protocol in place in case of an attack on Famine's labs that we need to know about?"

"No," Junior said, shaking his head. "You know the Boss's temper. Who would be crazy enough to attack Famine?"

Famine was a temperamental, spoiled brat that blew up at the slightest provocation. Unlike Death, who became whatever people believed Death to be, Famine claimed nothing. Famine was neither male nor female, just Famine. You could call Famine Boss, them, or they. A personal attack on them could be a disaster for the world.

"God, what would Famine do after this?" I asked.

"Famine? What about my Mistress?" Eugene added from the front. "Isis, this is the kind of stuff that triggers the apocalypse."

The ambulance got very quiet. We all looked at each other while trying to process the information.

"Who would benefit from this?" I finally asked.

"When the apocalypse hits, we will make a killing selling gas masks," Eugene confessed softly.

"We will, too, selling MREs and canned-food products." Junior didn't even bother facing me.

"Are you kidding me?" I glanced at the spot between Junior and Eugene.

"Don't look at us like that. War is going to make the most out of all of us," Eugene clarified. "That horsemen will be selling weapons to every side in the conflict, making millions in the process."

"Are we going to make money from the apocalypse?" Shorty asked from the front.

"I doubt we will be discounting trips to the afterlife as part of our get-rich-quick scheme," I told Shorty, bursting his bubble. "I got it. When the real thing happens, the horsemen are going to ride into their glory and make money. But who would benefit now by pissing them off?"

"When you figure that out, we will find our culprits," Bob answered.

"Sorry to interrupt this philosophical debate but we have arrived," Shorty announced, parking the ambulance off the highway on an access road.

The Triplets opened the back door and helped Junior climb out. Eugene and Shorty met us at the back, as Bob and I dismounted the ambulance.

"What are we going to do with this thing?" I pointed to the ambulance.

"The CDC will be picking it up to decontaminate before returning it to the hospital," Eugene answered.

"Boss Lady, the fur man," Shorty announced, strolling over with the phone.

"Have you secured Junior?" Constantine asked.

"Junior is secure," I answered.

"Not wearing any underpants, but he is secure," Shorty added.

"Thanks, Shorty," said Junior, glaring.

"Hey, my man. You can't be going around flashing people now. I'm sure that is illegal in like seven states in the union," Shorty clarified for him.

"Before Junior gets arrested for indecent exposure, can we get back to business?" Constantine asked us.

"Sorry, boss," Shorty replied.

"Have you found Katrina?" I asked.

"Hi, Isis." Katrina's voice came through the phone a little muffled.

"Oh God, where are you?" I asked with a hand over my heart.

"Flying over Texas as we speak," said Katrina. "I was planning to head home, but Fort Riley and every major installation is on lockdown due to terrorist attacks."

"Are you okay, Colonel?" Bob asked.

"My chopper was shot down, but what is the point of being air assault if I can't rappel off one?" Katrina dismissed the whole situation like the super-trooper she was.

"We are redirecting her landing to us," Constantine told us.

"ETA is forty-eight minutes, and I will need a ride," said Katrina.

"We are on our way," I answered as Constantine disconnected the call. "You heard the lady. We need to head home in a hurry."

"Triplets, you know the drill," Bob told the guys. "Please drop Junior and Eugene at Reapers. Afterwards, swing by the airport in case we need backup."

"Why can't I go with you to pick up the ultimate soldier?" Junior asked, examining us.

"Because you are not wearing any pants," Shorty reminded him.

"Oh yeah." Junior eyed his legs and blushed.

"Are you sure you guys don't need me?" Eugene asked.

"You'd better go check on Ninth. This shouldn't take us long," I told Eugene.

"I guess I should," Eugene replied. "Please be careful."

The Triplets led Junior and Eugene over to their truck, and Bob and I followed Shorty back to his truck.

"Shorty, I'm afraid to say this but we need you to hurry." I bit my lower lip when I spoke.

"I live for these moments." Shorty jumped in his truck ready for the race of a lifetime.

Lord, please don't let us die.

I have given permission to the worst driver on the planet to go full speed. Katrina better appreciate the sacrifices we have made for her because we might not be in one piece when we arrive in Texarkana again.

Chapter Six

We had less than a minute before Katrina's ETA, or Estimated Time of Arrival. Why was everyone always talking in acronyms? Shorty's truck jumped the railroad tracks in front of the airport, and it was a miracle I didn't get a concussion. The Texarkana Regional Airport was a very small, but efficient, facility. They had three outgoing and incoming flights. The last flight out of Texarkana had left for the day and the last incoming would not be arriving until nine thirty. Ideally, this left the airport fairly empty.

"Shorty, go towards our private hangar," Bob told him.

When Constantine moved the location of the jet to Texarkana, he had a private hangar built, which included automatic doors for vehicles to drive in. Bob used an app on his phone to open the doors as Shorty barreled through. The doors leading to the tarmac of the hangar were always left open to give Shorty easy access to the runaway.

"What airline is she flying?" Shorty asked as he slowed down.

"None," Bob answered. "According to her text, she is flying in a C-130."

"She is coming in on a Hercules?" I didn't know why I bothered asking. Katrina worked for War and had access to any military equipment around.

"Right on time," Bob said pointing at the incoming four-engine turboprop military transport.

"Is that thing going to be able to land?" Shorty asked, glancing at the runaway.

"That's its specialty: landing in unprepared runaways. This should be a piece of cake," I explained to Shorty.

BOOM.

The ground shook and the truck was pushed forward at least ten feet. We all three turned to watch our private hangar go up in flames.

"I think this piece of cake just got burned," Shorty announced. "The fur man is really going to kill someone today.

"God, they are taking fire." I pointed at the runaway where a truck was shooting at the C-130. "This madness is never going to end. Bob, call Katrina and tell them to turn around."

Bob dialed as I watched the flames in the hangar reach at least fifteen-feet tall. The police and the fire department should be here soon. The airport had patrols all the time, and explaining that would be impossible.

"Bob, no way!" Katrina shouted.

"Katrina, you are taking fire," I yelled through the speaker on the phone.

"Isis, I'm not losing another plane and I'm not running from a fight," Katrina told me. "I'm coming down, so I recommend you find a way to catch me."

Katrina disconnected the phone as the C-130 started rising.

"What do you think she meant by that?" Shorty asked, watching the plane.

"It means that crazy paratrooper is about to jump," I told the boys, opening the sunroof in the truck. "Bob, hand me the SAW. Shorty, get on that runaway."

"You are kidding me," Shorty said as I climbed out of the sunroof into the bed of the truck.

"Damn it, Katrina!" I said to myself as I watched the toughest soldier in history jumping off the plane. "Shorty get moving!"

It took a minute for Shorty to comprehend the madness of the situation. Bob had passed me the SAW with several cases of ammo. By the time Shorty was moving, half of the fun was set up and the tailgate was down.

"I hope you have a plan," said Bob.

"Plan? Who needs a plan when your friend jumps off a plane into the middle of a fire fight," I replied.

The shooters were taking aim at Katrina. My goal was to create a distraction long enough to give her time to land. That translated to me shooting at everything that moved, and hopefully Death would forgive me if I sent her some customers along the way.

"Shorty, I need you to drive in reverse so I can face those guys!" I shouted from the back, getting in the prone position on the bed of the truck.

Shorty hit the brakes a little harder than necessary, but I didn't argue. He put the truck in reverse and charged at full speed towards the enemy's vehicles. I made the sign of the cross with my fingers and opened fire. Either our friendly neighborhood villains were not expecting a counter attack, or they underestimated us, but they were too slow to avoid the impact. Several direct hits to the engine and body of that truck had it blowing smoke everywhere. A few more hits and the thing went up in flames. My celebration didn't last long as two vans drove onto the runway.

"Shorty, time to get Katrina!" I shouted, standing on the bed of the truck.

"Two o'clock, Shorty," Bob told him.

I braced myself as Shorty put the truck in gear and headed towards the falling soldier. Katrina glided down expertly like an avenging angel. Bob gave Shorty directions as we maneuvered underneath Katrina. About eight feet off the truck, Katrina released her parachute and dropped. There was a reason she was a jump master. The girl had the perfect technique. I grabbed her arm to stabilize her, but she dropped right next to the machine gun.

"This one is for my men," Katrina said as she opened fire on both vans.

The idea of killing people made my stomach turn—even this group of horrible criminals. With real bullets, I rarely aimed for people. Katrina had been a trained soldier for over fifty years. One of the gifts of War to his Interns was youth for a hundred years while they served their term as his Intern. Katrina had seen many deaths, many wars, and she probably had sent many men to their final destination. Her blonde hair flowed in the wind as she destroyed the vans and everyone inside them. I dropped down on the bed as she rolled over to face the fading sun.

"This has been one awful day," Katrina told me.

"Who are you telling?" I replied. "Shorty, please take us home."

"My pleasure, Boss Lady," Shorty said.

"How are you?" I asked Katrina.

"I should be asking you that." Katrina sat up to look up me. "I'm War's Intern, so this is my everyday life. How are you holding up?"

"I'm here," I said, playing with my hands. "I was mentally prepared when I was in the Army. Now I'm just struggling."

"Constantine told me." Katrina did not elaborate. "We are going to get them back."

Katrina sounded so confident I had to look up. She was single-handedly one of the most beautiful women, and completely deadly at that. Her eyes changed color from blue to green giving her a diabolical look under the orange sky. There was a reason I left the Army. I was tired of seeing my friends die. This was not my idea of fun.

"I will make anyone pay if they hurt him," I told her in a cold voice.

"I know you will." Katrina smiled at me.

I leaned my head against the truck and watched as fire trucks and police cars passed us heading towards the airport. The flames were increasing. The firemen were going to have their hands full with the damage back there. The burning trucks on the tarmac were not helping the situation. I doubt that last flight coming to Texarkana was landing tonight.

Chapter Seven

By the time we pulled into the Nash Industrial park, the sun was down. There were burn marks all over Reapers, and metal pieces scattered around the area. Constantine's tree pavilion was leveled to the ground. My heart ached at seeing all the destruction. It was a miracle Reapers was in one piece and Constantine was alive.

"How is Reapers still standing?" Shorty asked the obvious question as we drove through the vehicle entrance in the back.

"This is not Constantine's first rodeo, as you say in the South," Katrina answered. "This building has more protection than the Pentagon. I doubt anything could take it out."

Once inside Reapers, we dismounted the truck and headed towards the Loft. Each step up the stairs was like a dagger to my heart. The closer we got to our home, the more real it became that Bartholomew was not here.

We entered to find Constantine in front of the monitors.

"Boss, do you need me to come in?" Antarctica Bob asked.

I sauntered over to the conference area and sat on the couch.

"No, I need you to guard the jail," Constantine replied. "How long can you hold your position?"

"Without any reinforcements or supplies arriving? Seven days," Bob announced.

The camera moved to show a company of penguins with headgear operating machine guns. If we were not at war, that scene would have made me laugh. One of the penguins had opened fire at a strange shape that appeared out of the water.

"Damn it, Billy. That's a whale not a submarine," Bob shouted at his penguin, who continued to shoot. "How many times do I have to tell you? Boss, got to go."

Bob terminated the video call and the Loft went deathly silent.

"Great. Chickens and whales are going to be extinct this year thanks to these fools," Constantine announced.

"Whales have been an endangered species for a while, but why are chickens going extinct?" Katrina looked around the room. "Did I miss something?"

"Our enemies bombed every chicken plant and farm in the country," Constantine explained.

"Are you serious? Why?" Katrina asked, leaning against the glass wall that faced the downstairs of Reapers.

"Pestilence and Famine both have secret labs underneath chicken plants," I supplied the details for her.

"They were not taking any chances." Katrina nodded. "If this wasn't an attack against us, I would be highly impressed in their planning and execution. Unfortunately for them, now I want them all gone."

"Trust me, that makes two of us," Constantine told her. "I recommend you two go take a shower. I already sent Eugene and Junior to do the same. I'm ordering food. It's going to be a long night. Hope you don't mind spending time with Pestilence and Famine's Interns?"

"I'm sure I can take them." Katrina petted the top of his head before leaving the Loft.

Constantine actually let her. It was definitely a bad night if he was letting people touch him.

"Boss, we need to check on the underground," Bob told Constantine.

"I have secured several safe houses for all of our people," said Constantine. "The Triplets are staying with us tonight and nobody is allowed on patrol this evening. I have no idea how they are watching us, but until we do, I want everyone under cover."

"Thank you, Boss," Shorty told him, rubbing his eyes. "This place is not the same without Bart at the command center."

Shorty left the Loft in a hurry. The empty chair was a reminder my brother was missing, and even Shorty felt his loss. Bob squeezed my shoulder and left toward his apartment.

"I have trained hundreds of Interns, but having Bartholomew taken hurts like nothing else," Constantine confessed as he jumped over to the couch.

"Because Bartholomew is not an Intern; he is family," I told him, my voice cracking. "He is our family, and they made this personal, Constantine."

"The moment they attacked all the horsemen it was personal," Constantine reminded me. "Isis, you can be passionate, but you can't be emotional. Out-of-control emotions will get everyone killed. Can you handle that?"

"I don't have a choice," I replied, covering my face. "What do you need me to do?"

"Take a shower, regroup, and we need to take inventory of all the damage," Constantine answered.

I couldn't feel my legs as I made my way toward my room. The soft music started playing as soon as I hit the light switch, though this time it sounded like a funeral procession. I sat on the bed and my arms began to tremble.

Chirp. Chirp.

I looked around the room for the sound and found my spare cellphone on my night table. My regular phone went up in flames with Ladybug. Bartholomew made me keep two phones active at all times just in case I destroyed one. Another stabbing pain flitted through my heart at that thought.

"Hello," I answered the phone without checking the caller ID.

"Oh, thank God, sweetheart. I was trying to reach you all day." Godmother sounded out of breath and scared.

"It's been a long day for sure. Are you okay?" I asked, deflating as I sat back on the bed.

"The Order was infiltrated and we were betrayed," Godmother told me.

"What?" I jumped from my bed and started pacing.

I was becoming a horrible person. Why didn't it occur to me that Godmother could be a target? I never even checked in on her.

"How are you? We've been seeing the news reports," Godmother said. "While the civilians are not making the connection, the rest of us have."

"Godmother, I'm so sorry," I mumbled.

"Why are you apologizing?" Godmother asked.

"It's my fault you were attacked," I admitted.

"Isis, stop that," Godmother ordered. "This is not the time for you to become a martyr or narcissistic and think everything is about you."

"Ouch," I replied.

"I'm the high priestess of the Order, and I have made plenty of enemies," Godmother continued. "The horsemen have made their own share over the millennium they've been around. Do not take this guilt upon yourself. I know you are Catholic and you enjoy picking up things to feel guilty about, but this is not one of them. Do you understand?"

"Yes, Godmother." I hated it in that moment, but she made me smile. Even in the midst of our chaos, Godmother would make fun of things.

"We are heading your way," Godmother said after a few moments of silence.

"Is that safe?" I asked softly.

"I don't care if it's safe. Obviously our enemies are coming your way. I will be damned if I let them hurt you." Godmother sounded irate and was almost growling at the phone. "We are traveling by car because planes are out of the question. It will take us over a day to get to Texas. Promise me you will stay safe until then."

"I will do my best," I replied. "Godmother, I love you."

"I love you, too, sweetie. Now stop moping around." Godmother disconnected, and I held the phone for a few minutes.

This was awful!

I dropped the phone on the dresser and walked to my bathroom. My day started by being hunted by a boar, and less than twelve hours later we were being hunted. If only it was a bad dream and everything would go back to normal in the morning.

I undressed and climbed in the shower. The world was upside down and nothing made sense. I turned the water as hot as I could get it and stood under it, wanting the heat to burn my troubles away. Instead, the tears started rolling. The pain of watching Bartholomew being taken, the helplessness of not knowing what was going on, the pain, fear, anger, and everything else rolled into a big ball of water that filled my eyes and spilled over, mixing with the droplets from my shower.

It took me an hour to regroup, as Constantine asked me to do. Even after the longest shower of the century, I didn't want to leave my room. I didn't want to face the world and the millions of questions waiting outside. At the same time, hiding in my room was not going to get me any closer to finding Bartholomew and the rest of the Interns. I braided my hair and grabbed a fresh set of combat clothes. With the madness going on, I couldn't take any chances of being unprepared.

The Loft was packed by the time I emerged from my room. Another video conference was taking place. This time the four horsemen had dialed in from whatever secret location each one of them resided in. Constantine was on the computer table, facing the horsemen, while the rest of the team was scattered around the room. Bob, Shorty, and the Triplets stayed by the kitchen as far away from the action as possible. Eugene and Junior sat on the couch across from Constantine, while Katrina took the floor against the glass wall. I joined her there.

"What did I miss?" I whispered.

"Absolutely nothing," Katrina replied. "They have been arguing for the last twenty minutes about the merits of destroying the world."

"That's a valid argument?" I asked a little louder than I hoped to.

"They need a unanimous vote before they can ride," Eugene added from the couch. "Death is the only one holding out."

"You cannot argue that this was a personal attack against us," Famine shouted.

Famine, as Constantine liked to describe the horseman, was a gorgeous androgynous. Tonight, Famine was dressed to impress in a silver suit. If the apocalypse was happening, fashion was not being hurt.

"I have eight of my Interns underneath pounds of rock," Pestilence added.

Pestilence looked impeccable in a gold, strapless shirt. Her hair was fire-red today, and she was glamorous.

"Where is Ninth?" I looked around the room for the Intern.

"Napping," Eugene replied. "Nothing is going to change his napping schedule."

"The man is over a hundred years old. He can nap whenever he feels like it," Katrina defended the old Intern.

"You are only defending him because you are way past seventy," I teased her.

Katrina flipped her hair over my face but turned as soon as War started talking.

"My installations have been compromised!" War shouted, slamming his hand on a table. "Failure to retaliate to such an attack will make us look weak."

War was an imposing figure. It was hard to deny the strength that radiated from the man. As the main commander and chief advisor to every military force in the world, he took his job very seriously. Today, he resembled the wrestler The Rock, raised eyebrows and all.

"If you don't teach these mortals a lesson, the insults will escalate," Pestilence told her siblings.

Death was silent as she listened to everyone. While Famine refused to be nailed to a human form, Death was every form. Death appeared differently to every person depending on their beliefs. To me, Death was always a beautiful, tall brunette who resembled my mother. As her siblings argued the merits of killing everyone, Death only tapped her fingers on the table. Her long, silky hair was pulled back in a tight ponytail.

"My troops were killed today," War roared.

"There are worse things than death," Death said, and her siblings all went silent. "And at this time, my children are the ones experiencing it. I have already delivered yours to a glorious afterlife, my dears. I'm not even able to sense mine, so please do not lecture me on the toll we have taken."

Nobody in the Loft moved. I wasn't prepared to hear that Death couldn't track our people down. That left only a few places they could be held hostage.

"They are mocking us," Pestilence jumped in after the uncomfortable silence. "A lesson must be taught."

"What do you recommend then? Annihilation?" Death asked as she leaned back on the chair.

"A slow demise would be more suitable," War corrected her. "I will launch nukes to every major city in the world from their worst enemy."

"I will contaminate every water supply," Pestilence added.

"And I will kill all the crops, farm animals, and every bit of vegetation on this planet," Famine concluded.

"Are you mad?" It took me a minute to realize I was the one shouting at the horsemen and that I was on my feet doing it. "How will killing millions of innocent people teach a lesson to the ones that did this to us?"

"Interns don't get a say in this," Pestilence said, dismissing me.

"Why not?" Death asked, and her sibling stared at her. "They were the ones attacked. Why can't they have a say in this? At the end, they will be the ones picking up the dead after the world falls to pieces."

"Are you serious?" Pestilence hissed.

"Eugene, what do you think?" Death asked.

Eugene struggled to get out of the couch before speaking. "Death, I'm here to serve my mistress." I rolled my eyes at Eugene but let him finish. "But my family is down at that lab. I will do anything in my power to get them out or avenge them. I'm not ready to bury them yet."

Eugene sat down wiping tears from his eyes. It had taken everything out of him to defy his mistress.

"Junior, what do you think?" Death continued her questioning in a soft, motherly voice.

"I know I'm new here, and I will follow the orders of the Boss." Junior took a deep breath before facing the horsemen. "There are a lot of good people out there who didn't do anything to us. Maybe we could be more selective with our punishments."

That was efficient and diplomatic. Junior had the making of a great CEO or politician.

"Colonel, what do you think?" War cut off Death. "You know Death is going to ask you next?"

"General, I lost a lot of good men today and some very personal friends." Katrina didn't bother getting up from the floor, a strange move for a soldier. "I would like my chance at payback before you send them all to hell."

The room was silent. Slowly, everyone turned to face me knowing I was the last Intern present.

"What do you recommend we do, Isis?" Death gave me her undivided attention, and it felt like she was standing in front of me.

"Three days," I replied. "For every horrible, impossible mission we ever faced, the magic number has been three days. What do you have to lose by giving us three days?"

I crossed my arms and waited.

"Agreed." Death spoke for her siblings. "We won't make a move for three days."

"Hope you have a plan, or the fireworks you will see for the Fourth of July will not be in celebration," War announced.

"Guerra, can you hear me?" Constantine shouted at the horsemen. "I think we are losing you. Death, can you hear us?"

Before any of the horsemen could reply, Constantine terminated the conference call. The monitors went dark and the room was quiet.

"That was fun," Constantine told us.

"What did you do?" Katrina asked him.

"Nobody needs to hear their doom and despair speech," Constantine answered. "That conversation was not going anywhere fast."

"Three days?" Junior turned to face me. "You couldn't have asked for a week or maybe a month?"

"Let's not start arguing on this side as well," Constantine ordered. "I'm surprised they gave us that long. Nice job, Isis."

"Junior is right. Three days is not long enough." I took a seat on Bartholomew's chair. "We need a plan."

"I have a plan," Constantine announced. "Find them, eliminate them, and get our people back. All in favor?"

"I like it," Katrina told him from the floor. "Simple and to the point."

"I second that plan, Boss," Shorty cosigned from the kitchen.

"Saint Francis of Assisi once said, 'start by doing what's necessary, then do what's possible; and suddenly you are doing the impossible.'" Constantine made himself comfortable on the computer table. "Right now, we need to focus on the necessary. I need everyone checking on your areas. Take inventory of casualties, what was hit, and what we have available for resources. We will move to what's possible tomorrow."

"Yes, Constantine," the other Interns replied in unison.

Katrina, Eugene, and Junior all hugged me as they headed back to their new rooms. Bob, Shorty, and the Triplets followed quickly behind. Only Constantine and I were left in the Loft.

"Who do you need me to call?" I asked softly.

"All of our friends here in town," Constantine answered. "We need to know if anyone else was targeted or if it was only us."

"The Order has been compromised," I told him.

"How is Virginia?" Constantine rarely referred to my Godmother by her first name.

"Tough as nails. She is heading this way with her remaining members." I was learning how resilient my Godmother truly was.

"I feel sorry for those who betrayed her." Constantine hopped off the table.

"You do?" That was unexpected.

"If the horsemen have little mercy for traitors, your Godmother is pure evil," Constantine explained.

"I'm glad I have never seen that side of her," I told him.

"You should be," Constantine agreed. "I'll check on the elves. Don't ever doubt it when I tell you we have friends in many places, Isis."

"We are going to need them," I replied.

My list of friends, minus all the ones already at Reapers, was fairly small. This was not going to take long. I debated heading to my room to make the calls, and instead decided for the gym downstairs. With things as bad as they were, I needed something to punch. We had a large boxing bag downstairs for just the occasion. A few rounds of kicking and punching would come in handy.

Chapter Eight

Why do people have cell phones if they are not planning to pick up when people call?

According to the experts, my phone had more technology than the computers used to launch the first spacecraft to the moon. It could do anything, except make calls by the looks of it. I dropped the phone on the bench press and moved to the boxing bag. For the last fifteen minutes I had been on the stupid phone. I had called all the people I knew, left voice messages, and even texts. Nothing. Not a single soul replied, and I couldn't leave Reapers to find them.

I punched the bag several times and followed those with a couple of high kicks. Eric had developed a punching routine for me to speed up my response time. I closed my eyes and started the drill. Sweat was rolling down my back when I heard a noise behind me.

"God."

I opened my eyes and turned around.

"Junior, what's going on?" I asked softly, moving in his direction.

Junior was leaning against Bob's apartment crying. He slowly slid down the wall and hugged his legs. His face had no color and his normally-perfect hair was a mess.

"They took them," Junior mumbled.

"Who did they take?" Not the most helpful explanation Junior had ever given me.

"My sisters, they are missing." Junior sobbed loudly, and I dropped so I could hug him.

"Junior, I'm so sorry," I told him, holding him tight.

"They want me to leave Famine." Junior looked up at me. "If I want to see my sisters alive again, I have to walk away. Isis, they want me to betray the Boss or watch my sisters die."

I wiped his tears with my hand. I knew the pain he was feeling and the sense of helplessness that was reflected in his eyes.

"Junior. Listen to me. You do whatever you think is right to save your family," I told him.

"What would you do? Would you leave?" Tears rolled down his cheeks, and he reminded me so much of Bartholomew at that moment.

"I would trade places with Bartholomew in a heartbeat," I answered truthfully. "But they have the rest of Death's Interns. They won't let him go even if I turn myself in. This is a lose-lose situation. All I can do is protect the family I have here."

"If I left, it would unhinge the boss." Junior dropped his head on his lap.

"I think that's the plan. They are pushing the horsemen to attack without mercy." I sat in front of him. "But it's not your responsibility to hold Famine together."

"I don't know what to do." Junior sobbed again.

"Do you believe in God?" I asked.

"I was raised Christian, but I haven't practiced in years," Junior confessed.

"I'm sure He doesn't care how long it has been." I winked at him as I spoke. "Pray or meditate about it. Hope and faith is all we have left, so listen to that."

I wiped Junior's face again and kissed his forehead. Junior needed some space. Those were decisions that were best done alone. I headed back to the bench press to check my phone. Junior rose quietly and headed up the stairs.

Nothing, are you serious?

"God, where are my people?" I yelled at the phone.

Like magic, the pedestrian door to Reapers opened and in marched Abuelita, Angelito, Ana, Eric, and even TJ carrying bags.

"God, that was freaky," I said out loud. "A text would have sufficed."

"Do you normally talk to yourself?" Ana asked as I jogged towards her.

"Only when creepy things happen to me," I answered, hugging her tight.

"In that case you will never stop talking to yourself," Ana teased.

Ana was one of the coolest people I knew. She was the only human friend I had that didn't work for the Underground. She was only five feet four inches, but like Shorty, she was pure dynamite. Recently married, Ana was full of joy and smiles lately.

"Let me take a look at you," Abuelita said pulling me closer.

Abuelita was my surrogate mother in Texas. Taller than me and a beautiful full-figured woman and a witch, she owned the best Tex-Mex restaurant in town, which served as the hub for the supernatural community.

"I'm fine," I told her, rolling my eyes.

"Fine? Fine?" Abuelita scolded at me. "You have bags under your eyes, your skin looks pale, and your hair is a hot mess."

"Grandma, she looks like that all the time," Angelito informed her.

"Thanks," I told him as Eric and TJ giggled next to him.

"You are the only good-looking girl I know that goes out of her way to look like a hot mess," Angelito added. "How do you do it?"

The fact that I was enjoying listening to Angelito tease me was proof it was a horrible day. He was barely in his twenties and Abuelita's only grandson. A little over six feet, Angelito knew he looked good and enjoyed all the perks it gave him with the ladies.

"Seriously, how are you holding up?" Eric asked, acting like the adult in the group.

"I've had better days," I answered, trying to smile.

"Glad you are okay," TJ said softly.

TJ was one of the sweetest guys I had ever met. Handsome with brown hair, breathtaking hazel eyes, and tall, the boy was almost perfect. Minus the part where he lied to me. He failed to mention he was a shifter. For some awful reason, I had this strange obsession for tall boys with issues.

"I called and texted everyone, so where were you guys?" I asked instead.

"Calming the town," Abuelita answered.

"What?" I asked, and everyone shrugged.

"Let's eat first and then we will explain," said Abuelita. "Constantine has been waiting for food and is probably outraged because of that. Everyone, upstairs."

The troops rushed past Abuelita giving me side hugs.

"You didn't have to deliver the food, you know," I told Abuelita as she watched everyone marching up the stairs.

"Do you think I trust strangers with your food during these times?" Abuelita turned to face me. "If it is a war they want, it is a war they will get. Nobody messes with our family. They will pay dearly for what they have done, trust me."

Abuelita kissed my cheek and marched up the stairs. Between Constantine and Abuelita, whoever was behind this would burn. I marched back to the gym area and sat on the bench.

"Boss Lady, the fur man is asking everyone to come to dinner," Shorty told me rushing out of the apartment.

The Triplets wandered around him and headed up the stairs. Shorty made his way towards me with his hands in his pocket.

"I'll be right there," I said.

"You are not alone anymore, Isis." Shorty stood in front of me. "You don't have to carry this cross by yourself. We are here to help."

"I could get everyone killed." I didn't bother moving.

"In three days, we are all going to die anyway." Shorty gave me a bitter laugh. "So, let's find out who started this war and kick their teeth in before we go out."

"You have been hanging out with Constantine too much," I replied.

"No." Shorty kneeled in front of me. "I have a lot to fight for, Boss Lady. Nobody is taking this from me without a fight. Time to eat. We can't be missing meals here."

Shorty gave me a fist bump before skipping up the stairs. I took a deep breath and rubbed my eyes with my hands. I had too many raw emotions running through my veins. There was no way I could face everyone without freaking out. I couldn't go for a run to clear my head, but I needed something to do.

Push-ups.

My drill sergeant's solution to everything was push-ups. Two minutes. That was all I needed.

I took off my watch and set the timer. Like the physical fitness test I took in the military, I got in position. When the countdown hit zero, I pushed as hard and fast as I could. Two minutes were not long, except when you were forcing your body to the limits. All thoughts cleared, and all I could feel was the weight of my body, the air in my lungs, and the countdown in my head.

"Thirty, thirty-one, thirty-two..."

My arms were starting to burn as I forced myself to keep going. Sweat drops hit the mat as I focused on a spot in front of me to keep my form straight. Thirty more seconds.

The smell of Mexican food filled the air as soon as I entered the Loft. Bob handed me a plate as I walked to the kitchen area. Rice, beans, fried plantains, and avocados were piled high on my plate.

"Thank you," I told him as he handed me a glass of Horchata.

"Good luck finding a seat," replied Bob.

Our loft was definitely not designed to have this many people in it all at once. The Triplets and Ninth had confiscated the dining table. Eugene, Abuelita, Angelito, and Eric had the couch. I had no idea how they all managed to fit on it. TJ was reclining on Bartholomew's chair. Katrina paced in front of the monitors, while Constantine took his Sphinx pose on the table in front of her. Ana signaled for me to join her on the floor by the glass wall.

"I keep spending a lot of time in this corner lately," I told her.

"It's the only safe place in this room," she replied, holding my Horchata as I dropped to the floor.

"Have I missed anything?" I asked Ana after making myself comfortable.

"Not yet. Constantine has been ordering people to eat first." Ana took a bite of her taco.

"Who are we missing?" Constantine asked.

"Junior," Bob replied. "But here he comes."

Junior busted through the door. "I'm in."

"Yes, you are. Thank you for joining us," Constantine said, tilting his head as he stared at Junior.

"Not what I meant," Junior clarified. "I'm not leaving."

"I didn't realize leaving was an option," Constantine told him.

"They took my sisters." Junior leaned against the kitchen counter.

"Now we are talking." Constantine stood up on the table. "Continue."

"I got a message saying if I wanted to see them again, I had to leave Famine." Junior swallowed hard. "I'm not leaving. They want the Boss to snap. I won't give them the satisfaction. If we can't save my sisters, then I will meet then in heaven or hell. This is my family, too."

Junior looked at me and winked. Bob handed him a plate of food and a glass of Horchata. I patted the space next to me and Junior joined us on the floor.

"We will find them, Junior," Constantine told him. "Now, any other weird calls?"

"Everyone in Haven has been receiving messages all day," Abuelita announced. "They were warned that the horsemen are planning to destroy the earth. If they join them, they will be spared and be part of a new world order."

"Are you serious?" I asked with my fork hovering midair.

"For a small fee of ten thousand dollars per head, of course," Angelito supplied the last detail.

"Now that makes more sense," said Constantine.

"Isis, I think we found who would make more money than War from the apocalypse," Eugene told me from the couch.

"The offer was only made to the supernatural community and very selective rich humans," Ana added. "People are scared and confused. They have heard of the attacks."

"I don't blame them." Constantine took charge again. "What else do we know?"

"All my troops in the states are on lockdown," Katrina told him. "I can't get anyone to help us."

"Communications to the lab are out," Eugene said softly. "We have no way of knowing how severe the damage is or if anyone was hurt."

"My workers are safe, but oxygen will only last a few days," Junior informed us.

"Death is still not able to reach any of the interns that were taken." Constantine sat back down. "That means they could only be in two places."

"Two?" Junior asked with a mouth full of rice.

"Purgatory or hell," Constantine answered. "Heaven is out of the question. Those angels would spear any intruder on site."

"Can we get some angels on our team?" Shorty asked.

"We wish," I answered. "Gabriel has made it very clear on multiple occasions that they will not take sides."

"That is true. But if Jake decides to attack, the Almighty will unleash his forces on them," Constantine explained. "That battlefield will destroy whatever is left of earth."

"Humanity has been waiting for the apocalypse for the last two thousand years. Why now?" I asked the group. "Who would be crazy enough to push the horsemen?"

"Demons are at the top of my list," Katrina stated.

"You can add some vampires in there," Abuelita said. "They have always been pretty mad they can't roam the earth freely."

"Shifters have been pretty pissed too," TJ finally said.

"Don't forget all the witches the Order has oppressed," Angelito added his two cents.

"Basically, everyone is a potential threat," I summed it up. "Great."

"Death and her Interns have been policing the supernatural world for centuries, so it was only a matter of time," Constantine told us, licking his paws.

"But why now?" I pushed the issue.

"Because it is the first time in centuries the horsemen are getting along." Katrina leaned against the monitors.

"You call their constant bickering and fighting getting along?" I asked her as Eugene and Junior both nodded in agreement.

"I call this getting along." Katrina pointed at the room. "I'm the oldest Intern here. This has never happened in my lifetime, or the lifetime of many of my peers. We are a threat to any major power in the world."

"Katrina is right about that," Constantine said, analyzing the room.

"Not the answer I was hoping for, but fine." I gave up searching for motives. "Let's focus on what we do know and can do. We need to check purgatory and hell."

"Are you serious?" Junior choked on his food. "How can we do either one of those things?"

"Unfortunately, Isis has experience visiting both," Bob answered.

"And I thought my real family was dysfunctional." Junior took a gulp of his Horchata and leaned his head against the glass wall.

"Isis is right, and we need to inspect both places." Constantine looked at the computer monitor. "But we can't do either one of those things until we figure out how they are tracking us. I'm sure that was one of the main reasons they took Bartholomew, to stop us from searching it out, not just because he is Death's ward."

"Is anyone really good with computers?" Shorty asked as we all looked around the room.

"Would you mind if I try?" The silent Ninth rose from his seat. "I might not be as fast as our boy-wonder, but I can navigate my way through cyber space."

"Ninth, you're hired," Constantine told him as he pointed to the computer seat.

TJ switched places with Ninth and gave the old man a high five.

"Constantine, do you think we are bugged?" I asked after Ninth settled in front of the computer. "Bartholomew checked Reapers and the station on a daily basis."

"Not hacked, my young Isis, but we are being watched," Ninth answered instead. "To coordinate a synchronized attack across the globe, you would need resources and as much money as Constantine has. I have a theory they have been tapping the satellites to pinpoint our locations."

"Is that possible?" Ana asked in a whisper that unfortunately everyone heard.

"Oh, my dear, it is very possible," Ninth told her.

"That just sounds like it's out of a movie," she replied.

"When superpowers are concerned, movies have a way of explaining the illogical parts of the madness," Ninth continued.

"Can you confirm that and stop it?" Constantine moved closer to Ninth.

"I can but it will take me some time." Ninth started typing on the keyboard. "We could use a little help."

Ninth and Constantine both turned to face Katrina.

"What did I miss?" Eugene asked as the rest of us watched the interaction.

"I'm just as lost as you are," I told him.

"We don't have time for chasing rabbits," Ninth said. "When someone could just give us access to all the satellites."

"He is going to kill me," Katrina whined.

"He is planning to blow up the planet," Constantine chimed back. "What does he care if we use all his spy toys?"

"You do have a point," Katrina told him. "Let me call the General. This might take me a minute."

Katrina pulled her phone out and marched towards the door. Bob handed her a plate on her way out.

"No wonder nobody wants you guys getting along," Angelito informed us, chewing on his food. "You have unlimited potential."

"Unlimited potential that is now focused on one goal," Constantine told him. "Find and destroy the enemy. Until we figure out how they are watching us, nobody leaves Reapers."

I looked over at Ana.

"Don't worry, the hubby is locked down at the station," Ana told me with a smile. "At least I won't be home alone."

"TJ, do you think Roger will be okay?" Bob asked him about his strange roommate.

"Do you seriously think anyone would want to kidnap him?" TJ replied.

"Never mind," Bob answered. "Is he at least wearing pants today?"

Roger was an interesting guy who spent too much time high on pixie dust. Last time we saw him, he was rocking a pair of tube-socks and nothing else.

"No pants, but a really long shirt," TJ replied with a grin.

"Well, that's a start," I told him, shaking my head.

"Now that all those details are settled, Bob has room assignments." Constantine pointed toward Bob, who was holding a piece a paper in front of him. "Everyone, grab more food and get some rest. We are going to need our energy."

Constantine dismissed the room and slowly, everyone checked with Bob for their new bed assignment. Abuelita, Ana, Angelito, and TJ were sent to the back of the Loft. Everyone else was split between the other loft and Bob's apartment.

"You don't think Bartholomew will mind if Angelito and TJ sleep in his room?" Constantine asked me softly.

"Not at all. He likes them both," I answered. "You could have my room as well."

"You need your rest, Isis." Constantine hopped off the table and moseyed towards me. "Abuelita and Ana will have my room. I will take the couch in case anyone tries to contact us."

"I can keep Ninth Company," I said, trying to avoid heading to bed.

"You could, but tomorrow is going to be busy." Constantine placed a paw on my face. "It's been a very long day, Isis, so go to bed."

Fighting Constantine was pointless. He was right. I rubbed his head and slowly rose to my feet, handing Bob my plate on my way to my room.

"Thank you, Bob," I told him.

"Try to sleep, Isis," Bob replied.

It had been months since I had a nightmare, but I feared I would be facing some tonight. I marched into my room and didn't bother turning on the light. Instead, I dropped on my bed fully clothed and wrapped my arms around my pillow. It had been a horrible day.

Chapter Nine

My pillow felt damp when I rolled over. I had the vague sensation of dreaming but at least I didn't remember anything. If having nightmares wasn't bad enough, having to remember all the horror details once you woke up was even worse. In the past, I used to spend half of the day reliving the events in the dream. It was a never-ending cycle.

I stared at the glow-in-the-dark stars before realizing I wasn't alone. There was only one person that could be so still I didn't see her right away.

"Hi, Death," I finally told her.

"Good morning, Isis," she replied.

I rolled over again and turned on my night lamp. Death was sitting on my chair wearing an all-white Chanel suit.

"Nice suit," I told her. Normally I just admired in silence.

"I figured you would appreciate it." Death smiled and straightened the jacket's collar.

"You know I'm way over my head," I said, turning back to face the stars.

"Twenty-five hundred years ago, I was told a prophecy." Death settled back on the chair. "That I would find a young girl who would unite the horsemen and save the world."

"Are you serious?" I rolled over to glare at Death. "Let's just keep piling on the pressure now."

"Do you believe in prophecies, Isis?" Death was great at avoiding my questions today.

"I don't know." I decided to answer, unlike some people. "Nobody has ever given me one."

"I tend to place prophecies and fortune telling in the same category," Death told me. "Not very useful and full of nonsense."

"That's harsh," I replied.

"Not really." Death leaned closer to me. "The human mind is an amazing creation. What the mind believes, it will bring to reality. So, what would happen if I told the young girl she was destined to save the world? Would she do it out of free will or because I already told her she would?"

"That is too deep for five in the morning." A lot more than my poor brain could handle after a bad night's sleep.

"Obviously, you are that girl, and I have been looking over you your whole life," Death leaned back. "Why do you think I didn't tell you?"

"Hopefully, not to creep me out," I joked but Death never laughed.

"I wanted you to have free will," Death said softly.

"Then why tell me now?" Why bother at all with the revelations?

"Because regardless of what happens, you have already fulfilled the prophecy multiple times." Death smiled this time. "This one is just another drill."

"No pressure then?" I giggled to myself.

"None, my dear. I'm very proud of you." Death brushed my matted hair away from my forehead. "Trust in your friends, Isis, and follow your heart. This, too, shall pass."

"I hate that saying," I told Death, watching her stand from the chair.

"I know." Death walked towards the door. "The next days are going to be brutal, so make sure to sleep and eat."

"Do I look that rough?" I brushed my hair with my hands, but I had a giant bird's nest on my head instead of hair.

"'Rough' might be a little harsh. You look tired," Death added as she disappeared out the door.

Normally by five am, I would have been getting ready to go for a run. Everything was out of sync and I just felt wrong. The idea that we were on a countdown to the apocalypse was terrifying. I jumped out of bed and headed for my shower. There was no sense in staying in bed because I was sure we had work to do.

It took me less than twenty minutes to leave my room and enter the common area of the Loft. Constantine was still sitting on the computer table and Ninth was in front of the computer.

"Please tell me you two haven't been up all night," I told them. "I'm feeling guilty here."

"Don't be, my dear. I'm going to be out most of the day," Ninth told me, stretching in the chair. "You can take over from here. Teamwork."

"How did it go?" I asked as I stepped towards the computer area.

"Do you know how many satellites we have circling the earth?" Constantine asked after yawning. "Way too freaking many."

"Even with War's access codes, we had to hack into each satellite and reprogram it," Ninth said, rubbing his eyes. "It had been years since I had a challenge like this. It was exhilarating."

"We need to work on your definitions," I told him.

"Don't mess with genius," Constantine told me.

"Good news. Our little enemies won't be hacking those systems for a while," Ninth announced.

"Ninth, I have your café con leche," Eugene said as he came into the room.

"Why are you up this early?" I asked.

Eugene crossed the room carrying a large mug. The aroma of coffee filled the room, which made my mouth water.

"Hi, Isis." Eugene handed Ninth the mug. "I didn't know you were up or I would have brought you one, too."

"Too late now," I told Eugene, marching back to the kitchen. "I will make my own before I steal Ninth's cup."

"You would die a very painful death for trying, young one," Ninth told me holding the mug close to his body.

"I had a feeling you would kill me." I gave him a sideways glance and started the coffee maker. Bob always left water and coffee in the machine the night before so it was ready to go the next day.

"Thank you, Rookie," Ninth said before taking a sip. "Maybe I should call you Eugene?"

"No, sir," Eugene shook his head. "I will be 'Rookie' until I earn my next rank."

Ninth tapped Eugene in the arm. "I think my mission is done here for now, unless you still need me, Constantine?"

"Get some rest, Ninth. I think it's time for us to get to work." Constantine saluted the old Intern.

"Are you going to be able to sleep after drinking all that?" I asked Ninth as he shuffled in front of me.

"Dear, caffeine doesn't affect us," Ninth reminded me, since no poison or toxin on earth could harm any of Pestilence's Interns. "I just love the taste."

"Sweet dreams, Ninth," I told him.

"You can have my bed, sir," Eugene told him. "I changed the sheets already."

"You think of everything, Rookie," Ninth told him as he exited out the door.

"That was so sweet of you," I told Eugene, pouring the elixir of life into my cup.

"Ninth is brilliant and has been training me," Eugene confessed. "I really admire him, and he is the only one I have left." Eugene's eyes turned misty, and I wasn't ready for any more emotional breakdowns.

"Coffee?" I handed him my mug.

"Thank you," Eugene replied and took the cup.

"Constantine, are we allowed to go outside now?" I looked back at the computer area.

"Yes, but nobody roams without a battle buddy," Constantine answered.

"What's a battle buddy?" Eugene asked.

"We are going straight Army for this one," I told Eugene. "It means nobody goes out alone. At least two people will be together at all times."

"This is war and I'm not losing anyone else this week." Constantine made his way towards us. "What do you have in mind?"

"Let's start crossing places off our lists," I told him, pouring some coffee in another mug for him. "I think we need to check purgatory."

"I'm not Catholic but that sounds awful," Eugene said, raising his hand.

"We can't technically go into purgatory," I clarified. "We need a powerful witch to open a portal there, and my Godmother won't make it here fast enough. We are going to check with those who can enter."

"Who exactly can enter purgatory?" Eugene asked, holding his mug very tightly.

"The dead," Constantine replied, licking his coffee. "Both Catholic Churches are closed at this time."

"Yes, but Sacred Heart's cemetery is open," I told him.

"Eugene, my mad scientist, looks like you are going on a field trip," Constantine announced. "Each of you take a phone from the box by the computer. They are encrypted and Ninth finished programming them all. I'm not taking any chances."

"Will do," I replied.

"Isis, I know how you feel about shooting humans but don't let them kill you," Constantine said sternly.

"Don't worry about that," Eugene jumped in. "I have no issues shooting anyone. I've got her back."

"I'm not sure how safe I feel now," I told them as I made my way to the computer area. "Eugene, what color you want?"

Constantine had a collection of assorted colors for his newly-issued phones. I didn't think the brand mattered since they were all programmed the same.

"Can I have dark-blue since we are in Cowboy country?" Eugene replied.

"Since when are you a Dallas Cowboys fan?" I didn't know Eugene watched football.

"After spending so much time in Texas, it's hard to avoid," Eugene replied.

Sports fans were a committed group. They would follow their team for years even if they never won. I threw him a phone that he caught with one hand. Midnight-blue was my color, but not for the same reason. I picked a red one instead. Hopefully, I wouldn't lose it.

"Okay, Constantine, any last-minute orders?" I asked.

"Don't get shot," Constantine replied.

"We'll do our best," I told him. "By the way, what car should we take?"

I forgot that I was on foot since Ladybug had been blown to pieces.

"Take the Deathmobile," Constantine answered. "They want the horsemen to ride, so let's give them what they want."

"Is Death going to be okay with us taking the car?" Eugene asked, glancing over his shoulder towards the door.

"We are at war," Constantine answered. "Trust me, Death understands."

I saluted Constantine and placed my mug in the sink. Eugene and I marched out of the Loft and headed towards Death's Mustang. If the yellowish-green car didn't make a statement, very few things would. We were pretty sure every supernatural citizen in Texarkana knew the car belonged to Death. We were definitely at war, and only one side was going to be victorious.

Chapter Ten

Sacred Heart Church owned two cemeteries, one on Texas Boulevard and one attached to their current church. We were heading to the one next to the church on Elizabeth Street. The streets were deserted this early in the morning. The few drivers that passed us were probably heading to the Army depot for the six-thirty start time.

Sunrise would not be happening for at least another thirty minutes. I parked as close to the cemetery as possible to avoid drawing too much attention from early risers in the neighborhood. Most of my weapons were in the back seat, so I reached back to grab a machete and my scythe, securing both to my cargo pants. Texas heat was in full swing this time of the year, and even this early in the morning, it was in the seventies. I kept my jacket on since it provided protection for both bullets and spells. A custom-made piece for Death's Interns.

"Ready?" I asked Eugene as I handed him a 9mm and tucked another in my holster.

"We are going to a cemetery before the sun is out and you are asking me if I'm ready." Eugene took the gun and slipped it into the inside pocket of his jacket.

"Yeah," I replied.

"Nobody is ready for this, but let's go." Eugene exited the Deathmobile looking a bit like a gangster. All he was missing was a fedora and the look would be perfect.

We entered the cemetery and a cold fog spread around our feet. It didn't matter the time of the day; the weird fog was present anytime Father George roamed the grounds. We searched the cemetery for him. Father George was in his late sixties—at least that was how old he was when he died. He was the resident guardian of this place and had the best white hair I'd ever seen.

"Isis, is he alive?" Eugene stopped moving as Father George walked through a headstone towards us. "I hope not, but how can I see him?"

"You are standing very close to me and my powers are helping you," I replied softly. "Also, he could be allowing you to see him."

"Lucky me," Eugene told me, hiding behind me.

"Good morning, Father," I said, shaking hands with the friendly priest.

"This must be important for such an early house call," Father George replied.

"Unfortunately, it is," I agreed. "Father, this is Eugene, Pestilence's Intern."

"Good morning, young man," Father George told Eugene, and then he tried to shake hands with him, but his hands went right through Eugene's. "I always forget that each Intern has a different gift."

Father George gave Eugene a small bow instead. Eugene mimicked the gesture.

"Nice to meet you," Eugene said in a soft voice.

"How can I help you?" Father George led us into the cemetery.

"Have you heard of the attacks against the horsemen?" I asked, keeping pace with him.

"Yes, many faithful have come to pay their respects to their departed." Father George pointed at the graves. "Fear and anxiety are running wild."

"They have taken my people," I told him. "Death can't find them. We need to know if anyone has entered purgatory."

"Purgatory is secure." Father George stopped and looked around. "Do you hear that?"

I stopped moving and focused on listening. The wind had stopped blowing and nothing moved, but I could hear scraping sounds all around us.

"What is that?" Eugene asked turning in circles. "Holy cow!"

"What?" I screamed, but it was too late.

Corpses were rising from their graves. Hands and heads were pulling themselves out and hissing at us.

"Holy Jesus Christ, what is going on here?" I asked, grabbing my gun.

"There is a necromancer in our midst," Father George explained.

"I understand why Death hates necromancers," I told them. "There is something totally unholy about this."

"Isis, they are everywhere." Eugene moved closer to me.

"Thank you, Captain Obvious." I took several shots at the corpses and nothing happened. "Of course bullets are not going to hurt them when they are already dead."

"Wait." Eugene held me back with his left hand. With his right hand, he made a green ball of fire which expanded to the size of a bowling ball.

"When did you learn to do that?" I asked but Eugene didn't reply.

He launched the ball at three corpses heading our way. The fire hit the closest one straight in the chest and spread over his body. The flames ate his bones, and when it was done only his clothing remained, which dropped to the ground with a whoosh.

"WOW!" I shouted.

"Flesh-eating bacteria, or in this case bones," Eugene explained.

"That was impressive. We need more." I pointed at the corpses moving slowly towards us.

"I c-can't," stuttered Eugene.

"WHAT?" Was he serious?

"I can only do one. I'm still in training," Eugene said a little shyly.

"Are you freaking kidding me?" I shouted at him. "You have one trick and you used it on the first corpse you saw. Talk about a one-trick pony! Why didn't you use it on the necromancer?"

"It was a gut reaction," Eugene told me, shuffling his feet.

"Here." I handed him the machete. "Looks like we are doing this the old-fashioned way."

I pulled out my scythe, and with a click of the secret button it expanded. With the fully extended scythe, I made quick circles in front of us. The first set of corpses charged us, and I split them in half. I felt horrible, since those were the bones of a pure soul. I just didn't have enough time to worry about it. During the next five minutes, Eugene and I chopped and cut at everything that moved our way. Sweat dripped down my body as we stood shoulder-to-shoulder.

"I think that was the last one," Eugene announced before the scraping noise started again.

"Eugene, we are in a cemetery," I reminded him. "I'm sure the necromancer has an unlimited supply of bodies to wake up."

Hands were climbing out of the ground again and blocking our path to the Deathmobile.

"We really could use your gift," I told him. "All I can do is talk to the dead. Wait, I can talk to the dead."

"Are you planning to talk to this group? They don't look very responsive," Eugene told me.

"Sorry, no," I said quickly. "I can only talk to the souls and there are no souls inside them. They are just a pile of bones. Cover me."

I handed Eugene my scythe and closed my eyes.

"Isis, this thing is a lot harder to use than it looks," Eugene mumbled next to me.

"Shh, let me focus," I said. "I have never done this before."

"Ahh!"

I opened my eyes and watched Eugene scream at the corpse before charging at it. We needed to work on his war cry. I closed my eyes again and expanded my awareness. Listen to me. I need your help. If anyone can hear me, come to me.

I opened my eyes in time to charge at a corpse choking Eugene from the back. I gave the poor lady a round house to the head, making her skull fly off in the distance.

"Disgusting," I said as I yanked Eugene back. "I'll take that." I held out my hand.

"Any luck?" Eugene asked, handing me my scythe. I chopped three more corpses and waited as the next round approached us.

"We will see," I told him.

"We are going to die!" screamed Eugene from behind me.

"What now?" I looked over my shoulder.

"More zombies coming, and these have faces and flesh." Eugene pointed at the ghosts heading our way.

"Nope, those are with us." I ran over to the group but Father George stopped me.

"Isis, do you know those souls are condemned? They are violent and trapped here for their crimes," Father George explained.

"Father, right now we need a few violent souls or we are going to be joining them," I said moving past him.

"You called," the leader of the ghosts told me, a tall man wearing an old sixties suit.

"Why are you stuck in this place?" I asked.

"We need to make atonement for our past lives," the man replied. "Can you give us that?"

"No," I said honestly. "I do not have the power to forgive your sins, but are you willing to do one good deed?"

"Isis, they are coming," Eugene whispered behind me.

The ghost turned to face his comrade. Eugene and I turned in the opposite direction and attacked the new group of corpses charging us.

"Eugene, we need to find the necromancer or we will never get out of here," I told him, slicing my scythe over his head.

"I can't see anything with this weird fog and all the bodies," Eugene admitted.

"I can," Father George told us.

"Can you see the necromancer Father?" I asked, dodging an incoming corpse.

"I'll find him." Father George disappeared.

"Isis, watch out!" Eugene's warning came too late as a corpse hurled me ten feet in the air.

I landed hard on top of a headstone. Too bad my gear did not provide any protection against blunt impact. Three more corpses were on me and I had lost my scythe in the fall.

"God help me," I mumbled.

"He is not here yet. Just us," a female ghost said from behind one of the corpses.

She decapitated the first one, while her friends pulled apart the other two. I took a deep breath and the ghost extended her hand towards me.

"Thank you," I told her.

"Thank you for letting us help." She turned to attack the next batch.

I ran back to Eugene, jumping over broken bones on my way. Eugene was following Father George at a weird angle.

"Did you find him?" I asked them.

"Three o'clock by the statue of the angel," Father George replied.

"Isis, I can't see anything," Eugene told me.

"Neither can I but you better shoot it," I replied.

"What?" Eugene whined. "You are a better marksman than me."

"Probably, but somebody has to cover the other against those corpses and I'm a much better fighter." I knocked two more corpses away, then charged forward with my scythe in front of me.

"Yes, you are," Eugene conceded. "Father, guide my aim. Isis, ready?"

"Let's get this over with," I told him, blocking more of our dead enemies.

Eugene pulled his gun out and took aim. Nothing happened the first three pulls of the trigger, but with Father George's further instruction, finally shot number eight did the trick.

"Bingo," Father said. "Oh my Lord, forgive me." Father George did the sign of the cross with his hand, and the dead collapsed in heaps around us.

"I'm a man of God and should never rejoice for the suffering of others," Father informed us.

"Don't worry Father, we will rejoice for you," I told him as I gave Eugene a high-five. "Did you kill him?"

"No, but he did wound him," Father George explained.

"See, Father. Nobody died," I said. "Unless you count all the dead ones in pieces outside their graves."

The cemetery looked like a scene from a haunted house. Bones were scattered everywhere.

"What are we going to do about this?" Eugene asked me.

"I have no idea." Crime scene cleanup was not my specialty.

"We will do it," the first male ghost told us. "We will lay them back to rest."

His companions were already busy picking up body parts. Through the fog, Death appeared, and she was still wearing the fabulous white suit.

"You have been granted access to go home," Death told the ghosts, who stopped working.

"We can't," said the female that saved me.

"Why not?" I asked her. "Your sins have been forgiven. Don't you want to move on?"

"Yes, of course we do, but the gates will be unsecured," she answered.

"Why do you care?" Eugene asked.

"If the world ends, many of our family and friends will be condemned to hell. They need time to repent," the first ghost told us. "We can wait a few more days."

"I will be back when you are ready," Death told them, then she turned to face us. "I recommend you two hurry."

"Thank you," I told the ghost. "Father, send word if anything happens."

"I will and good luck," Father George said as he faced the ghosts. "We have a lot to clean up, so let's go."

"Eugene, that's our cue." I turned to find Eugene leaning against a headstone. "What's wrong?"

"That blast took a lot out of me, and the battle didn't help." Eugene wasn't able to stand up straight.

"We need to work on your powers," I told him, helping him get steady on his feet.

"How does the Army handle this?" Eugene asked. "How do soldiers do this much stuff before nine am? This lifestyle would kill people."

"You did well, my friend, but you need a nap now." I draped Eugene's arm over my shoulder and helped him tread towards the Deathmobile.

Eugene was barely able to keep his eyes open once secured in the car. He looked so innocent it was hard to believe the boy knew how to make flesh-eating firebombs. It was going to be a day full of surprises for sure.

Chapter Eleven

Eugene was rambling as he fought to stay awake. The conversation made absolutely no sense. I wasn't sure if he was singing or reciting poetry to me. His rambling ranged from unicorns not being extinct but prisoners of Pestilence, to the proper way to boil water. I had no idea there was an incorrect way to boil water, but according to Eugene's dissertation, I was failing miserably.

I parked the Deathmobile in its designated space, hopping out and rushing to the other side to help Eugene get out. He was in a worse state than a brand-new drunk private. If Eugene started puking, I was going to slap him.

I pulled him out of the Deathmobile and managed not to drop him.

"Isis, have I told you how pretty you are?" Eugene said, playing with my hair.

"Not today, Eugene," I said, going along with the madness.

"You are." He giggled.

God, please don't let him puke on me.

"You have the cutest little dimples that only show up when you are mad." Eugene tried to poke my cheeks but missed, his finger landing in my eye instead.

"Let's leave the demonstrations for later. Just come on." I struggled to open the door to Bob's apartment with the weight of Eugene.

Fortunately for me, Bob never locked his front door. The first room in the apartment was a living room. I maneuvered Eugene to a couch and gently dropped him. Bob had a blanket over the top, so I covered Eugene with it.

"Get some rest, my little mad scientist," I told him after pulling off his shoes.

"Isis, I love you," Eugene shouted.

"I love you, too, Eugene. Now sleep." I left the apartment and closed the door behind me.

Eugene was going to be out of commission for at least a few hours. I ran up the stairs and to the Loft. Constantine was sitting on the kitchen counter next to Bob and Katrina.

"You look like hell," Katrina told me.

"I was told this is my permanent look," I replied, stepping over to the fridge.

"One hour. You were only gone one hour. What happened?" Constantine asked.

"You are not going to like it. They have a necromancer," I said as calmly as possible, pulling out one of Eric's healing shakes.

"Damn the devil to hell, are you kidding me?" growled Constantine.

"I wish," I answered. "And I completely understand why necromancers are on Death's hit list. What they do to those poor corpses is not natural."

"They raised the dead?" Bob was at the edge of the counter.

"I'm pretty sure who ever it was raised the entire cemetery." I took a seat on top of the kitchen counter.

"You are out for one hour and have a battle with an army of zombies without me," Katrina pouted. "How is that fair?"

"Trust me, you can battle the undead anytime," I told her. "You can have that group."

"Where is Eugene? Katrina asked.

"Napping on Bob's couch," I explained. "He used a lot more energy than he expected."

"Please tell me you found anything in purgatory?" Constantine asked.

"I wish, but no," I answered a little less cynically. "The gates are secure, and nobody will be getting in with the souls that are guarding it. I just don't know if the necromancer was waiting for us or trying to get in?"

"Waiting," Katrina and Constantine said at the same time.

"They are probably watching both churches," Katrina explained. "It's only logical we go to inspect both purgatory and hell."

"Does that mean we go to hell next?" I asked, biting my lips. I really did not like hell and would avoid the place at all costs if I could.

"That is the next logical place to go," Constantine answered. "Katrina, you know what you must do."

"Why can't Isis make the call?" Katrina whined.

"Hey, I just battled a cemetery full of zombies," I told her. "You can take one for the team and call Jake."

"We do need to spread out the taskers, and Isis has other stuff to do," Constantine added.

"I do?" I turned to face him.

"Yes, we need to find out who the necromancer is," Constantine clarified. "You and Bob will be visiting the dark wizard."

"Not that guy again. He hates us." It was my turn to whine. "I take it back; I'll call the devil."

"Ha, ha," said Katrina. "Whose turn is it to take one for the team?"

I stuck out my tongue at her, and Constantine rolled his eyes.

"Boss, Isis is right," Bob jumped in to help me. "He does hate us."

"Maybe if you two stopped breaking down his door he might be nicer," Constantine chastised us.

"It was only once," I argued.

"It cost me fifteen-hundred dollars to repair that door," Constantine continued.

"Damn, what kind of door did you buy him?" Katrina asked in disbelief.

"Nothing worth fifteen-hundred dollars if you ask me," Constantine told her. "No more damage to private property. I'm not in the mood to be replacing more stuff this week. At the rate we are going, I'm considering leasing our next vehicles."

"With our reputation, do you think anyone would rent them to you?" I teased.

"That could be a problem." Constantine wiped his face with his paw.

Shorty ran in the door followed by Junior, whose hair was all over the place, very unlike the perfect style he normally sported.

"Fur man, everyone is accounted for," Shorty reported. "The station is still on lockdown but our people are ready to move in as soon as it opens."

"The lockdown procedure is for twenty-four hours, so we still have a few more," Constantine told him. "That will give us just enough time to figure out how to secure it before it opens again."

"Do you have any ideas?" I asked him, but he shook his head.

"That's the problem. We don't need anyone to take over the gate to hell," Constantine said.

"I thought it was a one-way elevator?" Katrina asked.

"Yes, but after the last little incident, we installed an override on this side to stop the doors from opening," Constantine explained. "If they take control of the station, the doors would be open for anyone."

"How deadly does it have to be?" Junior asked from the door.

"As lethal as possible. Something that would hold for at least for the next three days would be perfect," Constantine replied. "We don't need any authorized personnel getting past the entrance steps."

"I think I might be able to help," Junior said, rubbing his hair. "It might require me to contact the Boss, but we should be able to come up with something. Once ready, I will need to get to the station to test it."

"I can make that happen," Shorty volunteered.

"Junior, do your magic," Constantine gave him his blessing. "Shorty, stay with him. Get the Triplets to start gathering our forces. We need everyone ready for battle."

"YES, BOSS!" Shorty shouted before he saluted Constantine and ran out the front door. Junior followed quickly behind, but Katrina stared at the door for a few more seconds.

"Is it safe to leave Junior with Shorty?" she asked Constantine. "Junior might pick up some horrible habits from him."

"As long as they are survival skills, I'll take them," Constantine replied. "In the meantime, stopped stalling. GO. CALL. JAKE."

"FINE," Katrina yelled back.

Katrina marched out the door and headed across to her loft.

Constantine shook his head before turning to glare at me. "What are you two waiting for?" he barked.

"I need a shower before visiting our favorite wizard." I hopped off the counter. "I'm covered in dirt, grass, and dead bones. I'm sure I would offend him even more if I walked in his house like this."

"You actually do have a point," Constantine agreed.

"Bob, give me twenty minutes," I told him.

"Not a problem. I'll go get my gear on," Bob replied. "I'll meet you at the Camaro. I'm driving."

"You have no faith in my driving skills?" I placed my hands on my hip and tried to look offended.

"I saw you carrying Eugene in." Bob motioned towards the cars.

"That was not my fault." I waved my hands quickly in front of me. "Did you know Eugene does magic? Not a lot, but he still can do a wicked trick."

"Is he getting better?" Constantine asked.

"You knew?" Both Bob and Constantine nodded. Was I the only one who didn't know? "He made this bad-ass green fireball that ate right through flesh and bones."

"Now that is useful." Constantine stood on the counter.

"Don't get too excited. He can only do one and then comatose state hits him," I corrected him.

Constantine dropped down and said, "Pestilence needs to get better at distributing her gifts. That could have been an awesome weapon."

"That's what I thought," I said.

"Now you are stalling," Constantine told me, tapping his claws on the counter.

"Right, twenty minutes," I rushed to my room.

As much as I didn't enjoy talking to angry wizards, if this would help find that crazy necromancer, I was all in. Anyone who could control corpses and used them as weapons was on my list of least-favorite people. I barely had time to acknowledge the music playing in my room. The great thing about busy was there was very little time to think or mope around.

Chapter Twelve

The dark wizard lived in a pristine brick house with immaculate landscaping in Red Lick right next to the middle school. The idea of having a practitioner of the dark arts next to a school seemed dangerous. At the same time, it wasn't like he was a deranged criminal on the loose. Being perfectly honest, of all the citizens in Haven, we had never had a report against him, or any issues in this area for that matter.

Bob parked the Camaro across the street from his house. Since it was the middle of summer, we didn't have to worry about schoolteachers being terrorized by our gear. Bob and I both had on black combat fatigues. I had my machete strapped to my leg and my M16 across my chest. After my little morning ambush, overkill was my new motto.

We marched across the grass to the side door of the house. Bob and I stared at each other before I gave in and knocked on the door.

"Why not?" I told him.

It took a few minutes before the door opened. David, the dark wizard, was standing in the center of the door wearing an apron with little spoons. He had a large bowl with a spatula under his right arm.

"I was wondering if you were actually going to wait or just bust down my door," said David.

"Not this time," I replied. "Constantine gave us strict orders to avoid any damage to your property."

Bob and I waited politely outside the house.

"It's about time someone in your organization starts practicing manners." David moved to the side and waved us in. "I'm sure you are not here for my cinnamon rolls, so what can I do for you?"

"You are baking cinnamon rolls from scratch?" Bob decided that was a more important question than our actual mission.

"Only way to make them." David showed him a freshly-baked batch on top of the oven. "I'm finishing the glaze and they are going to be heavenly."

"What kind of glaze?" Bob continued his culinary inquisition. "I smell orange."

"You are good," David replied. "I have a vanilla-orange glaze that is divine."

I cleared my throat before the two of them started exchanging recipes.

"Sorry to interrupt, but we are still on a tight schedule." I tapped my watch. "You know, with the end of times taking place in three days, or maybe more like two and three quarters."

"Sorry about that." Bob moved next to me.

"Interesting. So, the rumors are true?" David put the bowl on the counter and leaned back. "What do you want?"

"We have a necromancer loose in Texarkana and we need a name," I told him, not wasting any more time.

"We have a lot of things loose in Texarkana lately, but I haven't heard of a necromancer." David looked around the room, playing with his dark hair.

For a dangerous, dark wizard, David was very handsome. His deep-blue eyes made a gorgeous contrast with his hair.

"Could you help us out?" Bob asked him.

"It would be my pleasure," David replied, pushing away from the counter.

"Why are you being so helpful?" I put my hands on my hips before continuing. "You don't like us at all."

"True, you are not my favorite group of people," David admitted, searching one of his cabinets. "But in the grand scheme of things, I prefer you guys over the fools that came over the other day."

"Do you know who they were?" I asked.

"Some two-timing wizards promising world changing events and the destruction of the Order. Blah, blah, blah." David made little circles with his hands. "All the stuff I heard before and nothing impressive. To be frank, the Order doesn't bother me in my little piece of Texas. Since you made us Haven, nobody bothers me at all."

Bob and I looked at each other. Last time we saw David, he had no clue who we were. Today, he was very well informed on who was running Haven. We were moving up on his chart.

"Sounds like we are a better alternative to your lifestyle," I told him, glancing at his cinnamon rolls.

"I'm too old and too independent to be bowing down to hacks who want to be an emperor." David came back with a business card. "I'd prefer the Order and the Horsemen in charge as long as I keep my freedom. I'll make some calls and let you know what I find out. Goodbye."

"Don't you need our number?" I asked David as he ushered us out the door.

"Got it right here." David flipped the card around. "Reapers Inc., and it came with the check to fix my door."

"Of course, it did," I said, standing outside his house. "Please don't take too long."

"Yes, I heard you've got less than three days." David slammed the door in our face.

"He really doesn't like us," I told Bob.

"No, he doesn't, but at least we didn't break the door down." Bob admired the beautiful new door.

"I don't think we were going to knock that baby down." I ran my hand over the door.

"Only if we shoot it first," said Bob.

"It is a fifteen-hundred-dollar door, so I'm pretty sure it's bullet-proof." I gave the door one last look and headed towards the Camaro.

Not a bad meeting compared to most we've had lately. Too bad the Camaro was being used as a park bench when we walked back. Three tall, angry shifters were sitting on the car cleaning their claws and knives.

"Look who decided to come out of hiding." One of the shifters with blond hair spoke first, while the other two laughed.

"Get off the car," Bob told the guys as he stretched his neck.

"Or what, old man? What are you going to do?" blond mocked.

"You have thirty seconds to get off the car or you will find out." I kept moving towards the car, not taking my gaze off the little, blond boy.

"We have a message from our leader," the shifter growled as she started to change.

I ran across the grass, pulling my scythe in the process. First corpses and now shifters. I was just not in the mood to be threatened. Before blond boy could finish turning, I hit him over the head with my scythe. The boy dropped to the ground like a squashed watermelon. Bob shot the other two with tranquilizers as they tried to jump over the Camaro.

"I have a message for your boss." I leaned closer to the Shifter. "We are coming and there will be hell to pay."

The Shifter growled, and Bob shot him straight in the chest. All the hair on the Shifter fell to the ground, including his facial hair.

"Ouch," I told Bob.

"Didn't think you would mind if I used Eugene's special ammo," Bob said, pointing at the hairless guy.

"Not at all," I replied. "We are at war. All ammo is fair game."

"Good." Bob put his gun away and picked up the blond, tossing him across the grass.

"Have you been working out?" I asked Bob surveying the guy he just moved more than ten feet away.

"Don't underestimate the old man here. You are not the only one that stays in shape in this group." Bob flexed his arms and his bicep muscles were showing underneath his shirt.

"Look at you." I gave him a high five as he walked past me.

Bob didn't bother picking up the other two. Instead, he dragged them off the Camaro and left them on the street.

"Is that safe?" I asked, climbing inside the Camaro.

"If they have people following us around, I'm sure one of their friends will pick them up," Bob explained. "Where to?"

"Let's drive around." I buckled my seatbelt and opened the sunroof. "It's about time people see us around town."

"Are you trying to instigate a fight?" Bob turned the Camaro on and drove away from the Dark Wizard's house.

"Not this time," I replied. "But the citizens of Haven need to know we are not hiding. Our enemies need to know we are not afraid. What kind of music does Constantine have here today?"

"Everything. I think he was blasting Imagine Dragons last week," Bob answered, opening the middle console and pulling out Constantine's A&ultima SP2000 Portable Audio Player.

Only the wealthiest cat on the planet had a thirty-five-hundred-dollar audio player to hook up to his car. I connected the slick device to the sound system in the Camaro. Everything in this car was top of the line, and the sound was flawless. I turned on the music and let the Devil Went Down to Georgia fill the car.

"Take your time, Bob," I told him. "I want everyone in town to know we are here."

Bob slowed down, turned the flashers on, and made himself comfortable. I leaned my head against the window and closed my eyes. Nobody was running us out of our town, and I was ready to bring the war to them. Bob turned the music louder and tapped his fingers along with the beat. First step in every war was psychological warfare. Today, we would play with their minds and make them question what we would do next.

Chapter Thirteen

It was mid-morning by the time Bob parked the Camaro inside Reapers. The place looked deserted. Bob and I made our way up the stairs in silence. We still looked like action heroes covered in the weapons we refused to take off.

"Isis, we are going to hell," Katrina announced as soon as I entered the room.

"You are the only person I know excited to go there," I told her. "In case you forgot, I'm Catholic. I could end up there."

"You work for Death, so the only place you are going to end up is in an inflatable tube sipping piña-colada down the river Styx," Katrina reminded me.

"You are right. I forgot," I conceded after a long pause. "But that river is in the same vicinity of hell, and it doesn't look pleasant."

"Whatever," Katrina continued. "You will hang out with the rest of the Interns waiting for Judgement Day, while I and the rest of War's Interns wait frozen. How is that fair?"

"Our horseman has a better retirement plan!" Constantine shouted from the computer station.

"He does have a point," I agreed with my guardian.

"Let's go," Katrina pulled me away. "We are meeting Jake at Abuelitas to get our passes."

"Wait." Junior came running inside the Loft. "Give me your hand."

"Junior, I'm a little old for you," Katrina teased him.

"Maybe, Grandma, but you are not leaving without being branded." Junior grabbed Katrina's right hand before she could walk away.

"You do know that the sign of the beast is branded on the right hand, right?" I asked from behind Katrina.

"We are going to see Jake, so that should be very fitting," Katrina stated.

"I'm not joining a Jake fan club," I announced as I stepped away from Junior.

"Very funny, you two," said Junior, pulling out a thin rod from his pocket. "This is going to sting but not for long."

"Why are we doing this again?" Katrina asked, watching Junior press the rod against her skin. Katrina barely flinched.

"Wow. You are tough," Junior told her with admiration. "Shorty is still crying downstairs, and that was thirty minutes ago."

"Are you branding everyone?" Bob asked.

"Only those entering the station," Junior clarified.

"Perfect. Count me out," Constantine told him from the computer area.

"I found a way to target anyone not authorized from entering," Junior said very quickly. "Ninth helped me perfect it."

"Junior, dear." Katrina inspected her hand carefully. "I don't see anything."

"You are not supposed to." Junior pulled a small flashlight from his pocket and shined it at her hand. "Only with a black light can you see the mark. We don't need everyone wondering why we all have skulls on our hands."

"Clever," Katrina complimented Junior. "What does your new defense system do?"

"Shrivels people to death," said Junior.

"That is so Famine," I told the group.

"Your turn, Isis." Junior waved me towards him.

"A skull?" I asked.

"Very death like," Junior said with a wicked grin.

"You and Bartholomew have a morbid sense of humor," I told him, thinking of the engraved jackets with skulls Bartholomew had ordered earlier this year.

"It runs in the family." Junior wiped the top of my hand with his sleeve. "Hold still now."

Before I could complain, Junior branded me with the rod. It was a searing-hot sensation that quickly changed to freezing pain. The feeling moved down my arm and all over my body. Goosebumps formed everywhere the heat and cold traveled.

"Ouch, that was different," I told him.

"How are you two so tough?" Junior asked us. "Why are all the men crying downstairs?"

"I'm sure they are exaggerating," said Bob, giving Junior his hand.

Junior quickly cleaned the area and stabbed Bob without warning. Bob didn't even flinch as he glanced at Junior, who was still holding the rod against his hand.

"How long is it supposed to take?" Bob asked.

"Sorry." Junior pulled the rod and glanced at Bob's hand. "Thank you, Bob."

"Is your faith in your gender renewed?" Katrina joked.

"I was starting to get worried," Junior admitted. "After everyone was in tears, I figured I was killing them."

"I have a feeling they were just trying to make you feel bad. They are fine," I told him, patting him on the shoulder. "We better go. No need making the devil wait."

"Be careful, you two," Constantine ordered.

"Always," Katrina replied.

"Bob, we will take the Deathmobile. You have the Camaro," I told him.

"Sounds like a plan," Bob answered. "Junior, we need to brand everyone in the Underground. We might as well get going."

Katrina and I left before Bob and Junior. Their project sounded a lot more intense than our simple trip to Abuelitas. Maybe we could get food while we were there. My stomach was starting to boycott itself now.

Jake had a way of clearing out a room. Every time he showed up at Abuelitas, the place ended up completely deserted. That was probably not a bad thing. Nobody needed special encounters with the devil in East Texas.

I parked the Deathmobile by the front door. Normally, I parked by the back near the employee entrance, but today, I wanted everyone to know I was in Haven.

I was still wearing my combat gear, which looked harsh next to Katrina's faded jeans and tank top. Her blonde hair was pulled back in a ponytail, making her look like she was in her early twenties. There were no weapons visible on her, but I knew she was packing. That girl carried more weapons than most of the Underground.

We entered the small restaurant. Only a couple of tables were located in the hole-in-the-wall establishment. The place smelled delicious. I wasn't a meat eater, but the smell of carnitas actually made me hungry. Jake wasn't hard to find. He was the only patron in the place and was sitting by the far wall near the window. Jake was rocking a Dolce & Gabbana metallic Jacquard suit that would look ridiculous on most men. On him, it was perfect, adding a flare to his golden-blond hair.

"You requested this meeting, so why do you keep me waiting?" Jake demanded, not bothering to get up when we arrived.

"Busy schedule?" I asked.

"I have a little situation in hell that I must address," Jake answered, staring at Katrina.

The two had a history together, one that made every encounter extremely awkward for me. They each had told me their version of their love story. For some strange reason, neither one addressed the elephant in the room with each other, though. They just glanced at the other one when they thought nobody was watching. We didn't have enough time at the moment to contemplate their situation, however.

"It sounds like we all have stuff going on," I told him.

"Are you telling us you are not involved in this 'end of time' scheme?" Katrina took a seat across from Jake.

"I have my own date with heaven. I don't need to speed up the timeline," Jake answered.

"Do you know who is?" I leaned across the table, trying to get his attention.

"It appears I have a few traitors in my midst." Jake eventually turned around, his stare radiating heat and hatred. I liked it better when his eyes were on Katrina instead of me. I was not ready to handle the devil's wrath.

"Coups in hell seem to be a very common thing," I said, slanting away from him. "This kind of thing happens a lot to you."

"I'm surrounded by demons and sinners, Isis." Jake took a sip of his glass. "What do you think they do all day besides plan takeovers?"

"You do have a rough crowd." I wanted to feel sorry for the devil, but that was impossible. "But can you help us?"

"Like I told wonder-woman over here"—Jake motioned to Katrina with his head—"hell is on lockdown until I find out who started all this. I can grant you access to get in, but getting out and safe passage will be for you to find."

"We can handle ourselves," Katrina told him.

"I've been remodeling the place, so can you try not blowing everything up?" Jake handed her a small business card from his pocket.

"Now, I can't make any promises about that." Katrina took the card from Jake and winked.

I was ready to gag. They were flirting. In a strange, traumatizing way those two still liked each other.

"Back to the potential apocalypse. How much time do we get in hell?" I asked, waving my hands for extra attention.

"No time limit this time," Jake answered.

"You are a bit too generous today." I looked at Katrina, who straightened in her chair.

"Yes, you are never this helpful. What's the catch?" she asked.

"Easy. I have demons making deals behind my back." Jake rolled the sleeves of his jacket up, making the motion look natural and sexy all at once. That was not fair. "I have vampires and all sorts of living things entering my domain without my permission. Having you two hanging out in hell should create all sorts of excitement. I'm looking forward to seeing who takes the bait."

"Now that's more like it," I told him. "We are bait so you can find your traitors."

"It's a fair deal, Isis," Jake said licking his lips. "You get to search for your friends, and I get to find out who has been playing king in my land. We all win. Just make it fast because I'm losing money every day my club is closed."

Jake stood up and adjusted his coat.

"I'm surprised you closed the Cave," I said.

"I will need to prepare for war if you fail at this little quest." Jake headed towards the door. "I don't need stragglers hiding at the Cave instead of picking a side. Been a pleasure, ladies." Jake bowed his head and vanished from Abuelitas as soon as the sun hit him.

"It is terrifying that he can manifest in plain sunlight," I said to Katrina.

"He is the devil, not a vampire. So, he isn't affected by sunlight like some of his creatures," she replied. "Knowing him, he probably came in through the front door."

"He did," Angelito added from the kitchen. "He was very polite and knocked before entering. We are a restaurant, too, so it's not like he needs permission to enter the establishment."

"I like it better when I believed demons could only come out at night." I played with my braid.

"How many times do I need to tell you that there is nothing simple about our job," Katrina told me, still staring at the door.

"A girl can hope." I stood from the table. "I'm grabbing lunch before we head to hell. Do you want some?"

"Why not?" Katrina answered.

I roamed around the door behind the bar that divided the kitchen from the dining room. Angelito was cleaning the bar, or at least pushing a rag back and forth. It didn't look like he had cleaned a thing. I strolled past him towards the kitchen area.

"Hi ,Abuelita." I gave her a kiss.

"I don't like it," she told me.

"You don't like what?" That statement could mean so many things.

"The fact that you are going to hell, or that you have to deal with the devil." Abuelita was stirring the beans very aggressively and spilling juice everywhere.

"If it makes you feel better, I don't like it either." I grabbed two plates, piling on the rice and beans.

"Be careful," Abuelita told me, adding a giant scoop of guacamole to my plate.

"Always," I said as I headed back to the dining area.

"One thing is for sure, Isis," Angelito said as I passed him, "you definitely have friends in low places. Really low places."

"You are not funny," I told him as he laughed at his own joke.

"I'm calling Constantine for instructions to get to hell," Katrina said as I slid her plate in front of her.

"Can't wait." I took a bite of my food.

Katrina and I had already visited hell once while searching for Ginny. One trip had been bad enough. A second was a horrible habit. But we had no choice so stressing about it would do nothing to help me in any way.

I made myself comfortable and enjoyed my meal as Katrina coordinated our next mission. If anyone could execute a crazy military expedition to the depths of hell, it was her. My assistance was not needed in that department.

Chapter Fourteen

As a master strategist in military campaigns, it did not take Katrina very long to coordinate our mission to hell. I wanted to give our trip a cool, fancy name, but there was no way of beating mission to hell. The plan was simple: get a ride to hell from the Boatman. We were using Lake Wright Patman as our body of water for our meeting point. Before leaving, we met up with Bob and Shorty by the boat ramp of the Lake. Bob delivered a few gifts for the Boatman and a few more supplies courtesy of Constantine. Bob was also going to take the Deathmobile back to Reapers. We were not taking any chances by leaving any of our vehicles unsupervised.

"Are you sure this is a good idea?" Bob asked for the third time.

"Going to hell is never a good idea," I answered, putting on the backpack he'd handed me.

Katrina was in the back of the Deathmobile changing. As cute as she looked in her summer outfit, it was not the most efficient clothing choice for hell. Was there such thing as appropriate attire for hell?

Shorty handed me a gift bag for the Boatman. The bag weighed at least fifteen pounds.

"What is in this thing?" I asked, trying to peek in through the tissue paper.

"Don't ask me," Shorty said, shaking his head. "I'm just making the delivery for the fur man. I don't ask questions about things I don't want to know the answers to. Gifts to the carrier of the underworld fall in that category."

Shorty was right. That was a lot more information than I cared to know. I moved the gift bag from one hand to the other and adjusted my holster on my leg. Between the machete attached to my leg, the three-gun holsters, the grenades around my waist, and the backpack full of holy water, I looked like a suicide-bomber. This was an extreme look for noon in East Texas.

Katrina climbed out of the Deathmobile looking almost exactly as I did. If we had spandex body armor, we could pass for stunt-doubles for the Black Widow.

"I'm ready," Katrina announced.

"Blending in is not part of the mission?" Shorty asked.

"We are going to hell. The fact that we are alive will keep us from blending in," I clarified for him.

"In that case, 'mad vigilantes' is a great look for both of you." Shorty gave us two thumbs up.

"Do you ladies need us to wait with you?" Bob asked.

"No need, boys. Our ride is here." Katrina walked towards the water where a speed boat was rushing our way.

"The Boatman will let us know when you are on your way back," Bob told me. "Be careful. The station should be opening soon. We are heading that way."

"Thanks, Bob," I said as I jogged towards the water.

Bob and Shorty saluted the Boatman, who made a smooth stop. He was a sight to be admired. A tall skeleton covered in a full-body coat with a hood. Normally, the only thing you saw of him were his hands and a bit of his face. Today, the hood was pulled back to reveal a cigar-smoking skull with glowing, yellow eyes.

"Hop in, little cousin," the Boatman told Katrina.

"How are you, DJ Bag of Bones?" Katrina had nicknamed the Boatman, and he loved it.

"Ready for war," the Boatman replied.

I hopped in the speedboat and managed to only get my boots wet. Shorty and Bob waved back from the shore. I handed the Boatman his gift bag and took a seat in the back with Katrina.

"What do we have here?" He squealed while pulling off seven layers of tissue paper. "Constantine is an angel."

The Boatman pulled an Uzi from the bag. I had to blink several times to make sure I was seeing the thing correctly.

"Your guardian angel sends you submachine guns as presents?" Katrina asked him.

"Don't be jealous," the Boatman told her, hugging his new weapon.

"I need Constantine to send me presents," Katrina told me. "Boatman, what happened to the Jesus boat?"

The first time we met the Boatman, he was riding in an old Galilee Boat full of souls. This top-of-the-line speedboat did not fit his demeanor. He pulled a CD from the bag and inserted it into a small device we couldn't see from the back. AC/DC's "Highway to Hell" raged from the sound system a second later.

"We are at war, little cousin, so there are no deliveries to the underworld," Boatman explained.

"Jake closed the doors even to the dead?" I looked at the Boatman for clarification.

"Especially to that group." The Boatman made little smoke circles with his cigar, a very impressive deed for a being with no lungs. "They didn't get to hell for being nice. You can't trust that lot."

"That is so true," Katrina agreed.

"Recommend you both hold on; it's going to be a bumpy ride." The Boatman accelerated away from the shore and headed towards the middle of the lake.

It was a pretty clear day, and we were in the middle of a dam. I looked around, trying to figure out how the Boatman was planning to get us to hell from here. He took one big puff of his cigar and let the smoke out. The small circles expanded into giant, gray clouds in front of us. The smoke covered the surface of the lake and continued to grow as the Boatman puffed out even more.

"It's a good thing he has no lungs or he would die of cancer," I told Katrina as I watched the smoke show.

"I doubt there is anything in this world that could kill DJ Bag of Bones over there." Katrina held one of the railings.

The Boatman increased the speed of the boat, making it bounce across the water. Having a large lunch had been a horrible idea, and I had a feeling I would pay for it during this ride. I leaned my head over the rail hoping not to puke on Katrina. The clear water changed to a muddy color as the day turned darker the further into the smoke we went.

The stench of sulfur and burning flesh was the first thing that hit me when I arrived in hell. The excruciating screams quickly followed. The Boatman's entrance to hell was right next to the fields of torture. Why any human would make a deal with demons was beyond me. Somebody should pass out videos of this place before any negotiations with demons. Too many gullible souls who believed themselves smarter than the beings in this land continued to sell their soul for nothing. A short span of power or fame did not measure to an eternity of suffering here.

The Boatman sped by the fields and down to the part of hell where the demons resided. It had taken me a while to comprehend that demons had a life in this place besides torturing the dead.

"Where are we heading?" I asked the Boatman as I inched closer.

"Rumor has it that humans have been seen at the strip," Boatman told me.

"'The strip,' like the Vegas Strip?" Katrina inquired, joining us by the steering wheel.

"Exactly like Vegas," the Boatman answered. "There is a replica down here, or was ours first?"

"Not surprised. Vegas is the city of sin," Katrina said softly.

"You two better act fast," the Boatman said, navigating the boat at full speed towards a cityscape of lights. "Once the demons know you are here, you're fair game."

"That shouldn't take long," I told him.

"Exactly." The Boatman made port at the far end of the strip in a desolate corner.

"Any ideas where on the strip the humans were seen?" Katrina hopped off the boat and pulled me out.

"Rumor mill said the Luxor," the Boatman replied, grinding his teeth.

"Even in hell they want to mock Death." I took a deep breath to calm myself.

"Which one is the Luxor?" Katrina asked.

"The pyramid," I replied, pulling out a water gun from my backpack.

"Of course," said Katrina getting out her own gun.

"Keep the boat running, Boatman. We won't be long," I told him. "Are you ready for a run?"

The Luxor was located on one end of the strip next to the Mandalay Bay and Excalibur. We were on the opposite end near the Stratosphere and Circus Circus.

"How fast is your mile run?" I asked Katrina as I adjusted my boots.

"How fast does it need to be?" she replied with a wicked grin.

"If the dimensions of this strip are the same as the one on Earth, we are at least four miles away from the Luxor," I told her as I pointed. "On a good day, I can do a five and a half minute mile. With all this gear, it'll probably be more like six minutes. Do we have twenty-four minutes to spare?"

"Your plan is to run full speed down the middle of the strip?" Katrina crossed her arms in front of her.

"Shooting every demon we encounter," I added.

"That's a given." Katrina just stared at me, a bit of humor twinkling in her gaze. "I thought I was the capricious one here. You continue to surprise me, Isis."

"Do you have a better plan?" I asked, stretching my legs.

"Nope." Katrina did the same. "My mission was to get us weapons and transportation. The rest we are going to wing-it."

"In that case, race you to the Luxor." I took off before Katrina had time to finish stretching.

Sneaking around in hell just seemed like a recipe for disaster. We had no idea what lurked in the dark, and the whole place was dark. If the demons could sense us, I wanted them to know we were not scared.

Too bad it didn't take Katrina that long to catch up with me. Fifty years of training had its benefits. She wasn't even breathing hard. In fact, it kind of looked like she was taking a jog around the block. I was going to have to step up my game.

"Are you done warming up?" Katrina asked, pulling her hair into a loose ponytail.

"Just waiting for you, Grandma," I answered, impressed my voice was not cracking.

"Let's go." Katrina picked up the pace and I followed suit.

There was a huge advantage between Hell's strip and Earth's: we didn't have any traffic. There were no cars anywhere to be found. The one thing they had plenty of were bike taxis. Too bad the taxi drivers were humans, or tortured souls as it were. What level of punishment was that?

With Katrina setting the pace, we made it across the strip in a little under twenty minutes. Sweat was running down my back and I had the desire to drink the holy water I was carrying. We hadn't encountered any demons on the way down. In fact, beside the tormented humans waiting around in the little bike taxis, we hadn't seen anyone.

"Shouldn't hell be a little busier?" Katrina asked me, and she wasn't even out of breath.

The idea of punching her crossed my mind. Were agility and endurance part of War's gifts? I would need to ask Constantine before I agreed to race Katrina again.

"I don't like it," I replied.

"You don't like anything about this place, so that doesn't help." Katrina was right. "Do you think Jake's lockdown has anything to do with this?"

"Do demons have houses?" I asked instead.

"No clue." Katrina shrugged. "We are here. Should we try the front door?"

"You read my mind." I held my water gun tight, and we marched straight through the front doors of the Luxor.

The front lobby had a reception desk with a lovely brunette standing behind it. I tramped straight toward her and placed my gun on the counter.

"Hi," I said cheerfully.

"Do you know where you are?" the brunette asked, inspecting Katrina and me.

"Is this not the Luxor in hell?" I asked.

"You do know you are in hell, then. In that case, how can I help you?" The brunette pulled out a small pad from a drawer.

"We need to find a few kidnappers, five of Death's Interns, and an angry thirteen-year-old. Have you seen them?"

The brunette blinked several times before answering my question. "You are not leaving here alive."

"They are here, perfect." I said, taking my gun back. "Which way?"

The brunette laughed and pointed towards the casino. "This should be interesting."

Not that many demons were in the casino area. A few groups stood around the gambling tables, and some others congregated in booths at the sides of the room. The lighting in the room was low, making it difficult to see.

"We don't have time for this." Katrina hopped on one of the empty tables and opened fire with her 9mm.

"That got their attention," I told her from the ground.

"We're looking for kidnappers. Where are you?" Katrina shouted, and the room exploded.

Demons flew at us from every table, their claws extended and jaws out as they shifted from pretty, little humans to monsters. Like Katrina, I was not in the mood to waste time. I squirted every one that rushed at me with holy water. The blessing of being friends with a priest meant containers of it were always available at Reapers. Fake human flesh peeled off the demons as the water touched it. Katrina was using her machetes, also blessed by our dear Father Francis, in hand-to-hand combat.

I dropped the empty water gun and pulled out my scythe. Two demons ended up decapitated with my first swing. For a small crowd, they were extremely persistent. A group in one of the booths rushed for a back door instead of joining the fight.

"Katrina, ten o'clock!" I yelled over the noise.

"Moving." Katrina carved her way down the table and over the heads of four demons.

Super fighting moves were definitely a gift from War. Katrina could do a somersault while shooting and still land on her feet. I was not even going to try that. I didn't have Katrina's skills or grace, but I had plenty of grenades. I pulled two from my belt, pulled the pins, and tossed them at the closest demons next to me.

"Grenades!" I yelled and took off running.

By the looks of the demons' reactions, that was not a common command in hell. In fact, one demon just stood holding it, though both grenades I chucked exploded, taking the demons, tables, and half of the ceiling with them. They weren't dead, but the collapsed roof had them pinned to the ground. I followed Katrina and the group out of the back door leading to the strip. Katrina was battling three of the kidnappers while two others dragged two men in hoods by their feet. I threw my machete at one of the villains. Since I had been practicing the stupid technique, I easily landed the throw. The guy dropped to the ground in pain, blood flowing everywhere.

By the time his friend noticed, I was mid-launch with my scythe extended. Slicing my weapon as I landed, the guy screamed right before he burst into a pile of ash.

"Katrina, these are not demons!" I shouted.

"I figured that out already." Katrina stabbed one of the guys who turned out to be a vampire.

"Duck!" I yelled, jumping over her and landing on the vampire blade first.

Ash was the only thing left after I pulled my scythe out. Katrina knocked out one of the kidnappers and dispatched the last vampire in the group.

"I see why Jake is pissed," I told Katrina as I moved to the hostages on the floor.

"He might have a point this time," Katrina said through gritted teeth.

I kneeled next to the hostages and pulled their hoods back. Jose, the South America Intern, and Will, the Australian—or more accurately the Australasia Intern—were both staring at me. Jose was bleeding from several places, including his head, lips, and leg. Will had a huge black eye but no blood.

"God, it's good to see you two," I told them, giving them a huge hug.

"I can't believe you are here," Will said with tears rolling down his cheek.

"Bartholomew said you would come," Jose mumbled, spitting blood on the ground. "Nobody believed him."

"They will now," I told them as I untied their hands. "Looks like you two put up quite a fight."

"We were not going to make it easy on them," Will said as he tried to climb to his feet but stumbled and fell back to the ground.

"It must run in your training," Katrina said from behind the guys.

"Katrina, meet Jose and Will. Jose and Will, meet Katrina. War's Intern." I made the introductions quickly and helped Katrina secure the two remaining kidnappers.

"Shifters," Katrina told me.

"Where are the rest of my friends?" I asked.

"You will have to kill me to find out," the conscious shifter growled.

"That can be arranged." Katrina shot the guy in the chest.

"Are you serious?" Jose said from behind me.

"Calm down over there," I told him. "We only knocked him out because he's coming with us. Can you guys walk?"

"Not very well," Jose admitted.

"There is no way we can drag these two and help them for four miles," I whispered to Katrina.

"I have an idea," Katrina took off running to the front of the strip. "How good are your biking skills?"

"You are brilliant," I told Katrina. I handed my gun to Will before following her. "Shoot anything that comes near you. We will be right back."

On the strip, Katrina had commandeered two bike taxis from two very passive human souls. Katrina jumped on one of the bikes, and I took over the second. We rushed back to the boys with our new form of transportation.

"All onboard," I told the Interns.

We helped Jose climb behind Katrina and Will behind me, placing an unconscious shifter in each of the taxis next to the Interns. It was the best way to make sure they didn't get away.

"Ready?" Katrina asked, but she took off before I could reply.

The strip was coming to life now. Demons were strolling through the area carrying swords and staves.

"This is going to suck," I said out loud. "Here."

I gave Will my backpack and the rest of the grenades. There was no way I could ride and fight demons all the way to the Boatman. Katrina and I didn't waste any time as we made our way down the strip. Will pulled out another water gun from the backpack and opened fire. Demons screamed as magic spells flew all around us.

"Isis, pedal faster!" Katrina yelled leading the way.

"What do you think I'm doing?" I responded as the top of my taxi went up in flames thanks to some green blast.

Demons were chasing us from everywhere. Jose joined Will and tossed grenades at the demons. I stood up on my bike and focused on pedaling as fast as my legs could go. I blocked the sound of the fighting, the explosions, and the screams to concentrate on avoiding the cracks on the streets the demons were creating. Biking was faster than running, and we were covering a lot of terrain. The demons were gaining ground, and I was getting extremely tired.

"Ladies, move!" the Boatman shouted from forty feet in front of us.

Katrina drove left, and I went right as the Boatman unleashed a missile down the strip. It hit the Stratosphere, taking the tower down. He sent another one flying and took out another hotel. Katrina and I didn't stop to see which one.

"That should keep them busy," Boatman announced when we reached him.

"Thank you, thank you," I told the Boatman, climbing off the bike with my legs burning. "I will take running anytime over this."

"Give yourself credit, you were pushing yourself and two other people," Katrina reminded me.

"Not fun at all," I said breathing hard. "Boatman, please help Jose and Will. We need to get out of here."

I trekked over to my unconscious passenger and dragged him off the bike. He was a lot heavier than he looked. My legs and arms were shaking. By the time I made it to the boat, I was hurting. The Boatman picked the shifter up with one hand and tossed him in the boat.

"Hope you don't mind the treatment?" Boatman asked, glancing over his shoulder.

"As long as he can talk, I don't care if he walks again," I replied, letting him help me down.

Katrina tossed her shifter over her shoulder without struggling, then she joined me on the boat, humming to herself.

"You are way too happy about this," I told her, leaning against the railing.

"Anytime we get to blow up a few buildings in hell, it's a good day," Katrina answered, tossing an arm over me. "Boys, what happened to the rest of your team?"

The Boatman started the boat before either Jose or Will could reply. "You might want to wait until later for that conversation. And hold on because we've got company."

"Everyone keep your heads down and grab something," I told the group. "Boatman, get us out of here."

The Boatman didn't waste any time maneuvering the boat away from the strip. Demons sent flames our way, but we were too far for them to reach us. The Boatman continued to accelerate down the dark waters, heading back to the fields of torture. This was not my favorite part of the trip, but I would take it just to get out of hell.

Chapter Fifteen

It was midnight by the time the Boatman pulled up to the boat dock at Lake Wright Patman. Hell had a way of distorting time that never matched the one on Earth. Bob and Shorty were waiting with the Camaro and the Deathmobile for us. Jose and Will were both passed out next to the two shifters.

"I gave Constantine a heads up that you were bringing company," the Boatman told me.

"Thank you for everything," I told him.

"We are family, this is what we do," the Boatman replied and helped me out of the boat.

Katrina and the Boatman got Will and Jose out of the boat. Bob jumped on while I helped the Interns to the Deathmobile. Their movements were becoming sluggish and painful. Jose wasn't able to bend his right leg, while Will's right arm was dislocated. Bob and the Boatman tossed the two shifters in the back of the Camaro.

"Can you two get back to Reapers okay?" Bob asked and Katrina glared at him. "Never mind. Shorty and I will take these two to the station."

"How will you get them in?" Katrina asked.

"Junior developed a special branding for prisoners." Bob pulled a small, red rod from his pocket. "That boy is a genius."

"Sounds like a typical Intern," Katrina said and strolled towards the passenger side of the Deathmobile. "Isis, we better hurry. These two are not doing well."

"Be careful," I told Bob.

"You, too," he replied.

We entered our respective vehicles and turned on the engines. Bob and Shorty left first. I drove slowly out of the dark, docking area, making sure nobody was following us.

"This sucks," Katrina said softly. "We have lost a whole day."

"That's the price for visiting hell," I said. "Are they awake?"

"I am," Will replied.

"Do you know where they took the others?" I asked him in a gentle voice.

"No, sorry," Will replied, wincing when he moved. "We were separated after we tried to escape the second time. They were not prepared to handle five Interns and Bartholomew. That boy never gives up."

"No, he doesn't," I said as tears tried to escape.

"He said the same thing about you," Will continued. "Isis, I don't think Jose and I will be very useful in a fight. They tortured us. Everything hurts. I know they broke several of Jose's bones. They wanted us to turn on Death."

"Will, I'm so sorry." I didn't have anything better to say.

"It's part of the job, but I wish I could be more helpful," he asked.

"You being here is helpful enough," I told him. "Rest now, we will be at Reapers shortly."

I drove as quickly as I could, avoiding sharp turns to not add any more pain to the boys. Katrina texted Constantine with an update. We were going to need medical attention fast. Will dozed off in the back. Neither Katrina nor I said a word the remainder of the drive.

Constantine was waiting for us on the first floor of Reapers. He was not alone. Iason the elven prince was standing with him. Iason was the twin brother of Genevieve, or Ginny as we all called her. In her infinite wisdom—which I questioned every day—Ginny made Iason and me the Godparents to her unborn child with Edward, a vampire. I thought that situation was complicated until this week. Now that seemed like the most normal relationship in the world.

"Your prince is here," Katrina whispered.

"He is not my prince," I hissed at her.

"Well, he doesn't look at me the same way he stares at you with those gorgeous aqua eyes," she teased as I parked the Deathmobile. "Come on, Isis. Six feet of bulging muscles and all that amazing hair. I'm jealous."

"Thanks, you can have him," I replied, getting out of the car.

"Hey," I said to Iason, who waved his reply. "Constantine, we need medical attention now. They are both seriously hurt."

"I can't get Death here," Constantine replied. "The horsemen are outraged. They've been getting threats and blackmail messages."

"That's insane. Why?" I asked.

"Just to make them mad," Katrina answered as she moved around me. "They know they can't kill the horsemen, but they are instigating them. Doesn't take much to make them snap."

"That's the understatement of the century," Constantine told her. "You need to call your General and give him an update. He should calm down once he hears we got some of our people back and took some prisoners in the process."

"Do you need help with Will and Jose?" she asked before leaving.

"No, we got it." Constantine dismissed her with a wave.

"Moving out." Katrina saluted him and jogged up the stairs towards her loft.

"Do you think Eugene or Junior could help?" I asked Constantine, glancing inside the Deathmobile.

"I don't think either one of them has enough training in internal injuries or saving people," Constantine confessed.

"Do you mind if we help?" Iason asked, stepping closer to the Deathmobile.

"Can you heal them?" I joined him at the door.

Iason closed his eyes and ran his hands over the boys without touching them. After several minutes, he stood up and met my eyes.

"Their injuries are too extensive for me," he said.

I opened my mouth to complain about false hope when Iason put a finger over my lips, his touch like fire on my skin.

"I can't, but Ulises is a miracle worker and can handle the damage." Iason signaled to someone behind me.

"Who is Ulises?" I asked, spinning to face another breathtaking elf with dark, curly hair. "Is every elf gorgeous?"

"I'm afraid so, Ms. Isis," Ulises answered in a soft, melodious voice. "The curse of the species, making beauty too common that it becomes boring. It's probably one of the reasons we are all so taken by humans and all your unique details."

"I think he just called us ugly," I told Constantine.

"I'm a feline, so I'm not included in your human dilemma," Constantine corrected me.

"Thanks," I told my unhelpful guardian. "Can you help them?"

Ulises leaned in the vehicle to examine them. "It's going to take me some time. I need a place to work."

"You can use our lab," Constantine told him. "Straight ahead."

"That will work." Ulises pulled Will out of the car.

Two more elves rushed to the vehicle and grabbed Jose. Neither of the boys were moving, and their skin had taken a greenish tint.

"Let me show you the lab," Constantine offered, leading the way.

"Thank you," I said to Ulises.

"Thank me after we save them." Ulises went toward the lab carrying Will in his arms like a small child.

"Your friends are in good hands. Ulises has been saving lives longer than I've been alive," Iason told me.

That was a huge statement since Iason was over five-hundred-years old if I remember correctly. How old was Ulises?

"What are you doing here?" I turned to face Iason.

"I heard you were having another spectacular 'end of the world' party and I didn't want to miss it," Iason replied with his hands in his pocket.

"That is not funny," I told him. "You should be in Cali protecting Ginny and the baby."

"Isis." Iason grabbed my arm and stopped me from pacing around the room. "Ginny is two weeks from giving birth, on bed rest with the best guards in the world. Do you think I could sit idly by and let her child be born to this mess?"

"Your people need you," I said softly. I didn't want to add another name to the list of people I was feeling responsible for.

"My people need a safe world," Iason told me, not letting go. "Don't worry, we left the Army guarding the kingdom and Ginny. Besides, Ginny would kill me if we didn't send help. Hope you don't mind that it's only me and my bodyguards."

"How many bodyguards do you have?" I pulled away from Iason and examined the room. I let my sixth sense take over and the shadows moved, making me jump.

"Nice job, you are getting better," said Iason. "In combat, six."

Iason had taught me how to use Death's gift to control my third eye to sense the supernatural world. My eye wasn't fully opened, but it created a sixth sense in a way. Three elves materialized from the darkness for a few seconds and disappeared back to the shadows. That was one of the coolest and creepiest tricks I had seen in a while.

"I'm impressed, and a bit scared all at once," I admitted.

"That's a smart girl," Iason told me, adjusting a strand of hair from my forehead. "Would you mind if we stay at Reapers?"

"Not at all," I answered, pulling away from his touch. "Constantine has been preparing for this day. We are officially a small armory."

"A new shipment of cots and mattresses arrived this afternoon," said Constantine, strolling back to us. "I can have them arranged anywhere you like."

"Do you mind if we take the lab?" Iason asked him. "I would like to stay close to my men while they work."

"Not a problem. We will get you settled in," Constantine said.

"Thank you." Iason gave Constantine a small bow and headed towards the lab. The three elves in the shadows followed behind him, all drop-dead gorgeous.

"Now we have seven elves in the mix," I told Constantine.

"I wouldn't dismiss them that quickly." Constantine slapped my leg with his paw. "Those seven are more deadly than an entire battalion of soldiers."

"You can't be serious?" If that was the case, those seven were more dangerous than three-hundred men." I guess I'm grateful they are on our side."

"Yes, be very grateful." Constantine sauntered slowly toward the Loft.

"What do you need me to do?" I asked going up the stairs behind him.

"Nothing major, besides eat something and take a shower." Constantine glanced over his shoulder. "You do smell like hell."

"You have jokes today, thanks." I poked him on the side before he could fly up the stairs.

"Seriously, get some rest, Isis." Constantine stopped at the top of the stairs. "This is only day one, and we have a lot of work in front of us. I don't need you passing out on me."

"That is true. Two comatose Interns is enough for this team." I didn't want to admit it, but I was tired. "Good night, Constantine."

"Good night, Isis." Constantine marched inside through the kitty door.

I decided to skip the food suggestion and went straight to my room. My hair did smell like sulfur. This time I wanted a long bath. My legs needed some soaking after the insane workout I pushed myself through. Constantine was right, too. I couldn't afford to pass out. Recovering was just as important as any crazy workout. I turned the light on and enjoyed the soft jazz filling the room. Closing my eyes, I reviewed the events of today in my head. We didn't get Bartholomew back or even all the Interns, but we rescued two. Our trip to hell wasn't a total failure. Progress was being made. And I definitely deserved some sleep after today's events.

Chapter Sixteen

Five hours of sleep was not enough time to rest and then wake up to function on. No way could anyone focus on saving the world from an apocalypse with so little sleep. But who could sleep with the weight of the world on their shoulders? My body was used to being up by five in the morning and running by five-thirty. Running was still out of the question due to Constantine's new rules. Staying in bed felt like a total waste of my morning. I was not a fan of weights, but strength training was better than nothing. I dressed and headed for the gym downstairs. With so many people in the building, earbuds were a must.

When I first started as an Intern, I was completely out of shape. Constantine and Eric developed over twenty different routines to get me back into fighting mode. They ranged from calisthenics, Pilates, and even hand-to-hand combat. I hadn't done any of them in a while. Today, I chose to run a few drills, starting with a plank routine to work on my core.

Twenty minutes later, I was dripping with sweat. The stupid Pilates moves had my legs sore, but my abs felt like they were on fire. How was it possible that such simple moves could have a person working so hard? Based on this routine, I was supposed to be moving into burpees, but I was tired already. I laid on the floor taking on the corpse pose. The pedestrian entrance opened not soon after, so I rolled to my side to get a glimpse of who was entering at this ungodly hour.

"I'm glad you are not running today," Eric told me.

"Running would have been a better plan than this infernal routine of yours." I fell to my back and stared at the lights on the ceiling.

"What are you doing?" Eric sat on the floor next to me.

"Sucking," I replied, unable to meet his eyes.

"I told you that you need to vary your workouts," Eric lectured me.

"It is too early for that. Tell me why you are here," I said, changing the topic.

"We got trouble," Eric replied.

"What now? That is not very specific, and we are already past the point of trouble. We are living in madness," I corrected him.

"Vampires have landed in Haven," Eric interrupted me.

"Are they friendly?" I sat up.

"If you are asking if they belong to Edward, I don't think so." Eric shook his head.

"Iason is here. I will ask him if he knows who they are," I told Eric, falling back to the ground.

"Your prince is here?" Eric asked, stretching out beside me.

"He is not my prince," I told him, shoving at his arm. "Why does everyone keep saying that?"

"I'm sure he is not here to see me or Constantine," Eric replied.

"Ginny sent him, that's all." I was sticking with that story.

"Sure, Isis. Whatever you say," Eric told me.

"Come on. Let's go find Constantine and give him the update." I dragged myself off the floor and reached down to pull Eric up. I did not appreciate it when he was this nice.

We headed up the stairs and Eric said, "You need to do more squats."

"If you say my butt is flabby, I'm pushing you down the stairs," I threatened him.

"Your butt is not flabby, but squats are great to work different muscles that running doesn't cover," Eric said, not sounding arrogant at all.

"Really?" I questioned his helpful tip.

"It's an awesome exercise for so many areas," Eric continued. "You need to switch things up to keep your body guessing and pushing the limits."

"I need a job where I can be lazy and chill on a couch," I said, walking through the Loft doors.

"I'm sure you could find one, but it won't pay as well as yours." Eric was speaking the truth. The fringe benefits of the Intern job were amazing as long as you didn't die.

"Constantine, Eric has news." Constantine was sitting by the computer watching the monitors with Ninth. "Hi, Ninth."

"Hi, Isis," the old Intern replied.

"Do we have another staircase I don't know about?" I asked them. "How do people keep getting up here and I never see them?"

"Probably because you do half of your exercises with your eyes closed. It's not very hard to sneak past you." Constantine was not being very nice today.

"It helps me concentrate," I defended myself.

"Whatever," Constantine added. "Pete called and said the prisoners were ready for interrogation. He wants to know if he should start or wait for you."

"Tell him to start. I still need a shower before leaving," I told him.

"Fine. But hurry up," Constantine shouted. "You know how easily distracted Pete can get with his interrogations."

"I'm hurrying." I left Eric with Constantine and Ninth and went to my room.

Death was sitting on my chair when I opened the door. Her hair was pulled back, and she had a black Prada pant suit on.

"Hi, Death," I said closing the door.

"Hi, Isis." Death stood from the chair. "Just wanted to thank you for getting Will and Jose back."

"Death, you don't have to thank me," I told her, taking a seat on the bed. "That's what family does. I just wish we had found everyone."

"Finding two was a huge victory," said Death. "It gave my siblings confidence you are on the right course."

"Your siblings are a tad bit bipolar," I added softly.

"You mean moody and demented?" Death corrected me with a smile. "Sometimes, we are more human than most. It's hard not to pick up your traits. Be careful, Isis. Our enemies are increasing each day."

"We do have a lot of them lately." There was no way around that.

"I will keep in touch." Death left the room.

I stood up and headed to shower. At least I would be able to get out of the house and maybe find some answers. As long as I made it in time before Pete, the Interrogator-Pixie, overdosed our kidnappers with pixie dust.

Constantine was the only one in the common area when I entered. He was focused on the computer monitors with headphones over his little ears.

"Bob left you food in the oven!" Constantine shouted across the room.

"You do know I can hear you?" I said back.

"What?" Constantine yelled again.

"Very funny." I opened the oven and found my all-time favorite: veggie quiche. "When does Bob find time to bake in the middle of this mess?"

"You work out. Bob bakes." Constantine was on the counter before I realized it.

"You are a sneaky one at times," I told the evil dictator who was at staring me down.

"I'm always sneaky," Constantine bragged. "It's part of my job."

"Whatever," I answered before popping a spoonful of quiche in my mouth. "Who is free this morning? I need a buddy to ride with me."

"Take Katrina and save her from the wonder-twins." Constantine pointed to the ground below.

"Who are the wonder-twins?" I chuckled a little.

"Who do you think?" Constantine shook his head. "Our mad scientists, who else? Now I understand why the horsemen never allow their Interns to mingle. They become dangerous when in numbers."

"You are overreacting," I told him, pointing at him with my spoon. "But what are they doing in the lab now?"

"They were supposed to be examining Jose and Will," Constantine stated, his voice full of sarcasm.

"But?" There was always a "but" when Constantine was this annoyed.

"Ulises did such a great job, there was nothing for the twins to do," Constantine informed me. "They moved Jose and Will in my room. Ulises said they are going to be out of commission for a few days. If we survive the apocalypse, they should be fine. What are those two boys doing? I have no idea."

"Well, I'm saving Katrina and heading to the station," I said, taking my quiche with me. "Call me if something happens."

Driving the streets of Texarkana this week was like being trapped in Grand Theft Auto. You had no idea what was going to happen and who would try to attack you. The only ones who were not chasing us down were the cops. I skipped down the stairs while enjoying my quiche, stopping in my tracks as I stumbled on Iason on the phone by the Deathmobile. He was wearing cargo pants and a tight T-shirt. It was the first time I'd ever seen him dress that casual, and he looked dreamy. I avoided staring at his well-defined abs. Even his biceps were exceptionally sculpted.

"Good morning, Isis." Iason waved, putting his phone away. "Are you actually eating?"

"Good morning to you, too," I replied. "And yes, I eat all the time. How many times do I need to explain that to you?"

"Just checking," said Iason, blinking his pretty eyes innocently.

"Were you guys able to sleep before the Interns took over the lab?" I asked, angling my head.

"Yes. We don't require a lot of sleep," Iason explained.

"Thank you for helping Will and Jose," I told him in my most humble voice. "I'm really grateful."

"We are here to help," Iason said softly. "We are heading out."

"You are?" I searched the area for his bodyguards.

"Edward is on his way," Iason continued. "We need to get things ready for him. Their house here is not secure, so we found another location. I know you have a hard time asking for help, but please call me if you get in trouble."

"Why would I get in trouble?" I felt like arguing with him today.

"Because trouble follows you like one of Pestilence's plagues." Iason lifted my chin and the electric shock from his hand ran down my entire body. "Call me."

I couldn't even speak, so I just nodded. Iason was satisfied and left out of the pedestrian exit. His six bodyguards appeared from the walls and who knew where else. I made sure all six had passed me before moving. An invisible, lethal soldier was a terrifying concept. Once the door closed, I made my way towards the lab. Constantine was right, Eugene and Junior were a menace together.

"What are you two doing?" Flames were dancing from beakers on the table.

Blood-red and orange concoctions boiled in glass spheres and the room had a salty, lemony smell. Katrina was sitting on the lab bed, kicking her feet like a five-year-old.

"Working?" Eugene replied, mixing green-and-blue liquid in a bowl.

"This is delicate stuff," Junior added, pouring gold drops in the bowl Eugene was working with.

"Is that quiche?" At least Eugene was easily distracted by food.

"I'm feeling generous." I placed the quiche on the lab table away from the fire. Eugene couldn't leave his work but at least he winked.

"They are trying to create a bullet to kill vampires and zombies," Katrina clarified for me when I stood next to her.

"Like they did in Underworld?" The boys were watching too much TV.

"Exactly," Katrina said with a fake grin. "They were trying to create a UV bullet that would set the world on fire."

"You two do know that Underworld is a movie and not a documentary?" I moved in closer to peek in the beakers.

"They have vampires, shifters, and the likes," Junior said, not glancing at me. "Let's just say reality is imitating art today."

"If you two can pull that off, I will be thrilled!" I exclaimed. "How is it coming?"

"Horribly." Eugene slammed the bottles on the table. "We don't have the right equipment or the proper ingredients to get this done. If I was at my lab..." Eugene stopped and moved towards the wall. His friends were still locked underground and we had a day and a half to get this situation under control.

"I know, but this is a shooting range," I reminded both boys. "Not an actual lab. It's not properly stocked and if Bart was here..."

It was my turn to stop abruptly. We were all used to having our family backing us up. The missing people made it feel like we lost an arm or leg. I moved around the table to stand next to Eugene.

"Keep trying, Eugene." I placed my head on his shoulder. "If anyone can figure this out, you can. Between you and Junior, you can make magic."

"Ebola pandemic is in full effect," Ninth announced from the door.

"We have an Ebola pandemic on top of everything else?" This week just kept getting better and better. "I thought you just made that stuff up."

"I did," Eugene defended himself.

"Relax, children." Ninth strolled in the room with a swagger. "We do not have a pandemic, but we needed to lock down this city."

Ninth pulled two small IDs from his lab pocket. He handed one to Katrina and the other one to me. According to the little ID, we were members of the CDC. That was such a scary thought that Pestilence's Interns could have this much power.

"Would you mind delivering more cards to the Station?" Ninth asked in that polite way of his. "I left a box on the bench press outside, then informed the CDC we have full control of the situation and to focus their efforts on Mount Pleasant. I will have Constantine contact the mayors of the cities and make it official. Civilians will be required to stay in their houses and should expect door-to-door visits from the CDC."

"That should buy us some time without civilians in the way," said Katrina, climbing off the table. "You are good, Ninth."

"We are all doing our part." Ninth adjusted his coat and moved around the table. "Now let's see what we can do with this project here." Ninth pulled up his sleeves and extended his hands in front of him, blowing on his hands. A foot-tall blue fire spurred to life.

"Wow!" Katrina moved away from Ninth. "Looks like the master came home to school you boys."

Eugene and Junior were both fixated on the flames and neither replied.

"I think I have an idea that might work," Ninth said to the boys as he tossed the flames from hand-to-hand.

"Want to come with me?" I asked Katrina.

"I thought you would never ask." Katrina led the way out of the lab.

I closed the door behind us. "I don't think the range is fireproof."

"We will find out soon enough," said Katrina, staring at the closed door with me.

"I fear you might be right," I concurred and walked away. "We need to hurry. Pete is going to be interrogating our shifter friends. It would be beneficial for everyone if we are there."

"Let's not forget Ninth's box." Katrina marched to the bench and picked up the small box.

"Why do you think he left it there?" I asked her.

"Ninth is pretty old," Katrina answered.

"Katrina, please, that box is tiny," I replied, and she just shrugged.

"Why are you questioning the madness?" Katrina asked as she headed towards the Deathmobile.

"I'm hoping something will start making sense," I answered.

"Hope is the last thing that dies, so keep at it," she teased.

"Get in the car," I ordered.

We climbed inside and headed out. Three days was not a lot of time to save the world. How did Bond or the Mission Impossible people pull it off?

Chapter Seventeen

The morning commuters were busy making their way around town. Once Constantine contacted the mayors and the police chief, this place would start to empty out. At least that was the goal. Texarkana, both the Texas and Arkansas side, were considered small towns, and in some sense even rural. For our current situation, they were not small enough. We had over thirty thousand potential victims cruising through both cities.

At least the drive downtown was uneventful. It would be nice if the rest of the day remained that way, but I highly doubted that would be the case.

"I'm so happy to be out of Reapers," Katrina said after a few minutes of silence. "I was starting to feel pretty useless watching Eugene and Junior creating their fireballs."

"I understand. Some days, that is exactly how I feel," I told her, focusing on navigating the Deathmobile down New Boston Road. "We all have our specialties but waiting is not one the two of us have."

"Not even close." Katrina leaned her head on the window. "It would be a shame if tomorrow was the end of the world and none of these poor people knew it."

"Would you like for us to make an announcement?" I teased her.

"I'm glad you have jokes." Katrina flicked my arm with her fingers.

"Ouch," I whined.

"Please, like that even hurt." Katrina was not buying my act as she made herself comfortable on the window again.

"Why can our job never be easy?" I glanced her way.

"Because it would be too boring," said Katrina, staring out the window again.

"I could do with a little boring this week," I admitted.

"Me, too," Katrina concurred.

By the time we arrived at Union Station in Downtown, there were fewer people around. The area was almost deserted, actually. Shorty had a couple of men in the front of the station with long jackets. They had a casual appearance to them, just sitting around the steps. The jackets helped to hide the rifle and multiple weapons they were carrying. Too bad those poor boys were going to boil to death in a few hours. Texas heat was a dangerous thing. I parked in the back of the building to use the private entrance.

Two more guards were stationed on that side, but they were not wearing jackets. The M16s they were carrying were on full display. Katrina and I dismounted the Deathmobile and made our way towards the building. I was barely up two steps when I felt Junior's security system. Cold shivers ran up and down my body, leaving me a little out of breath. I stopped at the fourth step to gather myself.

"I do not want to know what Junior did," Katrina told me as she grabbed a rail and held on while balancing Ninth's box in her other hand.

"That was intense, and we have the brand." I held up my hand. "Any intruder who wants to take a chance is going to have a rude awakening."

"If they make it long enough to figure out what they are doing." Katrina glanced over her shoulder.

"Morning, Boss Lady," David, one of the guards, told me.

"Good morning, David," I replied. "How did you get stuck on duty?"

"Jimmy and I requested it." David pointed at Jimmy with his head.

"If the barriers don't stop them, we will make sure they make it to hell before trespassing in our house," Jimmy announced, adjusting the M16. "You know, Boss Lady, I failed recess because I don't play."

Katrina couldn't contain it and giggled at Jimmy's comment. I, on the other hand, just tapped him on the back as I passed.

"You are a good man," I said. "Sound the alarm if someone tries to break in. I don't care if the barriers get them or not. We need to know they are trying to breach us."

"Yes, Boss Lady," both Jimmy and David replied.

"I love your people," Katrina whispered as we entered the building.

"I'm glad you are amused," I told her and led the way inside.

The station was buzzing with activity. Groups of people were moving around carrying weapons, ammunition, gear, and food. The cheerful station I was used to now had the feel of an army camp. Katrina looked at ease in the midst of the chaos. When we arrived at the lower levels, I opened the door to the viewing room without knocking. Shorty and Bob were mesmerized staring through the two-way mirror separating us from the interrogation room.

Katrina joined us after she closed the door. I stood next to Bob and Shorty, though I had no comment for what I was seeing. Pete, our six-inch-tall pixie, was pacing the interrogation table doing the Macarena. His wings shifted color with each step he took, pixie dust floating everywhere. The shifter from hell was shaking uncontrollably as Pete rambled a series of questions too fast for anyone to answer.

"Is that a normal procedure?" Katrina asked, inching closer to the window.

"There is nothing normal about Pete's techniques," I clarified. "This one I have never seen before. What is he doing?"

"Trying to break him," Shorty answered first.

"Pete has tried seven different combinations of dust on him, but he won't talk," Bob informed us.

"He is not looking good," I told them.

"Boss Lady, you can't imagine how hard it must be to do the Macarena while walking around shaking your wings," Shorty defended Pete.

"I was talking about the prisoner, Shorty," I explained.

"You are so right." Shorty turned to face the window.

Pete stopped dancing and flew up to the man's face. The rest of us in the viewing room moved closer to the window.

"You are too tough to break," Pete said softly to the man as he sat next to his ear. "But you have three minutes before the dust paralyzes all of your muscles. You won't die, but you won't be able to move or talk again. I recommend you give me something now if you want medical attention. It's all up to you?"

"You can't let that happen to me," the shifter told him, visibly shaking. "You are the good guys; you are supposed to be saving people."

"Well, at least we know he does know how to talk," said Shorty.

"He hasn't talked?" Katrina asked.

Bob shook his head. "Not a sound in the last two hours Pete has been working him."

"Saving people?" Pete howled. "You got the wrong department, fool. My only job here is to break you. If your body or your sanity does not make it, not my problem. You should have been a better person and not messed with the horsemen. Thirty seconds gone."

"I don't know much." The shifter pulled on the handcuffs holding him down.

"Then I recommend you stop wasting your precious time and spill your guts." Pete swung his legs back and forth like a little kid.

"There is a meeting scheduled between shifters and vampires." The shifter licked his lips. "A very powerful vampire named Marie is coming. This is her plan, and she has a score to settle with the horsemen."

"Good. See that wasn't so bad." Pete rubbed the man's cheek, which made him squirm. "Now give me the location and time. I would hate for such a nice guy like you to end up as a vegetable, though I promise you will be fully conscious the whole time."

"Pete is one scary little guy," Katrina told us. "I really like him."

"Of course, you would," I told her.

"The Fairgrounds at eight." The Shifter started convulsing and Pete flew off his shoulder.

"Could we get a medic here?" Pete asked in a very cheerful voice.

Bob and Shorty ran out of the viewing room toward the interrogation. Pete flew outside the room as Katrina and I exited as well. Bob and Shorty dragged the shifter out of the room.

"Good morning, Boss Lady," said Pete.

"Good morning, Pete," I replied. "Did you just put that man in a vegetable stage?"

"Of course not," answered Pete. "His muscles will be fine. Too bad he will have constant diarrhea for the next two days."

"You are evil," I told him, but I gave him a high five, too.

"That was impressive," Katrina complemented him.

"Pete, meet Katrina, War's Intern," I pointed at her as I made the introductions. "Katrina, Pete, the unsurpassed interrogator in all of Texas."

"Yes, he is," Katrina agreed.

"Not today." Pete dropped his head to his chest. "They are not breaking, Boss Lady. I don't know what is going on. They should not be able to last this long."

"We did drag them out of hell," Katrina told him.

"That is true." Pete flew in small circles around us while scratching his head. "I will need to up my game with these two."

"Pete, how much antidote do we need to give him?" Bob ran back in our direction.

"The usual." Pete flew towards him. "He will be fine, I just needed to scare him."

"Mission accomplished," Bob told him, his shoulders relaxing. "You scared us as well. We don't have facilities to house prisoners in vegetable conditions."

"That's good to know," Pete said. "I could use that in my routine."

Bob left back down the hallway. Pete went back to flying around in circles.

"Pete, are you going to be able to break the other one?" I asked him as I attempted to get him to stop moving around.

"I have to," he replied, squeezing his fingers together.

"I trust that you will." I gave him my vote of confidence. "I will be in my office while you work. As soon as you find something, let me know. Katrina, do you want to join me?"

"Do you mind if I stay?" Katrina replied.

"Not at all," I told her.

"I still need to give Bob and Shorty all the IDs." Katrina shook the box of IDs she was still carrying. "I'm also curious how Pete does his interrogations."

"It will be my pleasure to show you." Pete gave Katrina a low bow.

"Knock yourself out. I will be upstairs." I left them to their shop talk.

I had a stack of requests on my desk that I had been avoiding. If the interrogations were going so slow, leaving Pete to work was not going to hurt anyone. Paperwork was not exciting, but it had to be done. I climbed the steps two at a time towards the second floor where my office was located.

I lost track of time sitting at my desk. Nobody from the interrogation room had called with an update. The only one that called was Constantine to inform me that the city was on lockdown and the only ones allowed out were the cops, firefighters for extreme emergencies, and the CDC, or us. That had been several hours ago. I glanced at the clock on my desk and it was almost eleven in the morning. Two and a half hours of straight work and I still had half of the stack of papers to review. Why didn't I delegate this to someone?

Ring, ring, ring.

I picked up the handset on the phone on my desk.

"Hello," I answered.

"Isis, we have a situation." The words rushed out of Bob. "We have a supernatural attack at Kidtopia."

"Are you serious?" I answered, standing behind my desk.

"Yes, hurry," said Bob.

"I'll meet you at the parking lot," I replied and hung up the phone.

I had never been so happy to have an attack taking place. It wasn't like I was trying to run away from all the reports, requests for reconsideration on sentences, ban appeals, or the other fifty petitions I received per week. I was just anxious and needed something physical to do. Not to mention the fact that attacks during the day in the middle of the city were bad publicity. We had been lucky we were able to cover up all the strange incidents around town. I wanted to keep my amazing track record, at least until tomorrow. I double checked my pockets to make sure I had all my weapons before leaving my office.

Bob, Shorty, and Katrina were all outside by the time I made it to the Deathmobile. They were closer to the cars than I was, at least that was my excuse. Katrina had added a M16 to her arsenal and was ready to hurt someone. We all got in our designated vehicles and drove towards Kidtopia, the playground next to the public library.

The drive to Kidtopia was less than five minutes from the station. Katrina and I rode together in the Deathmobile, and Bob was with Shorty in his truck. A truck was important in case we had a prisoner or suspect to arrest.

The library had been evacuated, and the place was dark. I parked the Deathmobile in the library's parking lot instead of next to the park. With my track record, I couldn't afford some freak accident blowing up the Deathmobile today.

Katrina and I ran across the street from the library towards the playground. We heard screams coming from behind the playground and rushed over to that area. Katrina made her way toward the back, weapons on the ready, and I followed, my scythe in my arms and ready for whatever was to come. Katrina maneuvered her M16 to her front so she was ready to fire. When we came upon the scene, we saw the screams were coming from two teen shifters who were being attacked by two trolls.

"Get away from those kids," I ordered the trolls.

The two shifters turned to face me. They were in mid-shift, their faces contorted to their animal form and fur spreading all over their bodies. Instead of being grateful for our help, they charged at us with their teeth extended.

"Nice job, Isis," said Katrina, slamming the butt of the M16 on the head of the first approaching shifter.

"Hey, we are here to help," I said to the second one, but he just kept charging at me.

I wanted to give him the benefit of the doubt but that idea quickly faded when he lunged at me. Kicking the shifter in the stomach as hard as I could had him twisting, but it didn't keep him down as he came back for another round. I spun the scythe several times in the air trying to persuade the shifter from charging. That failed as well, so I stopped wasting time. With one hand I dropped the scythe over his head, then I nailed him twice in the side with the scythe. The demented shifter stirred a few more times and managed to stand again.

Bob shot him in the back twice. The poor boy landed head-first on the ground. Hopefully, that would keep him still long enough for us to figure out what was all the madness going on.

"Kill them," one of the trolls hissed.

"We are not here to kill anyone," I told the troll moving away from the two shifters.

"They tried to kidnap my daughter to take her to those torture camps." The troll hugged the smaller one standing next to him.

"What?" Bob asked, getting closer to the trolls.

"Check that box." The troll kicked the box towards Bob.

Bob and Shorty inspected it quickly. Bob pulled out several collars from inside, all large enough for the trolls.

"Are those what I think they are?" Katrina asked.

"If you are thinking shock collars then yes," Shorty replied, taking several more out.

"What is going on here?" I asked the group.

"They are taking our people," the troll answered me. "We are easy targets. Nobody ever thinks we need protection."

"I'm so sorry," I told the troll. "How many have been taken?"

"At least eight that we know of," the troll replied.

"We will find them," I told him, adding his friends to my list. "Are you guys going to be okay?"

"We are heading back to our colony," he said softly. "We are safer in large groups. Good luck, Intern. These enemies are ruthless."

The troll grabbed the hand of the smaller child and took off, headed away from the city. I marched over to the two unconscious shifters and kneeled.

"Take those two back to Pete. Maybe he will have better luck with them," I told Bob and Shorty. "We need more weapons."

"More weapons?" Katrina joined me next to the shifter. "What are you planning?"

"We are going to that meeting today," I announced. "I'm tired of always being on the defensive and feeling five steps behind. We are taking this game to them."

"Planning to charge a shifter/vampire convention," Katrina repeated. "That sounds like my kind of plan. Where are we getting these weapons from?"

"With Bartholomew missing, we are going to have to do our own shopping," I told her. "We need to get to New York and visit our favorite arms dealer."

"This is finally getting better," Katrina told me.

"Bob, are you guys going to be okay with this pair?" I gave the shifter a soft kick.

"We got them," Bob answered.

"Good," I said. "We are heading back to Reapers and checking to see what Constantine can do for transportation."

"If anyone can figure out logistics, it's Constantine," Katrina said.

"I hope you are right." I headed back to the Deathmobile.

Katrina quickly followed. The Deathmobile, for my sake, was intact. I still did a quick check around the perimeter of the car and underneath. I did not trust anyone anymore, and a car bomb would put a huge kink in our plans for today.

"Never a dull moment," Katrina reminded me.

"Not for us," I added. "I'm ready to give this group a little payback."

I started the Deathmobile and headed back to Reapers. I drove down several side roads to examine the number of people in the street. Finally, there weren't as many out and about. All we had to do was solve this little puzzle, get the evil out of town, and make sure the horsemen did not start the apocalypse this week. Simple, right? Not.

Chapter Eighteen

It was a depressing sight driving up to Reapers and peering over at the demolished Equinox Pavilion. If we ever made it out of this mess, I would help Constantine rebuild it. Regardless of the crazy memories it brought, it was a beautiful piece of art that shouldn't go down as collateral damage. I slowed the Deathmobile as I neared the rubble, my eyes spotting Constantine standing outside.

"Who is Constantine talking to?" Katrina pointed to the right.

"Dwarves," I replied as I stopped in front of Reapers.

Katrina and I climbed out of the vehicle and headed over to Constantine. Two small dwarves disappeared underground as we reached them.

"What are you planning, evil one?" Katrina whispered to Constantine.

"Searching for a way to stop Pestilence's back-up plan from being activated." Constantine strolled towards us. "The idea of losing eight of the best scientists in the world to a freezer does not sit well with me. Sending the dwarves to search both labs."

"Have you told Eugene and Junior?" I forced myself not to run inside to tell them myself.

"Not yet," Constantine replied softly. "I don't want to give them any false hope."

I dropped my shoulders and kicked a few rocks. There went my own hopes.

"Hate to add more bad news to your day, but we have a major vamp meeting going on tonight," Katrina told Constantine. "Our enemies are also kidnapping trolls and who knows who else to serve them."

"What?" hissed Constantine.

"We are going to that meeting," I announced to him.

"And you'd better teach them a lesson," Constantine added.

"That is the plan, but do you know a vampire named Marie?" I kneeled so I could meet Constantine's eyes.

"Can't be the same one?" Constantine paced back and forth. "Marie is a very common name."

"Based on what we heard, this one is an old and powerful vamp." Katrina sat on the ground.

"Let's hope it's not the same one," Constantine told us.

"Why?" Katrina and I asked simultaneously.

"Because if it is, we have a fifteen-hundred-year-old grudge and not enough fire power to handle it." Constantine stopped pacing.

"I'm not a spiritual person, but I will start praying that our luck is changing and it's not the same one," Katrina told him.

"Speaking of fire power, we need weapons," I told my guardian.

"Welch." Constantine looked me straight in the eyes. "He is the only dealer I trust not to betray us."

"Exactly who I was thinking," I told Constantine. "Any ideas how we can get to New York and back in time?"

"What do you think we have a jet for?" Constantine cleaned his face

"The same jet that went up in flames at the hangar." I slapped my hands together for greater impact.

"Do you honestly think I only have one plane?" Constantine strolled towards Reapers. "I own a whole fleet.

Meet us inside. Katrina, follow me."

Katrina stood up and followed Constantine towards the pedestrian's entrance, which left me no choice but to head back to the Deathmobile.

Of course, Constantine owns a whole fleet of jets because why wouldn't he?

I drove around Reapers towards the vehicle's entrance. The perimeter looked empty, but I didn't trust it anymore. Our enemies were accumulating a lot faster than our friends. Inside Reapers, Eugene and Junior had joined Constantine and Katrina. I parked the Deathmobile and met up with the group.

"We have tried everything and nothing is working," Junior told Constantine.

"We don't have enough equipment to make the necessary modifications," Eugene explained.

"Maybe what we need is different weapons," I told them.

Eugene and Junior both turned and stared at me. I wasn't sure if either one of them was even blinking.

"What kind of weapons?" Eugene said.

"I don't know. Something better than what we have for killing vampires," I replied. "I don't have enough time to show everyone hand-to-hand combat and how to use a scythe."

"They are really hard to use," Eugene told me.

"That's because those are designed for Death's Interns. They won't work as well if other people use them, and especially civilians," Constantine informed us.

"Now you say that." Eugene rubbed his temples. "Please tell me you have a plan."

"We are heading to New York to meet with Welch," I answered with a wink.

"The Welch?" Junior asked.

"You know him?" It was my turn to stare at Junior.

"The man is a legend, and he doesn't do deals with just anyone," Junior continued. "I have been on a waiting list for two months to meet with him."

"You should have told him you were friends with Constantine and Bartholomew," I told him.

"Not that easy. If Welch is a legend, Bartholomew and Constantine are straight myths," Junior said, rocking from side-to-side. "Proving that I know them means revealing I'm Famine's Intern, and that information is not available for disclosure yet."

"Can we continue this conversation later? We are running out of time," Constantine said, irritation lining each of his words. "Eugene, grab whatever you need; you are going with Isis. Katrina, I need you and Junior to drop them off."

"You don't want us going with them?" Katrina looked between Constantine and me.

"No," Constantine snapped. "I need you inspecting our security system and helping Bob increase the threat level. Ninth needs Junior back to help him with some tests. Why are you all just standing there? Move!"

"I'm ready," Eugene told me.

"Let's go," I replied. "Where is the plane? The airport?"

"Not this time. It's at the old Lone Star Munitions center in Hooks," Constantine said before heading up the stairs. "By the time you get to Hooks, George will be ready. Until we secure the airport and the hangar again, I can't risk any more planes going up in flames."

"Hooks it is." I saluted Constantine.

Katrina took the keys to the Deathmobile and marched to the driver seat. Eugene and I went to the back seat, and Junior made himself comfortable next to Katrina.

"If something goes wrong..." Katrina trailed off.

"Nothing is going to go wrong," I replied.

"Yes, let's keep that attitude," Eugene told her. "We have plenty of things to worry about. No need to add any more."

"True, but watch yourselves," Katrina ordered, and we nodded.

Katrina did not need directions to Lone Star. It seemed our super-soldier knew the location to every military installation in the world, both active and inactive ones. Constantine had texted the coordinates for the plane once we arrived at the old munitions center. Based on his instructions, the jet was somewhere in the back.

"Do you guys own this as well?" Junior asked, his eyes roaming the old facility.

"Knowing Constantine, I wouldn't be surprised." That was a really good question to ask my dear guardian once we finished this little mission.

A few miles off the entrance, stood a brand-new black jet. The name Reapers was stenciled on the side in the same red, gothic letters as our building. George, our pilot, was waiting on the tarmac for us. Katrina parked as closed to the jet as possible.

"We will be here when you land," she told me.

"I know," I replied and squeezed her shoulder. "Don't blow anything up, Junior."

"Me?" Junior's mouth puckered, and it made him look even younger.

"Yes, you," I replied, leaving the car.

Eugene and I made our way towards George as quickly as possible.

"Miss Isis, it's a pleasure to see you." George shook my hand.

"Is everyone okay?" I hadn't had time to check on them.

"We are hard to kill," George replied.

I let George's words sink in and expanded my sixth sense. Until now, I assumed George and the crew were all humans. After a few seconds, I had a new appreciation for Constantine's recruitment process. George was a witch.

"My Godmother will be glad to hear that," I told George.

"The High Priestess has my full admiration." George gave me a little bow. "The boss said we are short on time, so are we ready?"

"Yes." I waved one last time at Katrina and climbed the steps to the jet.

Eugene followed closely behind me. At the entrance of the jet, our friendly stewardess greeted us with drinks in hand. I let my senses examine her as well, finding another witch. We were in good company. Eugene and I took a seat on the soft, leather recliners and made ourselves comfortable.

"Ready to work on our shopping list?" Eugene asked as the jet started moving.

"How big is this list?" I asked as Eugene pulled out a small notebook from his pocket.

"We need enough weapons to handle all the potential enemies we have." Eugene opened the notebook.

"In that case, we need an entire arsenal," I told him.

"I hope Welch is as good as you said he is." He started writing down on his list.

I leaned closer to the table separating Eugene and me. This was going to be a busy flight. My stomach growled, and our flight attendant appeared with two trays of food.

"Lunch?" Her golden eyes sparkled as she gazed at me. "You are going to have a long afternoon, so you should eat."

"Thank you," Eugene told her, discarding his notebook. "How did she know I was starving?"

"I have a feeling she heard my stomach trying to eat itself." On cue, it growled again.

Eugene and I decided to multitask and work on our weapons' list as we devoured our food. The best part of having a private jet on call was the food was always delicious.

The three-hour flight was not long enough to get everything done that we needed. We had made rosters of potential enemies which included their weaknesses and strengths. We created rosters of our allies and ourselves, too. By the time we were done, our research looked more like a Dungeons and Dragon's lists of participants than real life. George navigated the jet to a private hangar in La Guardia. As the jet came to a stop, our sweet, little flight attendant pulled out an M4 from one of the cabinets.

"Is everyone okay?" Eugene asked her.

"We are at war, Mr. Eugene, so your safety is my first priority." With the friendly demeanor every flight attendant mastered, she opened the door to the jet.

"Should we pull out our weapons?" Eugene looked out the small window.

"No," I answered, heading out of the plane. "If they get past Killer-Barbie, George will have this jet in the air before getting clearance from the tower."

Eugene adjusted his lab coat and followed me outside. Three white vans were parked inside the hangar. My heart dropped and my hand hovered over the spot I kept my scythe, but the driver side of the first van opened before I could grab it.

"I hope you know how much I like you," said Welch, climbing down. "I don't do door-to-door delivery just for anyone."

Welch was handsome and of mixed descent. His mocha complexion had a slight glow, and he was styling a fabulous, gray suit.

"I'm honored," I told him with my hand to my heart. "Are all those yours?"

"We brought all the heavy hitters. With your adversaries, you are going to need everything I have." Welch clapped his hands and his men dismounted. "Vampires, demons, and shifters, oh my." Welch's impersonation of Dorothy was absolutely sexy and heat rose to my cheeks.

"Hi, I'm Eugene." Eugene extended his hand to Welch when I failed to make the proper introductions.

"Pestilence's mad scientist. It's a pleasure." Welch shook hands with Eugene.

"Is 'mad scientist' a compliment?" Eugene asked me softly.

"For an arms dealer, I think so," I replied, pushing him towards the vans.

My mouth dropped as we looked inside the formerly sixteen-passenger van. The vans had no seats, and instead were stacked with racks of arms on both side. Cases were also located in the center.

"What's in the cases?" Eugene asked as I played with one of the rocket launchers.

"Ballistic gear," Welch explained as his men pulled the cases out. "We made a modification to the design. They will repel spells and curses while being strong enough to withstand a direct blast from a demon, but you only get one."

"How about bullets?" Eugene asked as he picked one up.

"Bullets are the least of your worries," Welch said, pulling out a gun from his back pocket and shooting one of his guys in the chest.

"Holy shit!" Eugene screamed.

The man hit the ground hard. Nobody moved to help him, but he bounced back up after less than thirty seconds.

"How was the impact, Brad?" Welch asked him.

"Like a paint gun, boss, not bad at all." Brad returned to downloading guns from the van.

"If your enemies had guns, you wouldn't need any of these." Welch moved towards the racks. "We have added flame throwers to the launchers. Great for zombies and the recent dead. I heard you developed a special bullet for your shifter problem?"

"We did," Eugene answered while eyeing the flamethrower.

"You should also know if I've heard about it, so have your enemies." Welch opened another of the cases. "There have been large orders for body armor lately. After Constantine's phone call, I figured it was your friends loading up. I have some special ammo that might be able to help."

Eugene picked up one of the bullets and examined it, then handed one to me. The thing appeared more like a fat dart than a bullet.

"How does it work?" I asked Welch.

"The needle on the tip is made of silver," Welch explained. "The tip is thin and strong, enough to pierce any Kevlar and allow your formula to go through. That should give you an edge."

"You get me," Eugene told Welch rubbing his eyes.

This was one of the strangest male-bonding experiences I had ever seen. I left the guys to discuss ammo and weapons as I inspected the rest of the guns and crates.

"Weapons will not be enough." I turned to find a small man in his late seventies next to me. "The things you hunt are faster and stronger than you. You need magic to win this war."

Before I could reply, he walked away. I tried to follow him around the van but he was nowhere to be found. Welch and Eugene were still standing by the crates.

"Did he come this way?" I asked them.

"Who?" Welch asked.

"An old man, maybe in his seventies, with silver hair," I answered, trying to describe him with my hands.

"We don't have anyone that fits that description, babe," Welch replied, pulling out his gun as he went to search the area.

"That won't work on him," I said.

"Why?" he said.

"If I saw him and you didn't, he is already dead." I rubbed my temples softly. "We'll take it all. How much is it?"

"Already paid for," Welch replied. "Load it up, everyone."

The cargo area to the jet opened and Welch's men moved quickly to load everything in. Eugene grabbed a few of the grenades and flame throwers.

"Isis, take a few of the rifles and pistols," Eugene said.

"Are we doing target practice in the plane?" I asked, grabbing six.

"Just want to see how the rest of our ammo will work with some of these." Eugene was balancing seven different weapons around his body.

"Thank you, Welch," I said, unable to shake hands with him thanks to all my weapons.

"Always a pleasure." Welch kissed my cheek. "Don't die. I like knowing an Intern."

"I will do my best," I replied, backing away as fast as possible. I did not want to start blushing.

"You are good," Eugene told Welch, who only nodded back.

"Whenever everything is secure, we can go," I told George as I went up the stairs.

"Not a problem Ms. Isis." George put his 9mm away to inspect the cargo area as we climbed.

"You have the toughest crew I have ever seen," Eugene whispered.

"Constantine hired them," I answered. "Do you expect anything less?"

"That is so true." Eugene took his seat again, dropping all the weapons on the table.

Twenty minutes later, we were taxiing out and heading back to Texas. Eugene had dismantled several of the weapons when our flight attendant stopped by.

"Ms. Isis, you have an incoming conference call," she informed me.

"Thank you. Please connect us," I told her, expecting to see Constantine.

Instead of Constantine's furry face on the main screen of the plane, we had the fashionable-and-always-evil Pestilence staring at us.

"This better not be a shopping trip," Pestilence warned me.

"Mistress." Eugene almost fell to the ground in his attempt to bow.

"Unfortunately, your highness of evil, it was." I raised several guns for her to see. "Is this a social call?"

"Does it look like we have time for socializing?" Pestilence flipped her golden hair over one shoulder. "I need a status update."

"Mistress, we are trying to create a solar weapon that can be used against vampires but everything we have tried fails, and..." Eugene spoke so fast he forgot to breathe.

"Slow down now," I said softly.

"Are you trying to harness the power of the sun?" Pestilence asked, leaning closer to her screen. "Not bad, rookie. Unfortunately, human technology is not advanced enough to support that. I need to see your progress."

Pestilence's screen went dark. Eugene and I glanced around the room, making sure Pestilence was not behind us.

"Where do you think she went?" I asked after several checks of the jet.

"The only other place I can think of is Reapers." Eugene sagged back on his seat.

"We should warn Constantine." I reached for my phone.

"Too late," Eugene told me. "She is already there."

"He is going to be mad," I said. "Do you want some coffee?"

The jet was still taxiing, so I took the opportunity to get out of my seat.

"Yes, please," Eugene begged.

I didn't have to go far. Our flight attendant was heading my way with two cups of the divine elixir.

"Thank you so much," I told her taking the cups. "Here you go, Eugene."

Eugene took the cup in his hands. "Are you ready to work?"

"We have three hours. We can do this." I placed my cup on the table and started taking the rifles apart for Eugene.

We didn't have time to waste. If Eugene could find a way to improve our odds, I would assist in every way I could. The jet started to ascend, and I glanced out the window. Magic. The ghost said we will need magic to win. Besides my godmother and the elves, we didn't have magic. Or did we? Eugene's fingers were glowing as he played with the firing pin in his hand.

Chapter Nineteen

The sun was still shining when the jet landed in the back of the Lone Star center. What did the residence of Hooks think of this jet flying so close to them or did they even notice? I wanted to ask the flight crew, but it was close to seven pm according to my watch. We needed to hurry.

When the doors opened, we found Bob, Shorty, and the Triplets waiting for us with three trucks. The crew assisted us in loading all the weapons in the trucks. Thanks to Welch's great packing technique, moving everything took less than ten minutes.

"Thank you, George," I told the amazing pilot.

"If you need us, just call." George gave me a tight hug, and I wasn't sure if that was a bad sign.

"We will. Stay safe." I headed for Bob's truck.

"Always," George replied as he proceeded back to his team.

Eugene jumped in the truck with Shorty and the Triplets packed the last truck. Bob glanced at his rear-view mirror before taking off.

"Did I miss anything?" I asked Bob.

"Pestilence is at Reapers," he said, maneuvering out of the complex and heading east on Highway Eighty-Two.

"Glad I missed most of that." I adjusted my seatbelt in the truck. "How are Will and Jose?"

"Asleep," Bob replied. "Death stopped by and checked on them. Their injuries were extreme, but they are recovering. Interns are a touched bunch."

"A few days of sleep would be amazing," I mumbled. Wouldn't it be nice to miss the apocalypse?

"Minus the life-threatening injuries, of course," Bob added.

"Definitely minus those." I've had my share of injuries, and missing a few wasn't a bad thing.

"What's bothering you?" Bob asked.

"A soul told me we were going to need magic to win this war." I dropped my head against the window. "What kind of magic do we need?"

"You should ask Death," Bob said.

"That's a good idea," I agreed.

If anyone could figure out what we needed in this mess, it was probably Death. From the Lone Star center to Reapers was less than thirteen minutes on Eighty-Two. I barely had enough time to get my thoughts in order before pulling into the compound. The vehicles had to clear the security system one at a time. We were the first one through and I wasn't sure that was a good thing. The inside of Reapers was a beehive of excitement. People were all over the place, carrying things. Bob parked in his old spot, and Shorty took Ladybug's old space.

I really missed my car.

Pestilence and Death were exiting the lab followed by Ninth. Junior lagged behind, his hair in a mess and his coat scorched with burn marks. Whatever Pestilence had done in the lab had poor Junior wiping sweat from his face.

"Any problems?" Death asked as I hopped out of the truck.

"Not this time," I told her.

"Mistress." Eugene ran up to Pestilence as soon as he jumped out.

"Rookie," Pestilence answered. "We made some progress. But like I feared, the technology is not advanced enough to hold the amount of energy needed to burn a vampire down."

"I think I have an idea." Eugene did not dare look Pestilence in the eyes. "What if we created a grenade that was fueled with holy water and an accelerant? We have grenade launchers."

"That is an interesting idea." Pestilence snapped her fingers and the room went still. "Bring us as much holy water as you have and several cases of grenades."

The Triplets were the first ones to move and obey Pestilence. None of the other Interns were that excited to spend any time with Pestilence if it wasn't mandatory. Maybe it was the fact that they were fully human and had the least amount of exposure to the horseman. The rest of us went about our business.

"That's a great idea, but we don't have time to wait," Katrina announced. "The meeting is in forty-five minutes and we need to be there. Isis, you'd better get ready. We roll out in fifteen."

"Got it," I told her. "Death, do you need me?"

"If Marie is back, be very careful, Isis." Death crossed her arms over her immaculate white suit. "She is powerful and has been avoiding me for hundreds of years. Marie won't hesitate to kill you."

"She has been working hard at trying to kill me these last few days, so what else is new?" I asked. "Katrina, who is coming with us?"

"Bob, Shorty, and the Triplets if they stop serving Pestilence." Katrina watched the three men carrying more containers to the lab. "And five more troops."

"Is that enough?" For a regular house raid, that would be too many. For this, I didn't think so.

"Consider it a small recon mission. It will do." Katrina pushed me towards the stairs. "Now hurry."

I took the steps two at a time because I needed to change to my body armor to one similar to the one Welch had modified for us. Except that mine was blessed by my Godmother. The same person who was standing in the middle of Reapers with ripped clothes and messy hair when I entered. She was flanked by four other witches.

"God!" I shouted and rushed at her.

"Hi, honey." Godmother held me tight.

"What happened to you?" Godmother had bruises on her face as well as her arms. Her pants were ripped and not in a fashionable kind of way.

"It's been a long journey here," she replied, fixing my hair. "I really should be going with you."

"Are you serious?" I shouted.

"High Priestess, you are in no condition," one of her male companions told her.

"I agree with grown-up Harry Potter over there." It wasn't fair to make fun of him at a time like this, but I couldn't help it. He did look like Harry Potter.

"Your mouth is not going to save you from the threat that comes our way," grown-up Harry Potter told me.

"Anthony, please." Godmother calmed Harry Potter down. "We are all on the same team."

"Are we?" Anthony glared at me. "If it wasn't for her, they would have never dared to attack you."

"Is that what you all think?" Godmother asked all four witches. "Yes, I was attacked but not because Isis is my goddaughter. I was targeted because they knew I would never go against the horsemen. We are alive because of her. Or do you think the horsemen will forgive anyone who declared war on them?"

None of the witches replied, instead they sat on the dining room chairs. Godmother focused all her attention on me.

"Isis, please promise me you are going to be careful." Godmother held both of my hands.

"Godmother, don't worry about me. You need rest." I tried pulling away, but she held me tight.

"Promise me," she repeated.

"I promise," I told her. I could always try, but that didn't mean it was going to happen. "You can have my room."

"Constantine already made accommodations," she told me. "We've been on the run since I spoke to you. It appears the damage to the order was a lot deeper than I anticipated. We were hunted all the way here."

My heart rate increased, and I wanted to hold my Godmother tight.

"Relax, little one." Godmother gave me another hug. "You have work to do and so do we. I love you."

My Godmother kissed my cheeks and left the Loft. Her four minions followed her, none of them glancing in my direction. Not that I cared, but they could at least pretend to be polite in my house. I rushed towards my room to get dressed.

I'm in over my head.

I couldn't get the thought out of my mind. My heart rate was still elevated, and my hands were sweating. I paced the length of my room while taking deep breaths. Not even the soft jazz playing through the speaker system could soothe my soul. If my Godmother, who was hundreds of years old and super powerful, barely survived, how was I going to keep everyone alive? I needed to focus and quickly. I dropped to the ground and set my watch. Two minutes. It was only two minutes, but I did as many pushups as my body could handle. My mind started clearing around push-up number forty. By fifty-nine I could think straight again.

I laid on the ground and just breathed. I wasn't going to cry. I wasn't going to break down. We were going to find Bartholomew and make these fools pay for all our suffering. I was going to get them back if it was the last thing I ever did.

"Are you feeling better?" Death asked, startling me from my thoughts.

"When did you have time to come up?"

Death stood, moving to the bed and taking a seat closer to me. "You looked worried," she replied. "I didn't want to pressure you in front of the group. What is on your mind?"

"Everything," I replied. "The weight of the world. On top of that, I have a soul telling me I need magic to win this war. What kind of magic?"

I rolled on the ground to face the glow in the dark stars on my ceiling. My heart rate was starting to slow down, at least.

"You are battling supernatural creatures," Death answered after a few minutes of silence. "Human strength and willpower will not be enough. When the time comes, you will know what to do."

"That is absolutely not helpful," I told her.

"Neither is too much information," she replied. "Too much knowledge can have dangerous consequences. It can make you arrogant, and in turn clumsy. Or you can end up immobile with fear and terror. Focus on the present and you will find a way. You better hurry, though. Katrina is getting impatient."

Death pulled me from the floor and pushed me to the bathroom. If my options were clumsy or immobile, then Death was right. Too much knowledge was not worth the risk. Guess this giant mess was going to be tackled the same way I did everything else. I was going to make it up as we went along. Hopefully, other people were praying for us because we needed all the prayers we could get.

Chapter Twenty

The Four-States Fairgrounds was located on the Arkansas side, second exit off Interstate Thirty. It was no surprise the place was deserted and dark. There was nothing going on at the fairground this Thursday night. With all the Fourth of July celebrations having taken place the weekend before, there was not a soul in sight. We parked across the street from the fairground to avoid too much attention from potential witnesses. It was hard considering we were the only vehicles in the area. The group climbed from the vehicles, and we inspected our weapons.

"I recommend going around the back," Bob told us.

"I second that," Shorty jumped in. "We will have a few more places to hide."

"Lead the way then," Katrina told them.

We followed Bob and Shorty quickly across the field. Katrina unlocked the metal gate that was blocking our path towards the back. The Triplets were covering the rear, each carrying modified M16s. I didn't recognize any of the five guys with us. We had a lot of new recruits, and I was having a hard time keeping up with everyone. They were all young, and I doubted any of them were over twenty. They were a little fidgety, but they held their weapons steady even if their gazes jumped from shadow-to-shadow.

Lord, protect us.

We were going to need all the help we could get tonight, and silent prayers never hurt anyone. We made it to the back of the Fairgrounds, stopping right in front of the horse stables. The place was pitch-black.

"Are you sure anyone is here?" one of the young guys asked.

"They don't need light to see and they have exceptional hearing," Katrina told him. "Stay calm and try to not shoot any of us."

Katrina made a very valid point. If anyone on our team got trigger happy, we could all end up being collateral damage. Maybe I should have done a rosary before getting here. It appeared we needed a lot more prayers than the one I just sent up.

Katrina and Bob were the first ones through the doors. In a perfect military formation all in a V shape, we entered the fairgrounds in silence. Everyone donned their night-vision googles and moved deeper inside the area. The fairgrounds were the biggest event facility in Texarkana. With bleachers on both sides of the arena, the place could easily hold hundreds of people.

Bob stopped the group from advancing, then gave us a signal to remain quiet and move closer to the center. From our angle, the place looked desolate until I heard voices coming from the arena. The sounds were faint, and it took me several minutes to find them. Two massive vampires and three shifters stood around a female vampire who was sitting on a barrel. The arena this evening was set up for barrel racing, with some extra rolls of hay littering the place.

"We want the Americas," one of the shifters said.

"I'm not giving you both North and South America," the female replied in a sexy European accent. "Pick the countries you want, but you are not getting the whole thing. I already told you that before."

"Yes, but my people have no interest in claiming terrains overseas," the shifter replied.

It was very hard to see details with night-vision googles. Everyone had that strange aura that came with this type of surveillance.

"It will be great for you to see other parts of the world," the vampires added. "But I'd rather wait on victory negotiations until we know we have won."

"The horsemen will ride," the shifter told her.

"You said that two days ago and nothing," the vampire snapped. "We cannot take any chances. You underestimated the tenacity of Constantine and the will of his Interns."

"We shouldn't, since they are here," the vampire to her right motioned in our direction.

"Guess the surprise is over," said Katrina, charging at the small group.

The rest of us did not have any choice but to follow the super soldier to battle. This battle was like nothing I'd ever experienced. The vampires moved like shadows. One minute, they were standing in front of me, the next, they were gone. I pulled out my scythe and commenced assault maneuvers. The shifters didn't bother turning to their animal forms. They just transformed their hands into claws and charged at us. Within two minutes, our five young guys were knocked out on the ground bleeding from different places. I connected on a handful of punches before one of the shifters punched me in the chest. I landed a few feet away. Thankfully, it was not nearly as hard as Famine's punches.

It took me several seconds for my breathing to come back to normal. I took the googles off and decided to follow my senses instead. Battle was raging around me, as my team shot at the shifters without luck. It was like they were dodging moving bullets. I could hear the vampires but finding them was impossible.

"I'm going to kill you!" Katrina shouted, and I decided to follow her voice.

Laughter filled the arena. I couldn't hear Katrina, but I could sense her. By the time I reached her, she was pinned down by one of the vampires. His jaw was extended and moving towards Katrina's jaw way too quickly for my liking. I spun the scythe as hard as I could, but I was not fast enough. The vampire turned just in time and grabbed the scythe with one hand. The beast underneath the pretty face stared at me but only briefly.

That was the curse of Death's Interns; we could see the real beast. The fact that the real self only lasted a few seconds was a problem. It meant this vampire was old and powerful to maintain the glamour for that long. He extended his fangs and licked his lips. I grabbed the closest gun I had and opened fire. Bullets were useless with this monster, but they still served for shock value. The vampire bounced off Katrina a few feet away from us and released my scythe. I continued to open fire as Katrina got off the floor.

"Holy water is useless on them!" Katrina shouted, covering my back.

"Great" I yelled changing guns.

"Is this how you plan to die, little Interns," the female vampire spoke.

Her voice was close but we couldn't find her. She laughed, and this time, I looked up.

"Holy crap," I said. "She is on the ceiling."

The vampire was walking upside down on the ceiling of the fairgrounds right above our heads.

"That's a new level of crazy," Katrina told me.

"Now what?" I asked her.

"We have too many wounded. We need to get out of here," Katrina admitted.

"You can't leave," the female said from above. "We are going to have so much fun."

"Not if I send you to hell first." Shorty rushed at us.

"Shorty. NO!" I screamed.

Shorty let out his own evil laugh as he used the flamethrower he was carrying to set fire to the fairgrounds. The entire place went up in a blaze of smoke and flames. Bob and Shorty did not believe in overkill, but this was probably the exception.

"Bob, Triplets, grab the wounded," I ordered, running to the closest injured guy.

"What a pity," the female vampire said before flying from the building.

"She can fly," Katrina growled.

"Yes, and her little friends can dodge bullets," I told her, struggling to pick up the young man.

"Cover me. I got him." Katrina handed me her rifle and picked up the young man.

Without even breathing hard, she rolled the guy over her shoulder in a fireman-hold. The flames were spreading all around us and the smoke thickening.

"We need to go!" I shouted at my team.

"Isis, take point and Shorty will cover the rear!" Bob yelled from the back.

"Shorty, are you ready?" I asked, inspecting the area.

"Ready," Shorty replied, still sending flames all around him.

"Moving." I took off at a slow shuffle to ensure those carrying the injured could keep up.

Katrina was the fastest of the group. Carrying wounded was a basic drill in the military and she'd had years of practice mastering it. She moved with the ease of a runner even with her load. I didn't bother concealing our retreat. If any of the six attacked us, we were doomed. We rushed out of the fairgrounds and across the parking lot towards our vehicles.

We were not followed by either vampires or shifter, and that worried me. Katrina lowered the young man to the ground once we reached the vehicles. We both turned to face the road to provide backup for everyone else making their way to the vehicle.

"Did anyone follow you?" I asked Shorty as he ran in my direction.

"Nothing," Shorty replied, standing by my side inspecting the area. "I could feel something watching us inside the fairgrounds. But as soon as we left the arena it was gone."

"Why didn't they attack us?" Katrina asked, helping Bob and the Triplets with the wounded. "We were defenseless here."

"Because I was here," Death said from behind the vehicles.

"Now that makes more sense," said Katrina. "Thank you, Death."

"I might not be able to interfere, but I will not send you to a suicide mission if I can help it," Death told us.

"Was that the same vampire you and Constantine warned us about?" I asked Death, not lowering my gun.

"Yes," Death replied softly. "That is Marie, and she is more powerful than any vampire on this side of the ocean."

"Boss Lady, we need to go," Shorty told me. "Our guys are not looking good at all."

"We are heading to the station since it's closer than Reapers from here," I told them. "Death, are you coming with us?"

"Only to the doors. Once you are secure, I'll go." Death crossed her arms and stood guard. "I got this. Go help them."

I left Death and rushed over to Katrina. We had to stop the bleeding of all the guys before we loaded them in the vehicles. Blood was everywhere, and we had to improvise with dressings. Our first-aid kits did not contain enough bandages to cover all the affected areas. We ripped the guys' shirts, as well as the tank tops Katrina and I were wearing under our gear, to make more bandages. Since none of them were Interns, trying to have Death heal them could end up killing them instead.

"Isis, are you guys almost done?" Bob asked.

"Done," I replied.

We distributed the wounded troops between all the trucks. In their condition, they took up a lot more space than before.

"Good." Bob advanced to the front vehicle. "Shorty, you drive the second truck. Number one, take the third truck. Isis, you're with Shorty, and Katrina with number one. The rest with me."

"Boss Death, where would you like to ride?" Shorty asked as he glanced at all the vehicles.

"I'll take the top," Death told him, hopping on the bed of Bob's truck.

Death sat on the hood of the truck and crossed her legs, which made her look like a truck model waiting for a photographer.

"Bob, whenever you are ready," Death said softly to Bob.

Bob climbed in the driver seat and the rest of us followed, getting in our positions. Death leaned back on the hood of the truck and watched the surrounding night.

"Do you think that's safe?" Shorty asked me, pointing at Death.

I had to giggle. "You are actually concerned for Death's safety?" I buckled in to survive Shorty's journey.

"If Death goes flying off that hood, he'll be landing inside this one." Shorty swallowed hard.

"I'm pretty sure Death is not going to move from that spot," I told him.

Bob took off and Shorty followed behind. Like I expected, Death rode like a beauty queen in a parade, never bounced or moved regardless of the turns Bob took. Once Shorty realized he was safe from a Death-projectile, he picked up the speed. Now we just needed to make it to the station fast enough to not lose these five in transit. After all our work, that would be the worst ending ever.

Chapter Twenty-One

The station had medics on standby at all times. Our injured group was admitted and stabilized very quickly. After ensuring everyone was secure, we decided it was safer to split up. Shorty stayed at the station with the Triplets. Bob, Katrina, and I headed back to Reapers around eleven pm. The three of us had minor injuries, but nothing that we wanted our medics wasting their supplies on. Nobody said a word on the ride back. There wasn't much to say since we were outgunned and running out of time.

All the lights were on in Reapers when we parked the Camaro. We headed straight for the Loft like wounded puppies with our tails between our legs. Our friends were still up when we entered the Loft. Ninth, Junior, and Eugene were all sitting at the kitchen table with their faces down. Godmother and Anthony were on the couch avoiding the monitors.

The horsemen were having another action-packed video conference, this time yelling at Constantine, who was yelling right back while standing on a chair. If they were trying to intimidate someone, they picked the wrong guy. Constantine had increased to the size of a panther and was not backing down.

"How dare you tell me how to run my operations!" Constantine hissed. "If you were so brilliant why would you build a lab underneath a chicken plant and not create an emergency exit?"

"Listen here you furball for brains, don't you dare question my methods." Pestilence slammed her fist on her desk.

"Methods? What methods?" Constantine shouted back. "You're barely able to keep up with your inventory."

That was a low blow for Eugene, who slouched on the chair where he was sitting. Junior gave us a small wave while Eugene kept his eyes down.

"I told you we should have finished this off from the beginning," said Famine.

"You don't count," Constantine growled. "Your solution to everything is killing everyone off."

"Listen you..." Famine was getting louder.

I had a small throbbing pain developing behind my eyes, and this conversation was not helping. I marched over to the conference area.

"Enough!" it was my turn to scream.

The room went silent. All eyes were focused on me, to include the people in the Loft as well as the horsemen.

"What in God's name is going on here?" I placed my hands on my hips and tapped my foot.

"Listen here, little girl." War directed his undivided attention towards me. "We do not negotiate with terrorists and I do not get threatened in my own house by wannabes —"

"General, could you please get to the point?" I cut across him, ignoring the gasps coming from the Interns on my side. "I know your policies perfectly well. I was a soldier, remember? So, unless you have something useful to say, you can keep your comments to yourself."

"Attitude." Pestilence rolled her head to give War the stink eye. "Death, looks like your little girl is on fire."

"That goes for you, too, Pestilence." I directed my anger at her as well. "Is there a point to this?"

"Your little friends called us," Famine clarified. "To remind us of our current failures and the lack of progress for all of you."

"Did you actually get beaten up by three vampires and three werewolves?" War asked spitting all over the place. "That is a disgrace."

"We got slowed down by a fifteen-hundred-year-old vampire and some very powerful alpha shifters," I corrected.

"How are you planning to stop them?" Pestilence asked.

"If I remember correctly, we have until tomorrow." I rolled my head in the same arrogant manner as Pestilence. "That means we don't owe you a play-by-play on our progress. All you care about is your reputation, so if we fail tomorrow evening, you can correct that. Why don't you all go find something to entertain yourselves with? I heard The Witcher on Netflix is a killer."

"You arrogant brat." Famine disconnected his call.

"You have until eight pm tomorrow or the Fourth of July will be the spectacle you will never forget." War terminated his call.

"Death, I hope you know what you are doing," Pestilence told her sister and disconnected.

"Not bad, Isis." Constantine shrunk back to his normal cat size as Death appeared next to him.

"Constantine is right," Death adjusted her white suit. "You handled that very well."

"Handled what? Three angry horsemen?" I moved away from the screen and leaned on the glass wall. "They are right, though. Twelve of us couldn't even touch the six of them."

"We are fighting the supernatural with humans. How is that fair?" Katrina joined me against the glass.

"Why can't we call the Reapers?" Bob asked from the kitchen.

All the Interns turned to face Bob while Constantine shook his head.

"It's not that easy. In order to summon the Reapers from their slumber, we need a live one roaming the earth," Constantine answered Bob. "We haven't had a breathing Reaper in over twelve-hundred years."

"For those not following the Reaper conversation." Junior had his hand raised. "What is a Reaper?"

"A superhuman," Death told him. "With the speed and strength of a vampire but with my gifts and immortality."

"Now we are talking. How do we get a few of those?" Junior bounced from his seat and got closer to us.

"Junior is right, how do we get one of those?" I pushed myself away from the glass.

"Only Death's Intern can qualify as a Reaper," said Constantine.

"I have not made a Reaper in fifteen-hundred years and I'm not ready to make another." Death disappeared without another word.

"Constantine, what are we missing?" Katrina asked, searching the room. "The reputation of the Reapers skills and abilities are legendary. We could use them in this fight."

"The process is not as easy as it sounds." Constantine sat on the computer table. "Death has to share his essence with the Interns in order to make the transformation possible. The problem is, if the soul of the Intern is not a worthy one, the results are catastrophic."

"How bad can it be?" Eugene asked, not lifting his head from the table. "We are already surrounded by enemies and angry horsemen."

"A bad Reaper is worse than any vampire or wild monster around," Constantine said softly. "Death refuses to let that happen again."

"Is Death not willing to make more Reapers?" Katrina pushed Constantine this time.

"Death will not make them because if they turn out bad, we will be the ones ending them." Silence filled the room as Constantine's words hit home. "It's late. Everyone needs to get some rest."

Nobody moved for a few minutes. The events of the day weighed heavily on all of us. Godmother was the first to get up. It was odd for her not to have said anything. Her pride was probably shattered with the betrayal the Order suffered.

"Being one of the eldest here means I will lead the way." Godmother kissed my cheek. "Good night, Isis. Please try to sleep. Anthony, we have a long day ahead of us."

Anthony followed Godmother out of the Loft and towards Katrina's area. Junior tried to hold in a yawn but couldn't.

"Eugene, Junior, follow me. You two are about to crash," Bob told the wonder-twins.

"I'll be going with you as well," Ninth added.

That was a good thing since I was sure he had fallen asleep sitting on the chair. Katrina took a seat on the leather couch and made herself comfortable.

"You need rest," I told her.

"So do you, but I don't see that happening," Katrina told me.

"You both need sleep," Constantine added.

"Constantine, we didn't have a chance tonight." I went back to the original conversation. "How are we to battle a fifteen-hundred-year-old vampire that can walk on the ceiling?"

"She can?" Constantine stopped licking his paws and faced me.

"Not just walk. She can stroll like she was on a runway," Katrina clarified for me.

"The shifters were faster than anyone I had ever seen." I sat on the floor. "We were shooting and hitting nothing. It was like being stuck in The Matrix. How do we win against that?"

"There is always a way but beating yourself up is not going to help." Constantine turned to face the glass wall. "No one is going to sleep tonight. This air of despair is not what we need before our last day."

"It's hard to rest when the whole world is crumbling around you." Katrina tilted her head against the couch.

"I might be able to help." I rushed towards my room.

Our troubles were escalating rapidly but Constantine was right. We couldn't all be exhausted tomorrow if we had any hopes to win this war. I grabbed my guitar from the back of the room and ran out. Katrina and Constantine were both waiting for me when I returned.

"Are you planning to sing to our enemies?" Katrina pulled her legs closer to her body.

"Not tonight," I replied, sticking my tongue out at her. "Tonight, I'm planning to help people sleep. No more, no less."

"That is a really good idea," Constantine told me. "I'm sure some of our guests haven't had a good night's sleep in days."

"You are probably right. Do you need earphones Constantine?" I asked as I made myself comfortable.

"I can block you off pretty well by now," Constantine replied. "What do you have in mind?"

"I was thinking a lullaby." I turned on the intercom system.

My singing was not nearly as good as Katrina's, but then again very few people were as good as she was. My musical skills, on the other hand, were out of this world. With the help of Death's gifts, I could convey the most powerful feelings imaginable just by playing a song. I checked the cords in my guitar to make sure they were in tune. Then I slowly played the sweetest version of Go to Sleep Lullaby.

It didn't take long for Katrina to recline on the couch. Her eyelids slowly closed, and she was fast asleep. The movement across the other lofts also stopped, and the lights in Bob's apartment went out. I played for another twenty minutes to make sure everyone was really asleep.

"Now, when are you going to sleep?" Constantine asked me.

"My mind is all over the place, Constantine," I told him softly. "I miss Bartholomew so much."

"I know you do but burning out is not the best plan you've had all week," Constantine told me. "Isis, you are not going to be any help to anyone if you are falling down."

"I know you are right," I admitted to Constantine. "Just give me fifteen. I want to check a few things online before going down."

Constantine left the Loft through the kitty door. I took a seat in Bartholomew's chair and turned on his computer. Bartholomew's wallpaper was a picture of us—Bob, Constantine, him, and me. We were sitting on the stairs, all of us smiling. I missed him, and I would do anything to get him back. Bartholomew had a link to the supernatural dark web. I wanted to do a quick search on Reapers. What exactly did the rest of the world think of Death's superhuman creatures? Why was Death so hesitant to make more if it could mean winning this war?

Chapter Twenty-Two

The sun was barely out when I hit my second round of kicks and punches on the boxing bag. With the bag, my mind could focus all my energy and aggression on a solid object. After last night's research on the supernatural web, I was more confused than ever.

Reapers were the boogeyman of the supernatural world. They were powerful, deadly, and feared. The concept of Death wearing a hood and scythe came from the Reapers, since that was their original battle uniform. They rid the world of dangerous vampires and out-of-control monsters, but they destroyed cities and communities in the process. They did not care who was hurt or killed in their campaigns. The ones that went rogue were even worse. Their need for destruction had no end. Thousands of innocent people died at the hands of Reapers. It made sense why Death and Constantine were so hesitant about making more.

I closed my eyes and worked on my forms. The vampires glided like ballerinas when they moved. I needed to master their grace and speed. With my shoulders, I pushed the bag to add extra movement to my workout. My goal was to work on kicking a moving target just using my senses. Half of the punches and kicks landed on the bag, and the others just air. I did a somersault and released a roundhouse, but the kick landed on something softer than my bag.

"Ouch." I opened my eyes to find Iason completely red face.

"Oh God," I muttered. "I'm so sorry. I didn't know you were there."

"You didn't see me standing in front of you?" Iason pulled a cloth handkerchief and wiped the small trail of blood running down his nose.

"I was practicing a new technique." I wasn't lying.

"Have you ever considered it would be more effective to practice with your eyes open?" Iason chastised me.

"If you knew I had my eyes closed, why wouldn't you move?" I peeled the boxing gloves off me.

"I was hoping your sense of awareness was a lot better." Iason put the handkerchief away. "If you are not able to feel other beings around you, you really need to keep your eyes open."

"It is not my fault you are going around sneaking up on people." I was aiming to have the last word in this odd battle. "Why are you here so early?"

I looked at my watch and it was only six-forty-five.

Iason inched closer and stared me down. "What were you thinking?" He came even closer, now only inches from me.

"You might need to be more specific." By the sound of his voice, I had done something really serious. With my record this week, that could be anything.

"You attacked a group of ancient vampires with just humans?" Iason marched around me making small circles. "They have spread the word around all of Haven that they destroyed you last night and left you with tons of injured."

"Tons of injured?" Iason was making me dizzy with his movement, so I focused straight ahead. "We had five out of twelve. I wouldn't call that tons of injured."

"Why didn't you call me?" Iason's face was completely red.

"I didn't think we needed help." I bit my lower lip and looked at the ground. "We have faced vampires before. I figured between Katrina, Bob, and me, we could take on a few ash monsters."

"Isis, you have never faced an ancient vampire." Iason held me by the shoulder.

"Thanks. Kind of figured that out already." I took a deep breath instead of punching him in the guts for being overly dramatic.

"Isis." Bob and Shorty ran in through the pedestrian door, and Iason dropped his arms to his sides.

"What are you two up to?" I asked Bob, who handed me an envelope.

"This got delivered to the station an hour ago," Shorty answered.

"Is it safe?" Iason sniffed the envelope.

"It passed through all the detectors," replied Shorty.

"In that case..." I ripped open the envelope, relieved I wasn't going to be turned into a toad by a magical curse. "Damn, I think I was better off with a magical curse."

"Isis." Iason read the letter over my shoulder. "You can't."

I ran up the stairs without answering him. Bob and Shorty followed quickly behind. I burst through the door of the Loft where Katrina and Constantine were having coffee at the kitchen table.

"What is going on?" Katrina asked, putting her mug down.

I tossed them the letter and paced. Katrina pulled the letter over and read it.

"You are not doing this!" Katrina shouted, slamming her chair to the ground.

"Can someone please explain what the Boss Lady is not supposed to be doing?" Shorty asked, completely out of breath.

Bob wasn't far behind and leaned against the fridge.

"Trading herself for Bartholomew," Constantine told him after reading the letter.

"Hell no, she is not doing that," Shorty shouted as he, too, started pacing in the kitchen.

"Constantine, you can't let her," Iason demanded as he ran in.

"It's a trap. Please tell me you know that," Katrina said to me.

"Of course, it's a trap," I told her. "Do you think I haven't already figured that out? But what other option do we have?"

"Are we giving up? Is that what you are telling me?" Constantine pushed his mug away.

"This might be the only time for us to get them all together," I tried to explain. "I don't mind being bait if it gives us a chance. Make me a Reaper. That might be the magic we need to survive this war."

Shorty stopped and turned around. Bob pushed away from the fridge and stood up straight. Even Katrina and Iason did not move from their spots.

"Isis, you are full of anger and rage," Constantine reminded me. "If your soul is not pure, it will be up to me to rip your throat out."

"Was that really necessary?" Katrina smacked Constantine on the side.

"Isis, we can come up with a plan," said Bob.

"This is our best chance to win. Besides, am I really that messed up that you all think I wouldn't pass?" I had been very angry lately, but did they know something I didn't?

"You will be immortal," Iason answered. "Immortality is not what it's cracked up to be. Everyone you love, everyone you have fought for, will die before your eyes. You will witness them dying one-by-one, and you will be left alone."

"Hey, I will be here," Constantine argued.

"Semi-alone," Iason corrected himself.

"Is that why elves only marry other elves?" Katrina asked him.

"It's the reason we don't associate with other races," Iason said softly. "The pain is less when you don't have to face it over and over."

"You all heard it; we need a Reaper to raise the other ones." I faced the glass instead of my friends. "In less than twelve hours, it might not matter because the entire Earth will be destroyed. What do we have to lose?"

"You," Bob answered for the group.

"We need a vote," Katrina chinned in. "The wonder-twins need to be involved."

Katrina left the Loft to find Eugene and Junior.

"I'll go find your Godmother." Bob headed towards the door.

"Wait for me," Shorty told him.

"There is no turning back if you do this," Constantine told me. "Once the process has started, it cannot be stopped. If you don't pass the test, it will be a really short immortality."

"Great pep-talk Constantine," I tried to tease but it fell flat.

"I will give you an hour to think about it." Constantine hopped down from the table. "I must talk to Death."

Constantine left the Loft. Iason ran his hands through his hair and waited.

"Why are you doing this?" he asked softly.

"What would you do if Ginny was the one being held captive?" I moved closer to him.

"You know that already. Anything," he replied.

"I would do the same for Bartholomew," I told him. "I would never be able to live with myself knowing I had a way to save him and didn't try."

"Isis, this process is like Russian roulette," Iason explained. "On one hand, you have super-human powers and immortality. On the other hand, if your thoughts and emotions are not right, you will end up dead."

"But at least I tried." I kissed his cheek and strolled away because I didn't want to hear anymore lectures. Constantine said he would give me an hour, so the least I could do was show up to my funeral clean. I opened the door to my room to find Death by my bed.

"You know they are worried about you?" Death asked as she skimmed through one of my books.

"I don't want to worry anyone." I closed the door behind me. "I just want to do the right thing."

"Iason is right." Death put the book down. "It's fifty-fifty. It's not all good or all bad. You will have sacrifices to make if you become a Reaper, but you will also have infinite power. At first you will only see the good, but as your friends start dying, the emptiness becomes greater and greater."

"If I don't do this, everyone is going to die tomorrow." I sat on the bed.

"You don't know that." Death rose from the chair and moved towards me. "You are making a life decision based on an assumption. Are you willing to take that risk?"

"Do you think I won't pass?" I whispered to Death.

"That is not what I'm worried about." Death kneeled in front of me. "I don't want you to regret this decision and hate Bartholomew for it. If you decide to do this, it better be for all the right reasons and not because of guilt or shame. Think about it."

"Fine," I replied, my mouth dry.

Death left my bedroom and I sat on the bed motionless.

Why was I doing this? Was I trying to run away again?

I took several deep breaths and slowed my heart rate. Yes, I was angry Bartholomew and the other Interns were taken. Yes, I felt guilty that I was left behind while they were being tortured. Yes, I wanted those who did this to pay. But did I want power, revenge, or glory?

I didn't have answers for all my questions. Instead of wasting more time debating the meaning of life, I went to the bathroom. At least I could think about things while I washed my hair. The power of multitasking. All my best ideas always came in the shower.

Chapter Twenty-Three

The Loft was deserted when I emerged from my room. I still had five minutes left in my hour but there was no point sitting up here alone. My throat was still parched, but I feared I would puke everything up if I decided to drink something now. Instead of the fridge, I headed out the door.

Everyone was waiting for me on the first floor. Death was wearing a brilliant-red suit by Vera Wang. Godmother was wearing a dark robe and none of her minions were in attendance. That was a blessing since that group hated me. Katrina, Eugene, Junior, Bob, Shorty, Iason, and Constantine were standing in a semicircle around Death.

"This looks somber," I joked but nobody laughed.

I made my way towards Death and the group stood still.

"Have you made a decision?" Death asked as I stood in front of her.

"Isis, wait." Katrina strolled towards me. "Whatever you decide, please know that we support you. I love you, little girl, and I will be right here with you."

I embraced Katrina and didn't care if tears were rolling down my cheeks. Katrina kissed my cheeks and went back to her spot.

"Isis." Eugene stepped up.

"No, we are not doing this," I told the group. "I don't have the emotional energy. We are not saying goodbye. This is just a process, and we have done worse."

I strolled towards Eugene and hugged him. "I love you, too."

Speeches were out of the question. Instead, I made my way around the circle, hugging my friends and family one by one. Even Iason got a hug from me. He wiped the tears from my face and winked at me. I was grateful they were here but somehow it would have been easier to do this alone.

Godmother was the last one I hugged. She held me tight and kissed my forehead and both of my cheeks.

"The Goddess told me I would see you die one day," Godmother stated.

"That is not very reassuring, thanks," I told her, and she giggled.

"What I think the Goddess meant was I would see the death of your mortal form and the rebirth of your new one." Godmother wouldn't let me go.

"Nice recovery," I whispered in her ear.

"I love you like my own child." Godmother rubbed my cheeks. "Remember who you are. Kind, loving and brave."

I pulled away before I started crying again. Death was in the center of the semi-circle with Constantine standing by her side.

"Isis, remember why you are doing this," Constantine repeated to me.

"Are you ready?" Death asked.

"Let's do this," I replied, trying to sound cheerful but failing.

"It's going to hurt," Death warned before holding my head in her hands. "Breathe deeply."

I relaxed my shoulders and took a deep breath. Death blew in my face and her breath turned to smoke. The smoke wrapped all around me. At first it was light, like a fog, but slowly turned darker and I couldn't see anything in front of me. The smoke went in my mouth and my nostrils, burning all the way down. I wanted to scream but nothing came out of my mouth, instead more smoke came in. My knees buckled and I felt my body hit the ground. As my head smacked against the concrete, my soul lifted from my body.

Oh crap!

I was having an out of body experience. My body was on the ground thrashing. Constantine was whispering, or maybe shouting close to my ear, but I couldn't hear him. Godmother was praying, and Death kneeled by my side. Everyone else looked like shadows I couldn't see clearly.

"Why are you doing this?" a soft, sweet voice asked from behind.

My soul slowly shifted to find my mother next to me, her long, dark hair flowing in an invisible wind.

"Mom." I drifted closer to her. "I'm scared."

"I know you are, honey, but remember why you are doing this," she repeated in a gentle voice.

"For Bartholomew," I answered.

"Is that the only reason?" My mother played with my hair.

I turned and watched my body thrash over and over. Katrina leaned down, trying to touch me. Iason pulled her away. Eugene and Junior cried uncontrollably. Bob held Shorty as he wept.

"For them." I told my mother. "I want my family to have a long life, even if I'm not with them. I will trade my soul for their happiness."

Tears filled my vision as my mother embraced me.

"I'm so proud of you, sweetie." My mother kissed my forehead. "But it is time to work."

"What?" I asked in between tears.

My mother pushed my soul back into my body. I hit the ground so hard all my bones cracked and popped. I couldn't breathe, couldn't open my eyes, and the entire room felt like it was spinning.

"Isis, can you hear me?" Constantine shouted in my ear.

"Woah," I could barely utter the word.

"Good. Can you look at me?" Constantine demanded.

I followed the sound of his voice and moved my head. It was like dragging a fifty-pound bucket of lead. Everything hurt, and I struggled to open my eyes. When I finally got them opened, the light blinded me as pain crashed down my forehead. I rolled over and puked all over the floor. It was a blessing I skipped food before coming down.

"Isis, how do you feel?" I could feel Constantine's breath on my face.

It took all the power in my body to turn my head to face him. Our eyes locked, and Constantine jumped with joy.

"Glad you are happy," I mumbled. "I feel like I just got run over by Shorty several times."

"That's my girl," Constantine announced.

Death and Godmother kneeled in front of me. Godmother was wiping her face with her sleeve. Death slowly raised my face with her finger.

"Welcome to the world, my little Reaper." Her touch felt like an electric current all through my body.

"Thank you, God," prayed Bob.

"YES. Go, Boss Lady!" Shorty's voice was like a drum beating in my head.

Colors in the room were brighter, sounds more defined, and even my sense of smell was enhanced. That last one I could live without since half of the people in the room really needed a shower, including me after puking.

"She is alive. Thank you, my Lord!" cried Junior.

"Those are the famous Reapers' eyes," Katrina said leaning closer to me.

"What do they look like?" Eugene rushed over to see.

"Pure silver." Katrina reached for my hair.

"Don't touch her," Constantine shouted. "We have no idea how your essence could affect her new power. Last thing we need is to mix another horsemen's energy with Death's."

"Really?" Katrina asked, tugging at her hair.

"Constantine, she needs rest now," Death stated. "Unfortunately, if I do it she will be out for two days and all this will be for nothing."

"Can I help?" Iason volunteered.

"What do you have in mind, elf boy?" Constantine growled like a protective parent.

"We have a spell that speeds up healing and other things," Iason explained.

"Is it safe?" Eugene asked. "You wouldn't let us touch her. How is she going to handle Elf magic on top on Death's?"

"I'm not sure, Eugene," Death answered. "We are in uncharted territories."

"That only sounds cool in Star Trek." Eugene crossed his arms. "Right now, that is some scary shit."

"I second, Eugene," Junior concurred. "I vote we veto that idea."

"That's great, everyone, but that is not our choice," Katrina told them as she glanced my way. "What do you want to do, Isis? We will support you the whole way."

I love you Katrina. But I didn't have enough strength to speak anymore.

"Do it," I said to the floor.

"Listen here elf boy, if something happens to her I'm going to shred you to pieces," Constantine threatened.

"If you survive Constantine, I will skin you alive," my Godmother added her own deadly threat.

It was better for the world that they didn't join forces. The two of them together were terrifying. I felt sorry for Iason for volunteering.

"We don't need to tell you what the three of us would do, right?" Katrina told him as Eugene and Junior cracked their knuckles.

"You have more bodyguards than I do," Iason teased me. "I'm going to pick you up."

"Oh God!" I screamed as Iason lifted me into his arms.

My body trembled uncontrollably. The smell of cinnamon and vanilla coming off Iason was intoxicating.

"Careful," Death told him. "All of her cells are rebuilding."

"I'll be gentle," Iason told her. "I'm going to take you upstairs. Are you ready?"

Iason looked into my eyes and leaned down. Maybe it was the fact that he was carrying me like a baby, or that my mind was not fully working, but I didn't realize what happened until he kissed me. His lips tasted like honey as the throbbing in my head stopped.

"Sweet dreams," Iason whispered.

I fought to keep my eyes open, but it was a lost cause. My eyelids betrayed me, and the whole room was going dark. We were moving, and for a moment I worried if we were riding with the Boatman and the currents were taking us. My limbs felt lighter as the pain decreased. The world felt like it was rocking, and I was laying in something soft and warm.

"Rest, Isis," Iason whispered to me. "You've been through a lot."

"Where am I?" I asked, still unable to open my eyes fully.

"In your room." Iason moved my hair out of my face. "We need your cells to finish generating before you can go out and play. A part of you died today. I saw your soul leaving your body, and I wasn't sure if you were coming back."

"I didn't know that was an option," I admitted.

"That is always an option." Iason played with my hair.

"I'm never going to live that down," I told him, holding on to his hand.

"Live what down?" he asked softly, rubbing my hand.

"That whole sleeping beauty kiss thing." I cracked one eye open to find Iason blushing.

"The magic needs direct contact with your fluids to work," he explained, turning even redder. "Unless you prefer me sticking my fingers in your mouth."

"Gross," I replied. "I don't know where your hands have been. Or your mouth for that matter."

"Mouth is probably safer than hands," Iason joked. "I did cut a few vampires to pieces before coming here."

"Thank you," I said as my eyes closed again.

I felt Iason's lips kissing mine and the warmth from his body spreading all over me.

"What was that for?" I asked.

"For not staying dead." Iason covered me with one of my blankets.

My sheets smelled like Jasmine and I could hear every single note from the symphony playing in the speaker system. The smells were so intense I could taste them. Constantine never mentioned that everything was going to be enhanced with this transformation. I'd thought it would just be my strength. I wanted to stay awake and enjoy the feel of the sheets on my skin, but sleep pulled me away.

Chapter Twenty-Four

The air in the room shifted, and I didn't need to open my eyes to know Death was here. I rolled to one side and the pain was gone. My head wasn't spinning like a roller coaster.

"Hi, Death," I told her, proud my voice was back.

"I wondered how long you were planning to ignore me," Death said from her favorite chair.

"You knew I was awake?" I asked, opening my eyes slowly.

"At the same time you knew I was here," Death replied.

"How strong is this bond?" I wasn't ready for so much connection with Death all the time.

"A part of me is in you now," answered Death.

"Is that what replaced the part of me that died?" I still did not like knowing I had died.

"To some extent, yes." Death touched my forehead and examined my eyes. "How do you feel?"

"Overwhelmed," I confessed. "I'm grateful for the soundproof room, but even with it I can still hear sounds from outside."

"It's going to take a while to adjust to the new senses," Death sat back on the chair. "Iason's binding is fairly impressive."

"How so?" I asked, sitting up on the bed.

"Normally, it would take between twenty-four to forty-eight hours for the transformation to settle into your cells." Death examined my hands this time. "He did it in three hours. We let you sleep a few extra hours just to make sure, but you are ready."

"So, it is time to work?" I asked.

"Absolutely." Death stood from the chair. "The horsemen will be having a council in fifteen minutes downstairs. Make sure to grab a couple of shakes on your way down. You need some sustenance in your system."

Death disappeared. This meeting was urgent if Death didn't even bother walking out the door. I flipped the blankets off and climbed out of bed. The floor was freezing. These overly developed senses were going to be a pain to adjust. I proceeded slowly to the bathroom and turned on the light. My reflection shocked me. My nose and mouth were still the same, but my eyes were unnatural.

My eyeballs were different shades of silver. For the human eye, they would look like one solid silver ball. My pupils were a bit darker than my irises. Even my scleras were silver, creating a strange affect. The lines separating each part were there, but it was also a darker silver. There was no way to blend in with these babies. The dark circles under my eyes that had become a permanent part of my normal complexion were gone, so that was a plus.

I took off my shirt since it was stained from this morning's events. As I turned to face the mirror, I did a double take. I had perfect abs. That was impossible. I took off all my clothes and spun around in circles, checking myself out from all angles. Yes, the world was about to be destroyed but I was currently too busy checking out my newly-defined form. The transformation left me without an ounce of fat on my body, or even cellulite. That was an amazing perk.

After wasting seven out of my fifteen minutes analyzing my new body, I rushed down the stairs. Grace was not something that I'd inherited with this new transformation. I was not accustomed to my new speed and crashed into Shorty's truck when I tried to stop on the first floor. The side door of the truck now had two huge dents in the shape of my hands. If I wanted to make an entrance, I had accomplished that as well.

"Sorry about that," I said to the group of people staring at me.

The horsemen were all sitting on thrones made of precious jewels and metals. In front of each horsemen an Intern was kneeling, except for Death. I motioned to her, and she shook her head. Death crossed her legs and focused on her siblings. Shorty, Bob, and Ninth were standing back, watching the horsemen. Constantine sat on a chair on his back facing the ceiling. I walked instead of running towards Bob and Shorty to make sure I was able to stop. I didn't want a head-on-collision with them.

"Welcome back, Boss Lady." Shorty gave me a fist bump and I returned it.

"Thanks, Shorty. Sorry about the dents in your truck," I told him.

"That is the least of our worries," he replied with an evil grin.

"Looking good, Isis." Bob and I gave each other a high five.

"It's about time," Constantine told me instead.

"What did I miss?" I asked the boys.

"Long or short version?" Constantine asked from the chair.

"Short," I replied as the horsemen adjusted their capes. "Are they wearing capes?"

"That's part of the long version that you don't get," Constantine explained.

"Fair enough. I said 'short,' after all." I probably did not care to know why they were wearing capes anyway.

"The other three got jealous when they learned Death had made a Reaper," Constantine stated. "They cannot be outdone in this war, so they are here to make it right."

"Short version wasn't too bad," I told him.

Constantine rolled over to watch the horsemen. War cleared his throat and the rest of us focused on his announcement.

"Colonel, as a faithful and the most trustworthy of my Interns, and with the power granted to me by the universe, I hereby promote you." War stood from his throne.

"I thought he only had one Intern?" Shorty asked in a loud whisper.

"Do not confuse the madness with facts," Constantine hissed, and I had to hold back a giggle.

"I promote you to the rank of General." War snapped his finger and Katrina was wearing her army fatigues. Six Stars appeared on War's hand.

"Wow," I said louder than I intended. "Is that even a real rank?"

"That is actually the rank of the General of the Armies of the United States and only two other men have ever held the title, General John Jay Pershing and General George Washington, posthumously," Constantine lectured us in his most diplomatic voice. "It appears War is repurposing the rank as the General of the World."

"That is great, but not impressive," Shorty announced, and we all turned around. "Isis is immortal, so what are those little Stars going to do?"

War glared in our direction before continuing his speech. "You have command over all the forces in this world, and every military person is at your disposal. General, you are the ultimate warrior."

War placed the rank on Katrina's chest and the building trembled. Katrina rose and saluted War as his new ultimate General. We all clapped for Katrina.

"Now that part was impressive!" Shorty shouted. "Go, General!"

"You are going to get us killed," I told Shorty, slapping his chest.

"You mean Bob and I are going to get killed. You are now Immortal, Boss Lady, after all." Shorty did a little dance that resembled the Hokey Pokey.

War returned to his throne as Pestilence stepped down. Pestilence tossed her golden hair to one side, and her mane had sparkles in it. Did it always have sparkles and I just never noticed because of my human vision?

"Eugene," Pestilence announced, and we all stopped moving.

"Wow," Constantine gasped. "Pestilence knows the names of her Interns. That is a first."

"Like I was saying, Eugene," Pestilence spoke even louder. "As my devoted and faithful Intern, today I promote you to the rank of Enforcer."

"Hooray, Rookie!" Ninth clapped.

"What's an enforcer?" Bob asked me, and I shrugged. We turned to Constantine, who did the same.

"If you all will just let me finish you'll find out," Pestilence scorned us.

"Sorry," I apologized for the group.

"As my enforcer, you will carry my torch and powers." Pestilence kissed Eugene's forehead and green smoke covered his body.

"What is the deal with the kissing and all this smoke?" Shorty asked the same thing I was thinking.

"No clue, Shorty. But is his transformation going to hurt?" I asked Constantine.

"Doesn't look like it. He is still mortal." Constantine tilted his head to the side to examine Eugene.

"Rise, my enforcer," Pestilence commanded.

The smoke soaked into Eugene. He slowly rose from the ground, appearing a bit taller wearing a Prada suit. Pestilence paced around Eugene and inspected her work.

"Give it a try," Pestilence told him.

Eugene rubbed his hands together and green fireballs erupted in both of his hands.

"Marvelous," exclaimed Pestilence.

"Now that is impressive," Shorty cheered.

"Hey, Isis. I think I can handle more than one now," Eugene told me, juggling the balls.

"It's about time," I replied as I clapped for him.

Pestilence flipped her hair over her shoulder and strolled back to her throne. She looked over at Famine and told them, "Beat that."

"This family needs therapy," Bob told me.

"We are well past the point of therapy and have moved to needing medication," I added.

"I second that," Shorty said from his side.

Famine adjusted their suit before stepping down, making the process even more dramatic. I looked at my watch and we had less than six hours. The horsemen really needed to hurry this demonstration up.

Famine didn't have any fancy speeches for us. Instead, they reached for Junior and ran their hand down his face. A light mist covered Junior from head-to-toe as he fell to the ground. Famine raised Junior to his feet. With a snap of Famine's finger, Junior was wearing a brand-new Oscar de la Renta suit.

"I introduce you to my Shadow," Famine announced. "Do me proud, little one."

Tendrils of smoke rolled off Junior's fingers. Shorty, Bob, and I backed away from the smoke, knowing from experience those little things would suck the life out of us. With a snap of Junior's fingers, the smoke curled around his feet.

"Damn!" Shorty busted out. "Off the chart."

"Thank you," Famine told Shorty, heading back to their seat.

"That was good," Shorty told Junior.

"It appears like I won this round," Famine told Pestilence, sticking out their tongue at her.

"Punk," Pestilence replied and disappeared.

"I won." Famine adjusted their jacket and vanished as well.

"Children," Death told her siblings, covering her face with her hand.

"Do us proud," War told us. "You have until eight, so anything you don't finish we will destroy." With those last words, War was gone.

Death stepped down from her throne, shaking her head.

"Basically, in order to get the other horsemen to help, we had to make them jealous?" I asked Death.

"Competition is a strange motivator for some," Death answered. "In this case, it works great for my siblings."

"Did you know this was going to happen if you made me a Reaper?" I inched closer to Death, searching for the truth.

"Me? Of course not." Before I could ask any more questions, Death was gone.

"She did that on purpose," I told the group.

"I would put money on that one," Constantine agreed. "We have less than six hours, so what's the plan?"

"I need everyone to rally your forces," I told the team. "We are leaving Reapers at five. We have to be downtown at TRAHC by six pm and we can't be late. Gather anyone you can because we need all the help we can get."

"Where are you going?" Katrina asked me.

"I have a prisoner I want to visit," I replied. "Bob, Shorty, with me."

"Don't start a war without us," Eugene told us.

"Us? Never," I replied, copying Pestilence's hair toss. "To the station, Shorty, and make it quick."

Whoever had decided letting Shorty park inside Reapers was a good idea was regretting it now. He almost ran over every person, including Constantine. With my enhanced hearing, I could hear the cursing from outside the truck. Shorty just waved at everyone and headed for the exit. I enjoyed the feel of the car and realized Shorty was right. It was fun riding around in a fast-moving vehicle.

Chapter Twenty-Five

Telling Shorty to hurry was a dangerous thing to do, even for an immortal. Thank God for Ninth and locking down Texarkana, or the amount of injured people would have tripled on our short ride to Union Station. Shorty did not stop for traffic lights, emergency signs, or run-away shopping carts in the middle of the road. The only people out were part of the Underground and they knew better than to be in the way of their boss.

"Shorty, make sure to call everyone back to the station when we start," I told him from the back seat. "We don't need any more hostages."

"You are giving those vamps too much credit," Shorty replied. "You are assuming they consider any of our people a threat. That is going to be their downfall."

Shorty was right. Most affluent people in this country underestimated the transient population. If they only knew the power they had here in Haven, they would be terrified.

Security at Union Station had been tripled. Guards patrolled both the outside and the roof. Every member of the staff had a crucifix around their neck, as well as full-body gear complete with rifles and ballistics suits.

"How are they not burning up in this heat with all that gear?" According to the trucks thermometer, the temperature was over one-hundred degrees.

"Your Godmother's minions stopped by. They were feeling a bit useless," answered Bob. "They added a temperature-regulating spell to all the gear. Cool in the summer and warm in the winter."

"Smooth." I climbed out of the truck. "I might need to be nice to Harry Potter."

"Nah, that one is still an ass," Shorty announced. "Boss Lady, it's going to cost you to get those dents off my truck."

"Those are pretty bad." I examined my handprints on the door panels. "Send the bill to Constantine for that one."

"I'll wait until I put a few more in there so he can front the bill." Shorty grinned and climbed the steps.

"He is hopeless," I told Bob.

"You know Shorty is a hustler," he said. "What are we doing back here?"

"I have an idea," I replied, following Shorty inside the building. "Shorty, get the two prisoners in the interrogation cells together."

"But Pete has been working on both non-stop and still hasn't been able to get anything else," Shorty argued.

"Now," I ordered, and Shorty took off.

"You are a bit intimidating when you make demands," Bob said from behind.

"That bad?" The hallway was cleared, which finally gave me room to breathe.

"Different," Bob told me. "It's the same essence Death has. Not bad, just intense. It's going to take us a while to adjust to you having it."

"If we make it through tonight, we will have plenty of time," I replied and headed towards the interrogation rooms.

Pete was in the doorway waiting for us. His wings were pumping a mile a minute.

"Breathe, Pete or you're going to pass out," I told him, trying to duck around him.

"You don't trust my skills?" Pete asked, blocking my way. "By the Gods, what happened to you?"

"Long story, Pete. Let's get one thing done. And your skills are not in question," I explained. "Those two spent some time in hell. I don't think we are using the right motivators to get them to talk. I do hope you join me."

Pete dropped to my shoulder and exhaled. "You do?"

"You are the best, Pete. I need you here," I reminded him.

"We will break them, Boss Lady," Pete saluted. "By the way, your powers are radiating like a sun beacon. What are you now?"

"A Reaper." I pulled out one of the chairs and made myself comfortable in the room.

"By the Gods." Pete flew in front of my face and stared at my eyes. "I live to serve you, Boss Lady."

"Well, maybe it was a shorter story than I imagined. Pete, relax, you already work here," I told him, moving my head back as he flew closer to my face.

"I'm the first Pixie who has ever worked for a Reaper." Pete made circles over my head. "I will go down in history."

"You will go down to the dungeons if you don't stop spraying dust all over the place." I grabbed the flying, little maniac by the toes.

"Wow." Pete glanced at his feet and then back at my face. "You are quick. I never saw your hands move. That is amazing."

"Pete, focus or you are heading home," I ordered the little pixie.

"Yes, Boss Lady." Pete sat on my shoulder taking deep breaths. I could still feel the energy coursing through his body as he calmed himself down.

Two guards escorted the shifters from hell back into the interrogation room.

"What do you want?" the first shifter we interviewed asked. "We told you everything we know."

"Have a seat," I told them.

Neither one moved, but the guards assisted them in sitting down.

"Thank you," I told the guard. "You can leave us."

"Boss Lady, they are extremely dangerous," the guards argued.

"So am I," I replied, winking at them.

They both gasped when they saw my eyes and left the room in a hurry.

"Parlor tricks won't scare us," the second shifter told me.

"That is good to know since I don't have time for tricks," I informed them and leaned my chair back. "Are your parents alive?"

The shifters exchanged a quick look and closed their mouths.

"Boss Lady, can I help?" Pete asked, flying off my shoulder.

"Be my guest," I told him.

Pete sprinkled both men with green pixie dust. The men shook their heads trying to avoid Pete's dust, but it was too late. He had covered them both completely.

"We are going to play a game, and you will answer yes or no." Pete marched back and forth on the table between the prisoners and me.

"Prisoner one, that's you on the right." Pete pointed at the prisoner with his hand. "Is your mom alive?"

"Drop dead, you traitor," prisoner number one replied.

"Yes or no, dumbass," Pete corrected him. "Is your mom alive?"

"Yes," he finally replied.

"Prisoner two, is your mom alive?" Pete made his way to that side of the table.

"Of course, you fool," replied number two.

"Number two, is your dad alive?" Pete made right turns as he marched the perimeter.

"Yes, he is alive as well," he replied.

"Prisoner one, is your dad alive?" Pete never slowed in his marching.

"No, and I hope he is burning in hell," prisoner one answered.

"Both of their moms are dead, but their fathers are alive," Pete announced and both prisoners gasped.

"Nice job, Pete. See how I always need you," I told him. "Eventually, you will need to explain how you pulled that off."

"Lie-detecting dust," Pete explained. "Now, how is that going to help?"

"Give me a minute and I will show you." I stood from my chair and moseyed around the prisoners. "Relax, gentlemen, this is not going to hurt...much."

I placed my hands on their heads. My grip was stronger than both werewolves combined. If they tried to move, they would decapitate themselves. There was no way for either one to escape my grip. I took a deep breath and contacted the spirit world.

I'm searching for the mothers of these two werewolves. Your children are in trouble, please help me.

I flashed the images of the two shifters through my mind and waited. If I had an idea of who their mothers were maybe it would help. But this was the best I could do with very little practice using my new skills. The room turned cold. Fog covered the floor, and both shifters moved nervously on their chairs.

"We are here." I opened my eyes and two very stern, older shifters were facing us.

"Ladies, thank you for coming," I told them.

"Mom," prisoner one whimpered.

"Momma!" prisoner two cried.

"Why have you called us?" the souls asked me.

"Your sons have made a pact with some demons and will be losing their souls soon," I informed the mothers. "I figured you might want to have one last chat with them since you won't see them in the afterlife."

"You did what?" prisoner one's mom screamed in his face. "What were you thinking?"

Prisoner two's mom grew in size and her sweet, calm shape turned savage and feral. "I gave up everything for you, and you gave your soul to a demon?" she growled. "Have you lost your mind?"

"Momma, when the Antichrist comes, he will spare us," prisoner two pleaded with his momma.

"Spare you?" Momma number two slapped her son across his face, leaving claw marks. "You idiot. You will be spared to serve as his slave."

"Did you believe those lies as well?" Mom number one shouted at her son as she held his face down with her claws. "Did I raise a fool?"

"Mom, when we liberate him, he will owe us," he cried as claws dug deeper into his skin.

"Owe you?" Mom number mocked her son. "You will be steppingstones for his minions. Your father will pay for this."

"Mom, no. Please," prisoner number one begged.

"We are done here," Momma number two told me. "Do you still need us?"

"No, thank you, ladies," I bowed to both, and the souls left the building. "I don't think your mothers are very happy right now."

I sat on my chair with Pete on my shoulder. Both shifters were shaking. Blood trickled down their faces where their moms had marked them.

"You got nothing," prisoner one told me in between sobs. "The vampires will use your blood to raise the Antichrist."

"Why my blood?" I asked the prisoner softly.

"They need the blood of one of Death's Interns," prisoner number two answered.

"That doesn't answer my question. Why me?" I repeated the question. "They have two other interns with them."

"It seems to bring life into this world, a female is needed," prisoner one said and laughed.

"Wow, that sucks," I told them. "All this planning for nothing."

"You are going to die," prisoner two shouted.

"You are all a little too late. Been there, done that," I answered. "North America no longer has an Intern, only a Reaper. I will see you both in hell."

I knocked on the door and Shorty opened it.

"Put them on suicide watch. Both of them," I told Shorty. "I expect their mothers will be doing several trips to see them, and it won't be pretty."

"Yes, Boss Lady." Shorty ran down the hall to give the orders to the guards.

Bob exited the viewing room and met me in the hallway. "How did you know that would work?"

"That is exactly what I want to know," Pete added from my shoulder.

"During my transformation, or when I died to be more accurate, my mother came to me," I explained.

"You died?" Pete shouted in my ear.

"Softly, Pete," I told him. "I can hear for yards and you just destroyed my eardrum."

"Sorry, Boss Lady." Pete sounded sincere. "Back to your story."

"Thank you. During the transformation I spoke with my mother," I told them. "The things I couldn't explain to others or myself, I told her. Deep down, most of us want to make our parents proud."

"That is so messed up of you," Pete told me. "Those two are going to have mommy issues for the rest of their lives."

"Those two already had mommy issues," I told him. "We just exploited their vulnerabilities. Whatever they witness in hell will be worse than anything we can do. So, I just went a different route."

"I need to figure out how to use that with my interrogations." Pete flew away.

"Boss Lady, we have a guy named David here to see you." Shorty came running back.

"David who?" I asked, not recognizing the name.

"David, Dark Wizard David," Shorty repeated softly. "Is Dark Wizard a common last name?"

"Not his last name, but what he does," I clarified for Shorty. "Let him in and bring him to my office."

"Will do." Shorty ran back the same way he came.

"In the meantime, can you give Katrina a call, Bob, please?" I asked him as we walked down the hall. "We need her to set up a meeting with her boyfriend. We need to talk to Jake."

"Got it." Bob made a quick right turn down the hallway as I headed up the stairs.

Folders were piled five-inches high in my inbox. If the apocalypse didn't destroy me, these folders were going to eat me at alive. I scanned the top of a few hoping an easy answer would jump out. Nothing easy about domestic dispute and child custody. I closed the file and sat on my desk going through all the messages left on sticky-notes.

"Nice office," David the dark wizard told me.

"Thanks. Want to trade?" I asked.

"With the amount of files in that box, no thank you," he answered.

"I could hide the files," I joked, pushing the box behind me.

David's chuckle was cut short when our eyes met. "What happened to you? You are different."

"That's not very polite," I told him as I let him scan me. "What do you think?"

"I don't know." David moved cautiously inside the office. "I have never experienced anything like you, unless Death is around."

"I'm a Reaper," I said softly.

"By the moon, the legends are real." David reached for me.

"If you try to pet me, I will chop your hands off," I warned the wizard, who recovered his composure.

"The situation is worse than you explained if the horsemen brought back the mercenaries of death." David exhaled.

"I prefer Reaper," I corrected him.

"Absolutely," David replied.

"Please tell me you found something out and you are not just here to analyze me with your third eye," I told David, who kept squinting at me.

"I apologize about that." David rubbed his forehead. "It's hard to believe. I have studied the legends all my life. I expected a demon, or a beast trapped underneath the human form."

"What do you see?" I asked him, curiosity getting the best of me.

"Nothing," David told me softly. "You radiated power, but when I looked at you all I saw was power. No shape, no form, nothing but power. Like the real you was gone, and all that was left was death."

"That sounds about right," I confirmed. "Now what do you have for me?"

"Your necromancer is injured." David switched back to business mode. "He is a powerful witch, formerly a member of the Order. It appears that during your last encounter your friend managed to do some major damage. The Punisher is coming for him."

"The Punisher? Is that what he calls himself?" David nodded. "Like the movie The Punisher?"

"Don't give me that look. I didn't pick the name," David defended himself. "Tell your friend to watch himself."

"Thank you, David," I said, extending my hand to him. "Stay inside this evening, it's going to get nasty."

"I have people to protect in my neighborhood." David shook my hand. "Can you keep them out of Red Lick?"

"That shouldn't be a problem since they are heading downtown for the fun," I answered.

"I have a few friends, so we will watch the North side," David announced. "If you see the necromancer, aim for the right leg."

"I will pass the message along."

David, Bob, and Shorty met at the entrance of my office. David handed Bob a small index card, and Bob shook his hand.

"You two are passing notes to each other? Really?" I teased Bob.

"He just gave me his recipe for Red Velvet Cake." Bob held the recipe card to his chest.

"Is he expecting to die? So he has to pass along his deep-dark secrets?" I prayed that crazy wizard didn't see prophecies or the future.

"Very funny." Bob placed his recipe underneath my inbox. "I'm leaving this here for safe keeping."

"Trust me, nobody is ever going to move that inbox. Your recipe is safe." I patted the stack of files.

"Katrina got a meeting with Jake in ten minutes at Abuelitas. We need to hurry," Bob announced as he left the office.

"Only Katrina can pull that off," I told him.

Last time I requested a meeting with the devil for important Death business, I had to wait six weeks for an opening in his schedule. Katrina called with a vague request that might be important and he would see her in ten minutes. How was that fair? Hopefully, he was feeling generous and would volunteer to help us out. Then again, it was the devil we were talking about. Generous was not a word in his vocabulary.

"Shorty, secure the station," I told him. "We are going to be very close to here and I don't want anyone sneaking in this way."

"Boss Lady, nobody could sneak past us even if they used the tunnels," Shorty announced, and I stopped in my tracks.

"What tunnels?" I looked at Bob for clarification but he just shook his head.

"You know." Shorty pointed underneath us. "The ones that run all over downtown."

"We have tunnels in downtown?" I had never heard of this.

"Since when?" Bob asked, pacing the office.

"Since the prohibition," Shorty explained. "Rumor has it that all the old buildings were connected by underground tunnels. That way when the cops raided a location they just migrated their drinks and gambling parties to another. We have secured ours several times."

"Does anyone else know about these tunnels?" I leaned closer to Shorty.

"Anyone who has ever taken a tour at TRAHC," he answered. "One of the tunnels is supposed to be in that building. TRAHC used to be the old courthouse. It has lots of history."

"Could it be possible?" I said out loud. "Shorty, get ahold of Edward. We need him and his vamps to search all the tunnels."

"What is he looking for?" Bob asked.

"Anything or anyone," I answered. "I don't like the idea that Marie and her vamps could be moving around underneath us."

"Should we join them?" Shorty asked.

"No. If I'm right, Edward and his group might be the only ones strong enough to handle what is in those tunnels. Bob, let's go."

Bob clapped Shorty on the back and followed me out the door. My mind was moving faster than ever, processing information and jumping to conclusions. I didn't have time for guessing games. All I could do now was take it one step at a time. Next step was to meet with the devil.

Chapter Twenty-Six

Ten minutes was plenty of time to get to Abuelitas from Union Station. With the lack of traffic, we were there in seven. The Deathmobile was parked in the front. Shorty parked a few spaces away, blocking the entrance to the restaurant.

"Guard the door," I told Shorty and Bob. "We don't need any unexpected guests joining us here."

I entered the restaurant and found Katrina sitting alone in the middle of the restaurant.

"Aren't you supposed to have a buddy with you?" I took a seat next to her.

"Everyone is busy prepping for battle," she replied. Besides, I was on the phone the whole time with Ninth since he monitors all my movements. Constantine's new drone just arrived."

"Texarkana is not ready for another aerial assault," I told her as the front door opened.

Jake and Adam strolled through the door. Jake was wearing a navy suit while Adam had a gray one. Adam position himself to the right of the door as Jake inspected the restaurant. Jake took two steps towards us when the door opened again, and this time, Gabriel strolled in wearing full battle gear.

"Is this a set up?" Jake asked us.

"Please, don't flatter yourself," Katrina replied.

"Chips?" I asked Katrina, leaving our table to grab some chips and salsa from the bar area.

"That would be great, thank you," said Katrina, watching Jake and Gabriel size each other up. "Is this really necessary?

"Do I need to remind you two that if the horsemen ride we will unleash all of heaven upon this earth?" Gabriel asked us.

Gabriel was normally the sweetest Angel ever. Today, he radiated power, or my new senses were now taking in his full, glorious self. In his official capacity as the messenger of God, Gabriel was terrifying. The room became colder and his words echoed throughout the restaurant.

"How exciting," Jake mocked him. "Can't wait for the fireworks."

Jake walked in front of Gabriel, not paying him any mind. Adam relaxed against the door and adjusted his immaculate suit. Gabriel roared and headed straight for the kitchen.

"We need a better location for our meetings," Katrina told me as I sat down with the chips and salsa.

"What are you talking about?" I said. "And miss out on all the chips and salsa you can eat? Never. Besides, I'm sure the hosts in heaven are hungry, too."

"Are you two done?" Jake sat down across from us. "I don't have time for games today."

"Yes, you are a little busy planning a war, or is it finding a traitor?" I added more salt to my salsa before dipping my chip.

"A little of both," Jake replied, crossing his legs.

"You have a son." It was more a statement than a question.

"You saw the movies, and that's the rumor." Jake was being very vague.

"Well, it seems your little boy is planning a massive world take over with my blood," I announced to the group.

Katrina slammed her hands on the table. Adam stopped his casual slouching, straightening to pay full attention to us. Jake only licked his lips.

"Damn those muses," Jake said in a cold, soft voice. "If you ever get advice to have a child to expand your legacy, ignore it. Trust me, it will only bring headaches and problems. How many world-domination plots can one kid plan in a lifetime?"

"This happens often?" I asked, crunching chips mercilessly.

"At least twice a millennium." Jake kept readjusting his tie. "I'm going to ground that child until the real apocalypse happens. What do you want?"

"We need you to keep your evil spawn in hell," I replied.

"That's it?" Jake looked over at Adam, who was writing everything down.

"What else can you do?" Katrina joined the conversation.

"I don't know? Offer immortality or some big favor for finding my leak." Jake grabbed one of the chips from the basket.

"Too late. Already committed my life to Death." I blinked several times to show off my eyes.

"Reaper." Jake took a bite of his chip and grinned. "That's what I was sensing. At first, I thought it was the intoxicating aroma of self-righteousness coming from Gabriel. Interesting turn of events. Immortality is definitely off the table."

"Sorry, we can only serve one psycho master at a time," Katrina added.

"How about keeping your demons out of Haven?" I decided to push my luck.

"I can only keep the ones in hell there. Unfortunately too many were summoned already," Jake answered, not appearing sorry at all. "You will need to deal with those on your own. With your new-found power, that shouldn't be a problem."

"You are not very helpful today," I told the devil.

"Who said I was ever helpful?" Jake rose from his chair. "Ladies, happy hunting. Please make sure your temperamental masters don't set the world on fire. I'm still counting on a few hundred years to profit from this infernal rock."

Jake and Adam left Abuelita's in a cloud of sulfur. Katrina and I tried to clear the air in front of us with no luck.

"This whole entire thing was about setting the Antichrist loose on earth?" Katrina asked me.

"It was probably a side angle that just happens to fit into their plans," I replied. "Even with Jake's kid out of the picture, we still have demons, shifters, vampires, witches, and all sorts of craziness to deal with."

"Halloween all over again," Katrina said with a smile.

"Fortunately, this time we have a lot more friends," I told her.

"That's right," Abuelita announced from the bar window holding a shotgun in her hands. "Haven is ready. Anyone able to fight will be in the streets tonight."

"Just keep them out of downtown. It's going to be messy there," I informed Abuelita.

"You got it." Abuelita prowled around the bar and hugged me. "Welcome home, Reaper."

Everyone was taking this Reaper thing a lot better than me. Katrina and I hugged Abuelita and headed outside. Bob and Shorty sat on the hood of the Deathmobile.

"Why didn't you warn us that both Jake and Gabriel were coming in at the same time?" I asked them.

"Angels and Demons don't drive up to a place," Bob explained. "By the time they manifest, they are already at the front door. No time to warn anyone."

"He does have a point," Katrina concurred with Bob.

"How did it go?" Shorty asked.

"Gabriel didn't crucify the devil on the spot, and Jake is keeping his kid in time-out for the night," I answered. "Overall, not a bad day for dealing with beings from heaven and hell. Ready to plan a war?"

"Do we have a choice?" Bob asked.

"Not at all," Katrina told him trudging towards the driver seat of the Deathmobile.

I joined her on the passenger side of the Deathmobile, Bob rode with Shorty in the truck. There was no reason for Katrina to ride back alone if I was there. We still needed to maintain the protocol and keep two people together at all times. At least until all hell broke loose.

If you were preparing for a supernatural war, what would your command center look like? Probably a lot like ours, if you had unlimited resources and a five-thousand-year-old talking cat battle trained and ready.

We didn't bother parking inside of Reapers since all the vehicles had been moved outdoors. The witches and the elves were busy creating a force-field outside. Equal numbers for each—four witches and four elves—circled the perimeter of Reapers, casting spells. Katrina headed inside while I admired the work being done. It was glorious to see the layers being woven in the air. Threads of gold, fire, wind, and earth joined together to create a semi-glove of magic.

I had to force myself to look away and head inside. Godmother and Ulises stood by the door of Reapers supervising the progress.

"It's breathtaking, but are we expecting the battle to come to us?" I asked them.

"We are preparing for everything," Ulises replied. "I doubt they are just going to let you walk directly to your meeting. If it's a trap, they should know you won't be going alone."

"A little extra protection gives us more time to prepare instead of fighting right up to the last hour," Godmother added. "How do you feel?"

"Different." It was the best way I could think to explain it.

"Your cells are adjusting well to the transformation." Ulises was squinting at me.

"That's encouraging, I think," I told him.

I saluted both Ulises and my Godmother then went inside. People were everywhere inside Reapers. Welch's weapons were spread out across several tables against the walls. Father Francis, in his black, priestly garment, was busy blessing them with holy water. It was such a strange sight to see a priest praying over weapons and bullets. Too bad it was the only way to survive a war against demons and vampires. Members of the underground were replacing the weapons as fast as Father Francis blessed them.

Across from the blessing station stood Eugene and Ninth. They had a first-aid station going. With Pestilence's team it was hard to say what they were giving vaccinations for. I crossed the floor while trying to avoid tripping over machine guns and people.

"Ebola protection?" I asked Eugene.

"Among other things," he replied. "With the newfound gift the mistress gave me, my selection of deadly plagues and curses is infinite. I can't protect them from everything, since I have no clue what we are going to need, but at least some major ones."

Eugene stuck a poor young man in the arm with some strange bubbling liquid.

"Are the effects of that vaccine safe?" I asked Eugene as the poor, young man cried when the liquid was pushed in.

"For the most part." Eugene focused on putting a band aid on the young man.

"We have corrected some of the initial deficiencies," Ninth told me from across the table.

"You basically screwed up several times," I clarified.

"It's not like we have a manual for this kind of stuff," Eugene confessed.

"This is the reason human testing is illegal in most parts of the world." I poked Eugene in the side and he jumped.

"Do you need one?" Eugene offered one of the syringes to me but stopped after examining closer. "On second thought, I doubt anything I have could even touch you."

"She is pretty insulated already," Ninth told him.

"That is the best news I got all day. Don't kill anyone now." I wandered away from the mad scientists before they tried to run creepy experiments on my cells.

Near the shooting range—or working lab if you will—Junior was busy with a group of six Underground members. Sweat poured down their faces as Junior moved smoke around them. A poor, little blond passed out.

"What are you doing, Junior?" I jogged in his direction.

"Practicing," he replied, his face a little pale. "This is a lot harder than it looks."

"I wouldn't have a clue," I confessed. "But what are you doing?"

"Making the smoke move the same way the Boss does it," Junior explained.

"Give us a minute everyone. Go get a drink of water." The group of volunteers dispersed at once, dragging their falling comrades with them. "Junior, honey, you are never going to pull that off in three hours. Famine has had thousands of years of practice."

"Thanks, Isis. That's really encouraging." Junior's shoulders drooped. "Basically, you're saying I should give up now.

"That's not what I mean." I needed to work on my pep talks. "Don't try to be Famine. Just be you. If you were playing a video game and had Famine's powers, how would you use them?"

All the boys at Reapers played video games or tabletop games, so that was the best way I could think to describe our situation.

Junior was silent for a few minutes. "I would use an avatar." He beamed.

"Good," I replied.

"You have no idea what that means?" Junior asked me.

"None at all, but I don't have to," I answered. "As long as you figure out how to make your powers work for you, that is all that matters."

"Have you figured out yours?" Junior stared at my face.

"Some come more naturally than others," I confessed. "We will see how well the rest of them work for us."

I made my way towards the stairs when a pack of shifters jumped in front of me. Instinct took over. I disarmed the first two with a round house to the head. With a full-body flip, I pinned two more against a wall, pulling my gun out in the process. I was faster than the shifters, but I could see everything in slow motion. Every detail was ingrained in my head and I knew the location of all combatants on the floor.

"You have to be faster than the enemy!" Constantine shouted from behind me. "Thank you, Isis. Now, please let go of my recruits."

I slowly moved away from the shifters against the wall. The two men ran back to Constantine. All movement stopped inside the building and all eyes were on me. Constantine strolled forward.

"That, my friends, is what a new Reaper can do without warning. So, can you imagine what three-hundred trained Reapers will do to our enemies?" Constantine's voice filled the silence.

"Yes! Bring on the Reapers!" Shorty shouted from the doorway.

Cheers and clapping followed as everyone went back to their tasks.

"Thank you, Isis," Constantine said.

"Was that a test?" I replied as I noticed everyone keeping a good amount of distance between them and me.

"Not a test but a demonstration," Constantine explained. "How can they follow you if they don't know your capabilities? You took out four of their strongest alphas in six seconds without taking a breath. That is what they needed to see. You'd better get ready. We don't have a lot of time."

"Wow, he is right," TJ said coming down the stairs. "You are impressive."

"Hi." I wasn't sure what else to say after that compliment.

"You are so out of my league now." TJ stopped in front of me.

"What?" I asked him softly.

"Give them hell, Isis. I'm proud of you." He kissed my cheek and marched away.

"That's how it starts," Iason whispered, coming out of the shadows.

"Why are you lurking?" I chastised him instead.

"Things will change now," Iason continued in his overly-dramatic voice.

"It doesn't matter as long as they are safe," I cut him off. "I have to get ready. Stop being such a Debbie-downer and find something productive to do."

Before he could give me another crazy lecture, I jogged up the stairs. At least the Loft was quiet until Death appeared.

"It's going to be messy," she said.

"I wish I could tie them all up and leave them here," I told her.

"If only it was that easy." Death inspected me closer.

"It would be really nice if people stopped doing that to me," I said to Death.

"I wish I could keep you safe, but, obviously, none of us are getting our way today." Ouch. Death was not playing fair. "The blessing and curse of humanity is free will. Even knowing what is best for you, I can't force it upon you. Every choice has to be yours. Remember that it is their choice to fight for their survival." She rubbed my cheeks softly.

"I don't have to like it," I whined.

"No, we don't have to like it. Only accept it," Death informed me. "I came to wish you luck. Whatever happens tonight, I'm proud of you. Unfortunately, I have to wait with the other horsemen."

"Why?" I asked Death who rolled her eyes.

"I have no earthly idea, but we are supposed to stay together," Death adjusted her suit.

"Good luck." I would take battle anytime over dealing with her three siblings all at once.

"I'm going to need it," Death replied. "See you tonight."

Death vanished. It was time to change into battle gear. Weapons still had to be loaded, blessed, and stored. People had to be prepped and we needed as many hands on deck as possible. Time was not our friend now.

Chapter Twenty-Seven

Inhale. Exhale. Inhale. Exhale.

The Loft was dark when I opened my eyes. Constantine had sent me upstairs to find a way to center myself. I had too much nervous energy and was starting to make everyone fidgety. Constantine explained this was the reason Death was never upset or overly excited. Energy was contagious by the looks of it.

After thirty minutes of meditating, I felt calm, and maybe even refreshed. I shouldn't celebrate too much since it took me twenty minutes just to settle my mind and shut out all the outside noises. Blocking sounds and smells was like turning my third eye on and off. Except now I didn't need it because I could sense the makeup of a being without needing to switch. I did a few stretches and let my awareness expand.

Time to go. We have company.

Fear should have filled my veins from the amount of souls around us. Instead, anticipation and excitement coursed through my body. I grabbed my scythe, a long black robe Constantine gave me, and my machete—all standard Reaper gear—and was ready to battle. I left the Loft and, instead of taking the stairs down, jumped off the balcony.

Damn. I landed in a crouch with perfect form.

"Show off," said Iason.

"Just needed to confirm I could manage landing that or today is going to suck." I rose to my feet, adjusting my hair into a ponytail. "I also look really good doing it."

"Yes, you do." Iason took my robe and wrapped it around my shoulder. "I don't think this world is ready for Reapers."

"Is any world ready for us?" I asked as he tied the robe to the front of my fatigues.

"No, not at all." He left my hood down. "Ready for the apocalypse?"

"Not at all," I replied, leading us outside.

Our allies were minuscule compared to the host of beings outside the forcefield. We had about thirty members of the underground fully armed with blessed weapons, three packs of shifters, each with over twelve members flanking us, and seven deadly elves monitored our enemies while my Godmother and her four witches turned wands into swords. Not enough compared to the other side.

Hundreds of walking dead threw themselves at the forcefield. Dozens of shifters with guns, some fully transformed, paced the area. Every time they pounded on the field, the entire thing vibrated and turned a dark shade of red. Near the old rubble of the pavilion, stood Constantine with the rest of the Interns and group leaders. I made my way towards Bob and Shorty, who were off to the left of the group.

"It's going to be a messy one but at least we have the element of the sun," Constantine said to the group.

The group looked up as mysterious clouds moved over the sky. The sun was covered and light spread in all directions. In a matter of minutes, the clouds had covered the sun and turned the day to night.

"Well, there goes that advantage," Shorty told us.

"That is some powerful magic," Godmother confirmed, testing the air with her eyes closed.

"It seems the demons don't want to miss the fight," I told her. "It's five o'clock everyone, so time to call your back-up team."

"Ms. Virginia, Ulises, would you mind making a hole above?" Katrina asked studying her watch.

"When?" Godmother moved closer to her to stare at the sky.

"Now," Katrina answered. "ETA is twenty-six seconds for my men."

Godmother and Ulises signaled to their people. Two witches and two elves stepped forward and opened a ten-by-ten square directly above us.

"Will that be big enough?" Ulises asked her.

"Perfect." Katrina thanked them with a smile. "Make a hole."

The packs of shifters moved to one side, but the expressions on their face made it clear they had no clue what they were waiting for. Within seconds, fully armed paratroopers descended shooting at the masses outside the force field.

"Now, that's what I call an entrance!" Shorty shouted.

The first soldier released his chute and landed with ease in front of Katrina. The soldier saluted Katrina.

"Legio Patria Nostra," he said to her.

"Welcome, commander," Katrina replied back.

"The Legion is here to serve," he told her.

"'The Legion?'" Bob asked me. "As in the French Foreign Legion?"

"If you can command anyone in the world, you might as well bring in your A Team," I replied softly.

Over one-hundred and fifty Legionaries landed inside our perimeter. The witches and the elves closed the forcefield as soon as the last one came in. Katrina inspected her ranks, giving orders to the troops. The packs assisted the Legionaries in switching their ammo for the blessed ones.

"Eugene, hope you can beat that," Shorty told him.

"You are not helping," I told Shorty, who was grinning at Eugene.

Eugene stepped forward and pushed his sleeves up. I glanced quickly between him and Junior. They were both dressed exceptionally stylish for a war. They had matching black Dolce & Gabbana suits. Were they planning to go to a prom or a battlefield?

"Come to me," Eugene whispered to the night.

His hands glowed a dark-green color and energy rolled down his body. The witches near him moved several feet away, and even Junior gave him some space. The air shifted, and the sound of wings filled the air. Hundreds of bees, wasps, and flying insects surrounded Eugene. Around his feet, scorpions, venomous snakes, and deadly creatures slithered.

"He has a seriously unhealthy obsession with killer bees," said Constantine, moving away from the army of insects around Eugene.

"That is one scary sight," Shorty added. "I'm so happy he is on our side."

"I second that," Iason told him. "His control over those things is incredible."

"I'll let him know you are impressed," I told him.

"Okay, my man. You are next. Make us proud." Shorty pointed at Junior.

Junior moved away from the group and took a deep breath, then rolled his head several times. Slowly, he exhaled and smoke flowed from his fingers. Unlike Famine's smoke that curled and moved attacking people, Junior's smoke took form and grew. Within a few minutes, Junior had four human-smoke soldiers with swords and shields.

"My avatars," Junior told me from across the clearing.

"That is definitely more you," I replied to him.

"Boss Lady." Shorty moved closer to me. "Can you beat all of this? This is some seriously tough competition."

"We will see, Shorty," I answered, cracking my knuckles.

Constantine never explained how I was supposed to summon the Reapers from the River Styx. I moved over to the demolished pavilion and stood facing the rubble. Even from this position, I could sense everyone staring at me. Three hundred Reapers...that's how many I was supposed to summon. I barely managed to ask two old ghost ladies to come and see me at the station.

Ask! That's it. I just needed to ask.

I kneeled to the ground, closed my eyes, and placed my hand flat on the dirt. I expanded my senses and focused on the Reapers. Not the people that were Reapers, but the essences that felt like me. The connections with all the souls, the energy that was Death, and the power of thousands of years of existence.

I know you can hear me. Wake up. I need your help. You have been asleep for way too long and the world needs you. Will you help me?

I poured my will into those last words and pushed my energy as far out as it could reach. My body hummed with power, and slowly, the ground moved. I opened my eyes and watched as hooded Reapers sprang from the ground. The crowd gasped as silver scythes slammed to the ground all at once and made the earth tremble.

"Now we are cooking!" Shorty shouted. "Bow to the master."

"Leave it to Death to show us all up," Katrina announced, standing by my side. "Nice work."

I gave her a fist bump as silver eyes shone at us. "If I wasn't one of them, this would be terrifying."

"I'm not one of you guys, and this is terrifying," Katrina corrected me.

Three hooded Reapers walked towards us. Eugene and Junior stepped up to cover our left and right flank, hands glowing with power. I guessed my team was not sure what side the Reapers were on yet.

"Grim Reaper, you called?" one of the Reapers spoke.

"'Grim Reaper,' is that you?" Eugene asked, trying not to move his lips.

"No clue," I replied in the same manner.

"Of course, it's you," Constantine announced sneaking between our legs.

"Constantine?" the Reaper shouted, dropping to the ground.

"Sergius?" Constantine crawled slowly towards the Reaper.

The Reaper pulled his hood back to reveal the face of a young man, maybe in his late teens or early twenties, with curly, brown hair.

"If the end of times is happening, you knew Constantine was going to be right in the middle of it," the Reaper to his right said, taking off his hood.

"I missed you, too, Julius," Constantine told the Reapers.

"Wow! They are legends," Bob said from behind me.

"You know about these two," Katrina asked him.

"I heard a story about them," Bob said, backing away.

Constantine and the two Reapers were giving each other high fives and celebrating, when the third hooded figured stepped up.

"Do we really have time for all of this?" That scrappy voice was unmistakable.

"Boatman?" It was my turn to shout.

"Do you think I would miss the party?" the Boatman pushed his hood back to show off his glowing skull eyes and his huge cigar.

"A cigar-smoking skull? This is the best," Shorty said, poking his head between Katrina and me.

"Isis, this is Sergius, the first Reaper," Constantine made the introductions. "Isis was the former Intern of North America and the last Reaper."

"We have heard so much about the new world from all the deceased, so this is exciting," Julius told him.

"Too bad we don't have time for a tour." I signaled to the increasing number of enemies accumulating outside.

"I really wanted to try that food called Pizza," Julius said with a sigh. "Who is leading this fun, little group?"

"Marie," Constantine answered.

"Marie? My Marie?" Sergius stared blankly at Constantine.

"Well, the plot thickens," I told them. "It seems your girlfriend is hoping to sacrifice me to unleash the Antichrist."

"They are still trying to do that?" Julius jumped in.

"There are always trying to do that," the Boatman told him.

"The Antichrist is not our concern," Katrina interrupted the boys. "Jake is taking care of his kid. We still have an army of enemies and a few kidnapped people."

"That is so much better," Sergius told her with a fake grin. "Should we get going?"

Gun fire, horns, and screams erupted from the West side of the forcefield.

"Right on time," Constantine announced as he strolled toward the noise. "Ms. Virginia, Ulises, do you mind making a hole for us?"

"What are you doing?" I asked Constantine as an explosion hit the forcefield.

"Are you sure?" Godmother asked him.

"Now, please," Constantine replied.

The witches and the elves obeyed and opened a hole big enough for three men to pass on the west side. Smoke filled that side of the wall as more explosions rocked the field. Legionaries and Reapers moved into position to attack whatever was coming through. From the smoke, a Harley Davidson motorcycle crossed the field followed by eight of the biggest trolls I'd ever seen. The Harley did a quick one-eighty turn, and two lab-coated men opened fire at the opening after the last troll entered.

"Close it, please," Constantine ordered.

The witches and elves closed the perimeter as Second and Fourth sprinted at us leaving the Harley behind.

"Holy Jesus Christ," I said to myself as Eugene ran towards his brothers. "Constantine, you are good."

"Never underestimate the power of family," Constantine told me.

We moved towards the new arrivals. Second and Fourth's coats were ripped and bruises covered their faces, but they glowed with energy.

"Glad you made it," Constantine told them.

"Thank you for the assist," Second replied.

"We want some payback of our own." Fourth adjusted his ripped coat. "Nobody disrespects the Mistress. Enforcer, we are at your service. Love the bees."

"God, I'm so happy you are alive." Eugene rubbed his eyes.

"Mistress?" Sergius asked. "Is everyone represented here?"

"Pretty much, and we have less than three hours to stop these fools before the horsemen ride and the end of the world starts." I gave them the condensed version. "Constantine, man the skies."

"Not this time, little one," Constantine announced. "Ninth has that covered. I'm riding with you."

"You are kidding, right?" I replied. "We are fighting vampires and demons."

"I know." Constantine moved several steps back and shifted.

His Maine-coon body grew larger than a panther. His dark fur shifted to snow white. Once the transformation was complete, instead of an oversized, house cat, we had an enormous Saber-tooth tiger.

"Damn!" shouted Eugene.

"Never underestimate the fur man, little sis," the Boatman told me.

"I stand corrected. You are definitely coming," I told Constantine, who was now eye-level with me. "Is everyone ready?"

It was a rhetorical question. We didn't have a choice anymore.

"How far is the TRAHC building from here?" Junior asked.

"About five and half miles," Bob replied.

"Five miles through that?" Eugene stated. "For those of us without superhuman strength and speed, can we get a truck?"

"I thought you would never ask," Shorty told him. "Underground go."

The thirty members of the underground dispersed. Within minutes, a fleet of Ford F-150s rolled forward, all of them painted black with blood-red letters on their side. The messages ranged from Go Back to Hell, Time to Die, Reapers R Us, and my favorite Can't Touch This.

"When this is done, I'm going to make a killing selling those back to Orr," Shorty told me as he marched to the first truck in the line.

The driver jumped off and climbed in the bed. Each truck was equipped with a 50Cal and water hoses. They were not taking any chances.

"Eugene, you go with Bob," I started directing our assault team. "You need to find the necromancer and take him out. Aim for his legs."

"Roger." Eugene saluted and the two of them moved to a truck next to Shorty.

"Junior, you are with Shorty," I ordered.

"It will be my pleasure." Junior moved to the back of Shorty's truck while his shadow avatars positioned themselves around it.

"Godmother, pick your truck." She kissed my cheeks and moved silently towards the vehicles. "Everyone, it's going to be messy and deadly. Stay close. Reapers in the front, it is plowing time."

I moved to the front of the Reapers with Constantine on my side. Julius and Sergius flanked me on both sides. Our little army wasn't nearly as helpless anymore. I gave the group one last glance. Werewolves, panthers, tigers, and wild cats surrounded the trucks. The Legionaries positioned themselves right behind the Reapers with Katrina in the front. Second and Fourth were back on the bike, glowing with that crazy Pestilence power. Iason and Ulises were right behind me with their elves, golden swords out and magic flying from of their fingers.

"Ready?" Constantine asked me softly.

"Is it too late to send everyone home?" I replied.

Julius laughed.

"She's ready," Sergius answered for me.

"Now," Constantine growled.

The witches and the elves brought down the forcefield, and the floods of hell poured upon us. Time slowed for me. I charged at full speed with the Reapers and I could feel them. We could anticipate each other's moves as we reached for our enemies. Scythes were spun at double speed, sparks flying every time the blades hit the ground. The first line of our enemies didn't last three seconds when the Reapers hit them. Three hundred and one Reapers were a force to be reckoned with.

We cleared a path for our forces to move through. The Legionaries fought without mercy. Every zombie that crossed their path was turned into chunks of scattered bones. The enemies' shifters went for the weakest of our group, or at least they assumed. Werewolves and tigers charged at the Underground only to slam into the witches' forcefield. We had a long five miles, so hopefully, their powers lasted that long.

Chapter Twenty-Eight

It took us fifteen minutes just to make it to Abuelitas due to all the fighting. Highway Eighty-Two was a minefield. If leaving Reapers looked like the ending of the Infinity Wars, this part was straight out of The Hunger Games. I needed less-violent movies to compare my life to.

Neither Eugene nor Junior had been able to find the necromancer. I was sure he had emptied every cemetery in the four-states region. This place was loaded with cemeteries, and the zombies did not stop coming. Eugene's flesh-eating energy bombs had taken out at least fifty. The Reapers sustained minor injuries but nothing that could destroy their immortal bodies. The Legionaries, on the other hand, had a few wounded that the Order was mending. Losses did not stop those soldiers or their odds. Katrina was tougher than all her men. She single-handedly knocked out three werewolves attacking one of our shifters.

We didn't have time to stop but Abuelitas was surrounded. Vampires had joined the fight thanks to the ridiculous cloud blocking the sun. I decapitated two zombies trying to reach Abuelitas.

"We got this. Go!" yelled Abuelita from the front of the door.

Angelito was throwing spells next to her while Ana used a rifle. Trolls were on their left with shifters on their right. Trish took out a wolf by wrapping roots around its body. If those were their only foes, I would have listened. But four vampires were ripping their roof apart and about to drop down.

"In a minute," I replied and, using a parked car as a ramp, I catapulted to the roof. "Hi."

Four against one were horrible odds, and, unfortunately, I didn't feel like playing fair. Their monster faces flashed at me. I spun the scythe in front of me, chopping the arms off a vampire to the left. The vampire exploded into ashes covering his peers. I kicked the one on the right off the roof and smashed his face off the other two. The entire process took less than thirty seconds. I flew off the roof to finish the last vampire but Second had beat me to it. He had burned the monster to ashes.

"Nice job," I told him.

"We cannot be outdone by a bunch of Reapers," Second informed me. Even Interns like a friendly competition.

Eugene had sent his swarm of bees against the trolls. Two were on the ground rolling like mad dogs. Those trolls were paying dearly for picking the wrong side. The snakes and scorpions that covered them did not add to their comfort. Four more zombies popped out of the earth in front of the trolls.

"Did they just bury people everywhere here?" Eugene asked.

"Remember, this town is less than one-hundred and fifty years old," I explained. "Most of this was wild land."

"Great!" Eugene shouted after blasting the corpses with blue fire. "Junior! Get that damn necromancer."

"If anyone can point me in his direction, I will do just that!" shouted Junior as his avatar sucked the life out of two shifters.

"That was gross," I told Junior.

"Yuck," Eugene replied.

"What does he look like?" Katrina asked as she rode on top of the hood of Bob's truck.

"Limping?" I replied with a shrug.

"No help," said Katrina.

"I never saw him," I confessed, helping Trish knock out one more troll.

"I got this," Eugene announced.

He made circles with his hands and sent his bees across the entire area. Eugene climbed on Second's bike and followed the bees.

"Shorty, follow him," I ordered.

"We are on it, Boss Lady." Shorty put the truck in gear, running over any corpses or vampires that stood in his way.

The Underground members on the back fired at everything that rolled their way and Junior's avatar did the rest.

"I'm not sure if Junior is going to survive this," I told Second.

"He is a strong one," Second informed me.

"He is. But Shorty is a maniac behind the wheel," I clarified.

"Shit, we got him." Second ran off behind Shorty and Eugene blasted anything in his path.

"Isis, go." Abuelita gave me a hug and pushed me away. "We can handle it now."

I blew her a kiss and took off running. It was easy to pass a moving vehicle when you had Reaper speed. Past the Elks club, seven Legionaries and two shifters were surrounded by three demons. They were not even pretending to be human anymore. Wings extended, they were hell beasts in the flesh. Talons longer than my forearm slammed into our people. Scythe extended, I landed on top of one demon just as Constantine crashed into a second. The demons tossed me aside, slashing my arms and side. Blood trickled down but quickly stopped.

"Constantine, exactly what can kill a Reaper?" I asked, rolling to the side to avoid the demons lunging at me.

"Decapitation, like vampires," Julius answered, stabbing the demon through the gut. "So, don't lose your head."

"Good to know." I sprinted to the third demon and kicked it in the head.

Hand-to-hand combat with demons was not part of my training. Then again, I was only supposed to be collecting souls during the apocalypse, not trying to stop it. I cracked a few bones in the monster but the thing kept coming. Avoiding the Legionaries was becoming challenging since vampires had joined the fight. The demon had a dislocated jaw, but it didn't stop him from reaching for my head. I used the scythe to block the bite but venom dripped from its mouth.

"Not today, bitches," someone said from behind me.

Water soaked my face as the demon went up in flames. Julius slammed the monster off me as the Triplets sprayed the rest of the demons down.

"Have I told you three I love you?" I asked the Triplets.

"We know, Boss Lady," Triplet number one replied. "You'd better hurry. The fighting is getting heavy by Big Jakes. We got this."

Julius pulled me up to me feet. "Nice friends."

"Welcome to the family," I told him. "Race you."

I didn't wait to see if he followed. The feel of the pavement flying underneath me was exhilarating. Running never felt so good or so empowering when I was human. I didn't want to stop, but I arrived in less than a minute to Big Jakes.

"What took you so long?" Julius was leaning on his scythe when I stopped. "You need to stop thinking about running and focus on flying. You will move faster."

"Faster?" I let the idea sink in as I concentrated on the chaos in front of us. "What are we looking at?"

"Eugene found the necromancer on the roof of Big Jakes," Katrina explained, jogging across the street from the madness.

"Who set the trees on fire?" Big Jakes had several huge pines around the building that were covered in flames.

"That is a toss-up between Shorty, Second, or Fourth," Katrina confessed.

"Holy flames," Sergius said as he joined us. "What's going on?"

"Necromancer is on the roof," I told him.

"What's the plan?" Julius asked. "Besides setting the entire block on fire."

Dozens of corpses erupted from the ground. The trucks pulled back as the corpses attacked. Eugene sent his bees at the necromancer, but he exploded them with magic.

"Eugene is not going to be happy about that," I told the group. "We need to stop him."

"Great plan," Julius mocked. "How?"

"Everyone charge," I told them. "Confuse him until one of us can take him out."

"I'm in," Katrina said running across the street.

"Fly," Julius repeated and was gone.

By the time I blinked, he was on the roof dodging spells.

"Are you ready to try?" Sergius asked me.

"Not yet," I replied honestly. "I'll just run over."

Mastering flying was not something I had time for. With my luck, I would slam into the building and knock myself out. I ran at full speed and used Shorty's truck as a steppingstone towards the roof. Sergius and Julius were busy swinging at the necromancer. He was a lot stronger than I imagined. He used to be a member of the Order, so he was probably ancient. I joined the fight, and the necromancer brought even more corpses to the battle. One took me by surprise and pushed me off the roof. I landed flat on my butt on the ground and stuck the landing.

"That sucked," I mumbled as I rolled over.

"Help us," a girl in her mid-twenties told me.

I spun around and was surrounded. Over twenty people were closing in on me.

"Make him stop," a man in his seventies pleaded with me.

"God help us," I told them.

The necromancer wasn't pulling just empty corpses, he was pulling the bodies of souls who hadn't transitioned as well. This was super awful. Three more Reapers joined Julius and Sergius, but the necromancer only added more bodies. The souls screamed around me as the battle raged on. I had a horrible idea.

"Death, please forgive me," I told my boss, who I was sure was listening. "I command you. I free you from your bonds. Stop him."

I pushed my powers onto the souls and gave them form. The souls glowed and followed my orders, climbing up the building towards the necromancer. Julius swung his scythe towards the young girl.

"Don't hurt them!" I shouted.

"What?" Sergius asked.

"They are with us," I explained.

The souls surrounded the necromancer and plowed through the corpses. The Reapers jumped off the roof as the souls attacked the demented witch. The screams of the necromancer filled the night as the souls dragged him off the roof. I didn't know how to stop them as they dragged the live witch into the ground with them.

"That's disturbing," Katrina said walking towards me.

"What did you tell them?" Sergius asked, moving the dirt with his foot.

"To stop him," I whined.

"That's it?" Julius questioned me as well.

"Yeah," I replied, staring at the ground the necromancer disappeared into.

"We need to work on your commands," Sergius told me as he pulled me away from the newly-made grave. "You have a lot of power. You need to be very specific from now on."

"I'll add that to the list right next to flying lessons," I told the boys, who pushed me away.

"Well, the necromancer has been taken care of," I announced to Eugene and Junior.

"Great," Junior told me. "But is he coming back?"

"I'm pretty sure the only place we will see him again is in hell," Katrina answered.

"That's even better." Eugene joined me. "That bastard killed three of my swarms. He'd better burn for a long time."

"We need to work on your priorities," Julius told Eugene. "Then again, there is too much stuff to work on with all of you. I'm ready to get back to my floaty tube."

"Me, too," Sergius agreed with him.

"Should we get going?" Shorty asked us.

"Can someone please put those out first?" I pointed to the giant torches next to us.

"I got it," Junior volunteered. He extended his hands towards the trees and extinguished the fired.

"Impressive," Sergius told him. "How did you pull that off?"

"I sucked the air out of the fire," Junior told him as he climbed on the truck.

"Is it me or is this a lot of work just to get to a trap?" I asked the group.

"They are trying to wear us down," Katrina explained. "The weaker we are, the easier we are to finish off when we get there."

"Tired? I'm just getting warmed up." Julius stretched his legs. "Race you."

Julius was gone.

"Damn it!" Sergius shouted as he flew behind Julius.

"I'm not sure if I'm ready for you to be like that in twelve-hundred years," Katrina told me.

"That makes two of us," I replied and took off after the Reapers.

We barely made it past Wadley Regional Hospital on Texas Boulevard and Pine Street before hitting another roadblock. Witches and demons were reclining in the middle of MLK Boulevard.

"Should we be offended?" Julius asked.

"Yes," I told them.

"Didn't think you were going to make it," one of the witches shouted.

We didn't have time to reply when they opened fire on us. And just our luck, they didn't use guns. Instead, they assaulted us with pure magic. Sergius reacted faster than me and dragged me behind a building.

"We aren't immune to magical attacks?" I asked Sergius and Julius.

"No. This can definitely make your head explode," Sergius answered.

"Now what?" I asked.

"I think this is the part where you need us," Iason announced in my ear.

"Holy Christ, where did you come from?" I told him, not prepared for his arrival.

"He has mastered the art of fast running," Julius told me without a single ounce of surprise in his tone.

"Gentlemen," Iason said, straightening.

From the shadows next to us, four of his elves materialized. I peeked around the building as the elves created magical shields.

"You do know there are fifteen of them," I told Iason.

"Not my fault they don't have more people," he replied, marching towards his men.

"I really like him," Julius told me.

"Me, too," Sergius joined in.

"Did we miss it?" Godmother and Ulises dropped from the sky in front of us.

"Can everyone do the flying thing around here?" I asked Sergius and Julius, who only nodded. "Not at all, Godmother. I think they are just getting started."

"Oh, good," Godmother told me, taking off the cape she was wearing.

Godmother had a see-through mesh onesie that she rocked like a supermodel. I gasped, while Sergius and Julius whistled behind her.

"Can I marry your Godmother?" Julius asked as I tried to cover his eyes.

"Too late, little boy. I claimed her first," Ulises told him, joining my Godmother with a magical shield.

"That is so not fair," Julius whined.

"Is that going to make him your Godfather?" Sergius asked instead.

"No. It doesn't work like that." I punched both boys in the arm. "Now focus on the battle and not my Godmother."

"Going to be difficult." I slapped Julius over the head for that comment.

Iason was not kidding; the odds were not fair. The elves let the demons and witches shower them with bolts of magic that made the entire street shake. Clouds of lightning followed their attack, but the shields never failed. Iason and Ulises returned fire and evaporated the witches' shields.

"This is for the Order, you traitors!" Godmother sent her back-stabbing witches a blast that smoldered every building it touched.

The witches went flying with their clothes smoking. The demons were gone, and only ashes remained. Bob drove over to the unconscious group with Godmother's remaining members of the Order. Shorty was right behind him with Junior. The witches hit the traitors with another set of spells and Shorty shot them in the chest with tranquilizer darts.

"Is that really necessary?" Sergius asked them.

"There is no such thing as overkill," Bob explained.

"I like how he thinks," Julius told Sergius.

"How far are we?" Iason asked.

"About three blocks away," I answered.

"I told you. Halloween all over again," Katrina said, joining the group.

"Is it the same building?" Iason asked.

"No but run by the same people. Just a block closer," I said gazing down Texas Boulevard.

"Boss Lady, the TRAHC people are really going to hate us after this," Shorty verbalized my suspicion.

"Why is everyone taking a break?" Constantine growled coming to a stop next to us.

"Letting you catch up, old man," Julius teased him.

I could get used to Julius.

"We are here, so the wait is over," Constantine announced. "What's the plan?"

"Surround the building and do a synchronized assault on it," I told them.

"Works for me," Katrina concurred.

"In that case, we have three blocks to go so watch your backs." Constantine took the lead this time, and the rest of us followed.

Chapter Twenty-Nine

The city of Texarkana was going to be furious with us. Our path here was littered with destruction and massive damage. Constantine was going to be spending a fortune to rebuild the town and get everything back to a semi-functioning order. That was before we counted the damage that was surely going to be taking place at the TRAHC building after we were done with it.

We stood across the street from TRAHC and hid behind another building. Snipers were on the roof facing the perimeter of the building. There was no way for us to sneak in anywhere. It didn't help that the front had a steel, security door that was locked either. Why would you invite people over and lock your front door? Absolutely rude on the vampires' part.

The rest of our team slowly joined us. Most of the humans were out of breath, but they refused to give up. The Legionaries had taken major losses, but they still remained focused and unshakable. The Underground was making their way through in their trucks, half of them filled with victims they picked up along the way. Bob and Shorty made their way through the crowd to the front line next to Constantine and me.

"Any ideas?" I asked Bob as I pointed at the snipers on the roof.

"Ninth has one," Bob replied, handing me one of his earpieces.

"Ninth, my man, where have you been?" I asked using the earpiece.

"Somebody had to clean up the mess you guys left in your wake," Ninth replied softly. "Those damn things did not want to die. I had to reload the drones three times each."

"Tell that old man he better be careful with my drones," Constantine hissed next to me.

"Sure thing," I replied to Constantine before turning my attention back to Ninth. "Good job, Ninth. Completely forgot about the ones that were left behind. What can you do with this group?"

I had been so busy moving forward, I didn't consider how many enemies were still moving behind us. This battle was definitely a group effort.

"I think I can handle your little problem, dear," said Ninth. "I do have a little treat for you."

Bob and I glanced at each other before facing the building again. Two fully armed drones flew over us towards the building. The snipers facing the building took cover and opened fire on the drones.

"I'm going to rip them apart if they blow up my drones!" Constantine shouted. "That's the second set I bought this week."

The rest of our team took cover to avoid the crossfire. Ninth raised the drones higher doing evasive maneuvers. Before the snipers had a chance to reload, Ninth returned fire on the rooftop.

"Take that, you bastards!" Ninth shouted over the earpiece as two sets of machine guns dropped on the rooftop of the TRAHC building.

"Make it rain on their asses," Shorty encouraged Ninth from his headset.

Two minutes later, not a single sniper was visible on the rooftop.

"Mission accomplished, my friends. The roof is clear," Ninth announced. "Now unleash hell on our enemies. This is for the Mistress."

The drones circled the building in small figure-eight patterns to avoid hitting each other. From the speaker system in the drones, Ninth played Method Man's Judgement Day.

"That is a fitting anthem for this day," Katrina said from my right.

"Thank you Ninth. That is perfect," I told him, returning Bob's earpiece.

"We still need to get in, ladies, and we have five minutes before six," Eugene said stretching his back.

"I'm open to suggestion," I announced to the group over the music as we stared at the gates.

"Sounds like you need me." The Boatman stepped forward smoking his cigar. "I recommend everyone take a few steps back. This will get messy."

"What is he going to do?" Junior whispered.

"Good question," Katrina replied as we moved away from the Boatman.

The Boatman clapped his hands and the ground shook. Legionaries scattered as Reapers casually strolled around the sinkhole being created by the Boatman. As the ground parted, a boat made of bones pushed by the dead appeared. It probably came from the depths of hell, but I was not asking the Boatman to confirm.

"That is traumatizing!" screamed Junior. "I'm never going on a boat."

"You should see his battleship," Julius joked with him.

"I'll pass," Junior replied.

"Me, too," Eugene added.

"Are we ramming the boat at the gates?" Katrina asked the Boatman as she roamed next to him.

"Can bone crash through concrete and steel?" I asked, debating the logistics of that tactic.

"Don't be ridiculous," the Boatman told us. "This is a cruising ship, not one for ramming."

"We don't have all day, so please get this plan in motion," Constantine ordered.

"Yes master." The Boatman saluted Constantine before doing an about face towards the boat. "Napoleon, cannons."

From the bowels of the boat, a tall skeleton wearing a pair of ripped shorts ran up pushing a cannon.

"Where did he come from?" Shorty asked, leaning on the boat.

"We really don't want to know." I pulled him away from the evil contraption.

"Fire!" shouted the Boatman as he lit the fuse in the cannon by snapping his fingers together.

The metal gate, the wooden door, and part of the wall and windows were shattered by the cannon ball. Debris flew in every direction. I covered Eugene and Junior with my body. Bob dragged Shorty to the ground, while Julius protected Katrina. The area looked like it was hit by a bomb. I would never underestimate the power of an old-school cannon.

"Door is secure," the Boatman announced while jumping on the boat.

The Boatman placed one foot on the cannon and admired his work. If the owners of Captain Morgan needed a stand-in for their commercials, the Boatman would have been perfect. That was if you preferred your pirates demented and without skin.

"It's time for us to pay our respects to this little group of wannabes," Constantine announced traipsing slowly over the rubble.

"General, it has been an honor." I saluted Katrina hoping this wasn't our last time.

"Reapers, kill them all," Katrina started the old Eighty-Second Airborne's motto.

"And let God sort them out," I finished for her.

"Legionaries, cover the perimeter!" Katrina shouted at her men. "Anything that comes out, send it to hell."

Katrina jogged with her troops to take positions around the building. If the Reapers couldn't contain the situation inside, the Legionaries would do their best to stop them outside. If that was even possible.

"Isis, on your left," Eugene told me as his hands shimmered with blue power.

"I got your right," Junior stated, bringing three shadow soldiers to life.

"Bob, it's time," I informed him. "Get the fire trucks here and let it rain."

Bob saluted and took off, whispering orders into his earpiece. Ninth had increased the sound of the song and the hip-hop beat bounced off the building in downtown.

The citizens of downtown were probably terrified.

"Grim Reaper, on your command," Sergius told me.

I slammed the end of my scythe down making the ground tremble. All at once, Reapers got in their positions like runners at the start of a race. I slammed the scythe again.

"Now." The word was more a thought that rippled through the Reapers.

Without a sound, the Reapers charged the building. Some went in through the front door while others made their own way in through the walls and windows.

"Why did we blow up the front wall if they could just crash through the building?" I asked Constantine while staring at the hundreds of human cannonballs crashing at the building.

"For the psychological impact it creates," Constantine replied with all his sharp canines extended. "Should we go?"

"Follow me," I told him, sprinting to the building while dragging my scythe to create sparks in my wake.

Chapter Thirty

The first floor of TRAHC was a beehive of madness. Vampires dropped on us from the ceiling. The sounds of battle came from everywhere. The gallery halls in the building were pitch-black, but sparks appeared every time a scythe hit a sword. Demons blocked the stairwell to the second floor, and crossing the foyers was like crossing landmines.

"Never a dull moment with you." Iason appeared from behind me. "Allow me."

Before I could reply, Iason had launched a green ball of magic toward the demons on the stairwell. One demon blocked the assault and sent the ball of magic towards the right. The ball slammed against three vampires demolishing them.

"Guess they don't like each other as much as we thought," Eugene told me, sending his own balls of magic at two incoming vampires.

"Not at all," I told him, decapitating the first vampire that ran at me. "They each have their own agendas and their goals don't match. Not our problem. We need to get upstairs."

The fighting was not slowing down. For every vampire we took out, three more appeared. The demons cast spells at us, and we started to take casualties. A few Reapers were killed by demons as they ripped them apart. Iason and his men were busy helping Junior battle a group of vampires. Constantine was ripping vampires apart with his bare teeth but we were still not able to get close to the stairwell.

"Isis, move!" Godmother shouted at me from in front of the door.

Eugene pulled me aside since I was busy dodging demon spells directed at my head. Godmother sent a blast of energy across the foyer that melted everything it touched. Vampires, demons, and even a few of their shifters went down.

"Go now," Godmother told me, getting ready to send another blast out.

"Sergius, with me," I told him as I ran up the stairs.

Sergius and Julius followed closely behind as we made it up the semi-circular stairwell. Our feet never touched the stone as we moved. The second floor was dark and the doors to the Gable hall were closed.

"Our meeting is in that room, right?" Sergius asked.

"It's never easy," I told him, kicking the door off its hinges. "But I can get used to this much power."

"It doesn't take very long, trust me," Julius answered, strolling into the room past the broken door pieces.

The Gable hall was a scene out of a scary movie. Vampires were everywhere, against the walls, on chairs, and even walking on the ceiling. Demons were also in full attendance.

"Well, well, look who finally decided to join us," Marie said from the center of the room. "You are late."

"Traffic," I replied with a smirk.

"Do you think this is funny?" she hissed at me. "You will not be laughing when your brother pays for your insolence."

Marie moved from the center of the room to show off a beaten Bartholomew. His left eye was completely swollen shut and his lips were badly bruised. My body moved towards Bartholomew without thinking. Sergius pulled me back.

"Hi, Bart." I wasn't sure if he could see me.

"I knew you would come." His voice was so low that if it wasn't for my super hearing, I would have missed it.

"Marie, are you still playing these silly games?" Sergius asked.

"This is a pleasant surprise," Marie told him, playing with Bartholomew's hair. "Death must be running out of good help if he is dragging his little pets out of their slumber."

"You, on the other hand, should have stayed in hell," Julius jumped in to defend his friend.

"Now, Julius, is that any way to talk to an old friend?" Marie teased Julius.

"We were never friends and it will be my pleasure to dispatch you to your permanent death," Julius replied, spinning his scythe.

"We need to get Bartholomew away from her," I told the boys.

"You need to find better friends," Marie announced. "Junior, kill them if you want to see your sister."

Junior strolled in the room followed by Eugene. Eugene stopped at the door after hearing Marie's orders. Junior kept on marching over to stand next to me.

"I would do whatever I could to save my family," I told Junior.

Junior glanced at Bartholomew and then back at me. "Isis, I'm sorry."

Smoke covered his fingers, and the room turned cold. Sergius tried to pull me away but I wouldn't budge. I couldn't let Junior lose his family because I failed.

"Those are some pretty little clouds," Edward announced from the door, shaking off dust from his dark pants and jacket. "I recommend you save them for your group and not your family."

"The traitor has joined us," Marie told her brethren, who hissed at Edward.

Edward was the only vampire, not counting the really ancient ones that did not look like a monster. The blood he shared with Ginny had given him a soul again. Her magic had transformed his monster while keeping all the insane powers. He still couldn't walk in the daylight, but he was just as powerful as any of the ancients.

"Enough," Edward told the room. "I have made it very clear that I will always choose my family. This bitch, on the other hand, is planning to sacrifice you all to the Antichrist as soon as he crosses over. Who is a traitor now?"

"Lies!" Marie screamed. "He would say anything to save his own skin."

"Maybe." Edward strolled in the room and the other vampires watched him. "Or a very reliable source told me."

Edward ripped one of the curtains off the huge windows. The window faced the front of the building. Edward leaned against the frame and looked outside.

"I think his name was Carlos," Edward announced to the room, not even glancing in Marie's direction. "He didn't last long after we interrogated him. Too bad, he seemed like a nice fellow. Junior, your sisters send their love. Would you like to wave at them?"

Junior rushed to the window. Tears rolled down his cheeks as he waved uncontrollably out the window. Edward strolled back in my direction. Iason joined our group, shaking hands with his brother-in-law.

"You took your sweet time," I finally told him.

"You forgot to mention how many tunnels there were underneath this city," Edward chastised me.

"Sorry, I had no clue," I replied.

"I do, and I will gladly give you a blueprint after we are done," Edward told me. "You are immortal."

"A Reaper," I replied.

"Thank you, God." Edward squeezed my arm. "I don't want to explain to your soon-to-be God-child why you had to die. I love you, Isis."

"I wouldn't celebrate just yet. Do you think you will leave here alive?" Marie screamed. "Kill them!"

"Junior, get over here now," I ordered him.

Junior rushed back to our small group. Once he joined us, we stood in a circle with our backs facing each other to cover all of our angles.

"Thank you," Junior told Edward in between sobs.

"Don't thank me. It was Isis's idea," he replied, pulling out two swords from his back.

"Isis," Junior mumbled.

"I told you I would do whatever it took to protect my family," I told him, swinging my scythe from hand to hand.

"Do you all mind saving all the thank yous until we get out of here?" asked Iason.

Vampires and demons charged at us from all sides. Iason and Edward were the first to be attacked. It seemed the vampires had a personal hatred towards a traitor and the people he joined. Edward did not appear to be that upset when he decapitated two of the vampires attacking him. Iason ripped another one apart. Vampire ash sprayed everyone as demons dispatched magic balls at us. Eugene countered the attack with a few of his own, making the room shake from the explosion. Junior joined Eugene and together they sent smoke around the vampires in front of them.

"We have a lot of demons joining us," Sergius told me.

"They just keep coming," I replied. "According to Jake, hell was on lockdown."

"He needs better locks, because a lot of his kind are here," Julius added.

"They are preparing for the coming." Marie had moved to the far end of the hall dragging Bartholomew with her.

God, please let her be wrong. Jake, please keep your son in hell.

It was demented that I could be praying to both God and the Devil at the same time. In the midst of this chaos I wasn't very picky. Demons were reaching for my face. I stabbed a few with my scythe and eventually had to pull my machete from my holster. Standing this close to my group, I was more likely to stab my own people than the enemy. I shrunk the scythe and used the machete instead. Father Francis had blessed that as well, so any demon it touched would be sent back to Jake...in pieces, of course.

"Marie, he is not coming!" I shouted at the vampire.

"Is that what you believe?" Marie replied. "Just because your horsemen and your God won't send you help, it doesn't mean ours won't."

"This is nothing to do with faith, trust me," I replied, kicking a demon in the solar plexus. "He is not coming because his daddy has him in a timeout."

Marie laughed and her melodious voice vibrated in my ear. If she wasn't a murdering beast, she would have been a lovely lady.

"We need to get closer," Julius told me.

"He will come," Marie shouted.

"Not according to Jake," I answered her. "Iason, Edward, cover us."

"If that is true, then it makes no difference whose blood we spill tonight." Marie's fingers extended to claws and her eyes became blood-red.

"No!" I ran towards her.

Time slowed down and everything in the room became sharper. Sergius, Julius, and I ran across the hall toward Marie. Iason shot energy balls at the demons coming for us. Edward dispatched vampires trying to get past them. Sergius spun his scythe, slashing demons and vampires alike. Marie moved causally, her claws glowing against the darkness of the night. With one swift movement, she cut Bartholomew's throat open. My heart stopped.

I reached him in time to stop his body from hitting the ground. I covered his throat with my hands, but blood spurted in every direction.

"Stay with me Bart!" I cried.

Bartholomew touched my hand and our eyes met.

"I love you, Isis." Blood poured out of his mouth as he tried to speak.

"Don't talk. Please hold on!" I held him as tight as I could, but it did nothing to stop the blood from rushing from him.

"Isis, down!" Sergius ordered as he fought Marie behind me.

I covered the bleeding Bartholomew with my body. Sergius and Julius fought the powerful vampire. Marie was a skillful fighter, but Sergius and Julius had over a thousand years of training. They were not going to be defeated again. I needed to move Bartholomew but couldn't do it without letting go of the wound. More demons materialized, throwing spells at everyone.

"Time to die, humans!" one of the demons announced, throwing the biggest ball of energy I had ever seen.

The ball was the size of a large pillow and went directly for Eugene and Junior.

"No humans here," Eugene replied in a cold, deadly voice.

Eugene repelled the spell and sent the ball through the ceiling. Pieces of it rained down on us. Iason pulled me away before a piece landed on me and Bartholomew.

"Isis, we need to go," Iason told me.

"We need to take Bartholomew." I glanced down at my brother who wasn't moving.

"Let him go, he's gone," Iason pried my hands away from Bartholomew.

"No, I can't." I held as tightly as I could. "We can save him."

Iason pulled me away kicking and screaming. The hall was collapsing around us. I dug in my heels, making it impossible for him to drag me away.

"You are not dying here!" Iason told me, picking me up and tossing me over his shoulder.

The front door exploded right after Edward dragged Eugene and Junior away. Iason turned around and ran towards the large glass window. With an elven command, the glass exploded.

"Time to go, you two," Iason told Julius and Sergius.

From my awkward angle and in between tears covering my face, I could see Sergius and Julius. They pinned Marie to a corner of the hall. Debris kept falling and Marie fought like a wild cat, but the Reapers were not letting her go. I turned my gaze towards Bartholomew's body. Death was standing over him. She picked up her son and cradled him in her arms.

"Take me Death, take me!" I shouted at her.

"Not today," Iason replied and leapt out of the window.

My world crumpled as the TRAHC building fell to pieces. I dropped my head and cried, not caring who was around me.

Chapter Thirty-One

As a leader, I was doing a horrible job at this moment. I couldn't control the tears, and I was worthless to my team. The TRACH building was crumbling. The Triplets had three fire trucks pumping holy water to the building through every available hole, including the roof. Screams and howls filled the night as the holy water hit every diabolical thing inside. Constantine had cleared the building and our troops, the majority of them, were alive. Many were injured but most were breathing. The Legionaries terminated every vampire that tried to escape.

The few members of the Order apprehended the misfit's witches with the help of the elves. A magical barrier was placed around the witches. The shifters, on their end, had secured the leaders of the enemies' packs. With the help of the underground, the shifters were tied and lying flat on the ground. Everyone was busy securing the location and the prisoners, except me. I sat on the sidewalk, depleted, watching the building fall.

"Isis." Constantine was back to his normal cat size. He put his soft paw on my face and wiped the dirt and tears away, his feline eyes shining with unshed tears.

"It hurts so much," I admitted to him.

"I know," Constantine replied.

Lightning crashed in front of us and smoke filled the street. Constantine and I stood up. I pulled out my scythe and Constantine grew a few feet.

"This can't be good," I told him as our people readied to charge the smoke.

The smoke cleared and War, Pestilence, and Famine stood in the middle of the street in all their grand glory.

"I definitely don't have the patience for those three." I dropped back on the sidewalk avoiding the Horsemen.

"Congratulations, children. You did it," War announced like a presidential candidate.

"Who are you calling 'children?'" my Godmother told the arrogant Horsemen.

"Let him have it, Virginia!" Constantine cheered my Godmother on.

Those two were a deadly pair for the world. Now that they found a bond, not even War would be able to handle it.

"Humans just have a very short life span," War tried to explain.

"Then it's a blessing many of us are not human," Godmother corrected him. "I'm the high priestess of the Order of Witches in this world and demand respect. By the way, why are you here? To destroy what is left of Texarkana?"

"High priestess, my apologies." War gave my Godmother a short bow and the rest of us just stared in silence. "I'm only here to congratulate you all on a job well done."

"Nobody needs your congratulations. Not starting the apocalypse is good enough." Godmother walked away from War and back to her prisoners.

"Smooth, brother," Pestilence told him, covering her grin with her hand.

"Next time you get to talk first," War informed her before facing the crowd again. "General."

Katrina marched to the front and saluted her boss. War saluted her back and presented her with a medal.

"You have represented us well. And in meritorious service of your outstanding command, I present you this." War pinned the medal on Katrina, who never flinched.

"You have a medal for stopping the apocalypse?" Shorty asked as he pushed forward to inspect the shiny medal. "How often does the apocalypse almost happen for you to have a medal for stopping it?"

"You don't want to know," Katrina told Shorty, and Bob pulled him away from the horsemen.

"Legionaries, your services on this mission has been completed," War announced. "You are dismissed."

The Legionaries picked up their weapons and injured troops then took off running towards State Line. War saluted his siblings and disappeared.

"Where are they going?" Eugene asked.

"Home," War replied.

"On foot to France?" Junior added.

"On foot to the airport to catch their flight," Katrina explained.

"Should we tell them we could give them a ride?" Shorty asked.

"Good luck catching them," Bob told him.

The Legionaries were gone when Pestilence moved forward to stand in front of the group.

"Well, that was interesting," said Pestilence, fixing her black Alexander McQueen suit that probably cost a fortune. "Let's be honest. We all had our doubts whether you could pull this off."

"Do horsemen get points for honesty?" I asked the crowd.

"Not today," replied Shorty.

"Have you considered a shower? You are covered in blood," Pestilence asked me.

I considered throwing a rock at her, one of the millions scattered around me from the building. Instead, I just stuck out my tongue at her. Constantine and Katrina chuckled, while Eugene's face changed colors. Katrina joined me on the sidewalk and wrapped her arms around me. Words were not needed. She had lost soldiers and understood. We watched the devilish Pestilence address her Interns.

"As much as I hate agreeing with my sibling, in this case, he is right." Pestilence rolled her eyes. "You all have done an incredible job. It appears it's time to recruit a new rookie."

Katrina and I glanced at Eugene, who had been standing proud a moment ago and now had his chin low and his eyes on the ground. I was ready to pound that evil nut to the ground when Katrina held me back.

"You misunderstand me." Pestilence moved closer to Eugene. "We need a new rookie because you can't be both. I can't have my enforcer be the rookie. That is absurd."

"Mistress." In a momentary loss of conscience, Eugene hugged Pestilence.

"Oh my." Pestilence hugged him back, then peeled him away. "Let's not make that a habit, okay?"

"Yes, Mistress. Sorry about that," Eugene answered, blushing from ear-to-ear.

"Second, Fourth. Is everyone else well?" Pestilence asked the other two Interns.

"Yes, Mistress. Thanks to Constantine, everyone is secure," Fourth answered.

Pestilence directed her attention towards Constantine, who was cleaning himself in the most inappropriate places.

"It's called having a backup plan that doesn't kill everyone," Constantine told her in between licks. "You're welcome, Ursula."

"At least the bag of fur did something useful for once," Pestilence told her Interns. "We will start rebuilding tomorrow. Good night, my children."

Pestilence dissolved in a cloud of smoke. Second and Fourth ran towards Eugene and saluted him.

"Congratulations," Second told him proudly. "You are doing a great job so far."

"We are stepping up our game," Fourth said. "We have lots of training for you."

Famine was left alone in the middle of the street, shaking their head.

"Humans," said Famine. "Shadow."

"Yes, Boss." Junior moved around the crowd to face his boss.

"You made us proud," Famine told him. "We will need to find a new location for our lab. And your family needs a more secure home. Please make that happen."

"It will be my honor, Boss." Junior glowed with excitement.

Famine gave Junior a fist bump that ended in smoke bouncing off their fingers. With a wave of their fingers, Famine was gone.

"That was exhausting," Constantine told me.

"Where is our horseman?" Shorty asked, searching the area.

"Taking into account how much it's going to cost to rebuild this city," a masculine voice said from behind me.

I spun around to find a six foot tall, handsome young man in his early twenties standing behind me. His curly, brown hair was a mess but his eyes, they were Reaper's eyes. They were the same shape with the same mischievous look as Bartholomew, but he was a Reaper.

"Holy Jesus Christ!" I shouted and ran at my brother.

"By the Goddess," my Godmother said.

"It is a miracle! Thank you, God!" Shorty screamed at the sky.

"How is this possible? You are here." I searched Bartholomew's neck for his wound.

"I was only gone like thirty minutes people, relax," Bartholomew told everyone. "Well, technically, about four days, but still."

"You honestly didn't think I was going to let my only ward die like that?" Death asked me.

I had a Eugene moment and hugged Death. Unlike Pestilence, Death was not afraid of a hug and was glad to hug me back.

"I was grateful for your offer." Death wiped my tears away. "But unlike all other souls in this world, yours already belongs to me. Bartholomew said he wanted to go back home."

"I like the new look," Constantine told Bartholomew, who picked him up and placed Constantine on his shoulder.

"Some modifications were in order," Death explained. "I couldn't have him stuck in the body of a thirteen-year-old for all eternity."

"Look at these guns, Constantine." Bartholomew flexed his biceps. "My abs are even better."

"Don't you dare show those off," I told him.

"He will grow out of that stage...eventually," Death told me when I stared at her. "Now Reapers, are you ready to head back?"

"Yes," the replies came from all around us.

One-by-one, Reapers sunk back to the ground spinning their scythes in salute.

"We will save you two an inner tube," Julius told Bartholomew and me before disappearing.

"It was a pleasure, Isis." Sergius shook my hand.

"You wouldn't want to stay here?" I asked him.

"It was nice to be on Earth again, but our time has passed," Sergius explained. "We will wait for the end of times in the river. We have finally resolved the last of our unfinished business. We can relax in piece."

"Drinking margaritas and floating around," Katrina added.

"Absolutely," Sergius said with a huge smile. "We will see you again, Isis. Keep your head on."

Sergius sunk and we waved at the first Reaper of Death. The Boatman came forth still smoking the same huge cigar without any ash.

"Would you like to keep the boat, little sister?" he asked me.

I gulped before answering. "I think we are good for now."

"If you need it, just give me a shout." The Boatman clapped, and the dead pulled the boat back to hell. "Boss, it was a pleasure."

"Always a pleasure, Boatman," Death replied.

"Constantine, keep those records coming," the Boatman said as he started to sink. "I have a block party next week and need a new soundtrack."

"DJ Bag of Bones at his best," Katrina said as the Boatman vanished under the earth. "Now what?"

"Now you have a city to put back together," Death told us. "I don't need to explain how important handling the public relations of this incident will be."

"Public image and news is my specialty, so I got this," Junior volunteered.

"We will handle the CDC and the quarantine situation," Eugene offered.

"I will get the National Guard mobilized and declare Texarkana a state of emergency due to earthquakes and other natural phenomenon." Katrina was already dialing her cell phone.

"We got the funding," Constantine said. "The city could use an anonymous benefactor to assist with the repairs of all these historical buildings."

"We are definitely not good for the city," Bartholomew joked.

"Clean-up is going to be painful," Shorty told the group.

"Can we worry about that in the morning?" I asked. "I'm exhausted. I thought Reapers did not need sleep."

"Recently-made Reapers will need a lot more rest in the beginning," Death explained.

"How come Bartholomew looks so perky?" Bartholomew did not look like I did after my transformation.

"His process was different," Death told me. "Bartholomew was already dead when I made him. Constantine, you can handle things here?"

"I always do," Constantine replied, marching over to Bob.

"Good," Death said. "Time for bed, Isis."

I didn't get a chance to reply. Death kissed my forehead and the whole world went dark. I was falling into clouds of pink marshmallows and floating cotton candy.

Chapter Thirty-Two

The scent of jasmine and vanilla filled the air. I rolled over to my side and felt Death in the room.

"Good morning, Death," I told her. "Is it morning? And is it the fourth?"

Those were important questions to ask. Death was known for knocking me out for days at a time when I needed healing.

"Good morning, Isis," Death told me. "Happy Fourth of July, and yes, it is morning."

"That is unusual," I told her, not needing to turn on the light to see her.

Death sat on my chair holding one of my books. One of these days, I will actually check to see if she reads the books or just holds them.

"Healing is faster as a Reaper," Death explained while fixing her skirt. "In a few days, you will barely need sleep."

"Then why the early wakeup call?" I sat up on my bed.

"You have work to do." Death stood from the chair.

"That doesn't sound like fun," I said, running a hand through my matted hair.

"We were compromised, and I want to know how," Death informed me. "Marie was not the only one involved in this little coup. I want those who started this war found."

"What about North America?" I asked, playing with my sheets.

"You are no longer an Intern, Isis." Death sat back down. "Reapers don't have territories they watch; they manage the world. Since you hate our recruitment process so much, you get to select your successor. Bartholomew will be joining you in the search. He needs training."

"When do we leave?" I asked.

"Today," Death announced. "Constantine has the details. Keep a low profile and try to blend in. Also, do try to avoid destroying any more towns, please."

"That last one might be tough," I told Death.

"I'm proud of you," said Death softly. "I recommend you hurry since your friends are outside waiting for you."

Death stood from the chair and left the room. I glanced at the clock on the night table and it was only seven-thirty. Death didn't seem too worried, so at least it was not bad news that was waiting for me. I jumped out of bed with more energy than I'd felt in years.

Should I take a shower or just go out and check on everyone? A glance at the mirror answered that question for me. Shower won because I looked like roadkill.

It didn't take me long to get ready. By the time I stepped out to the common room, the smell of coffee had reached me. I wasn't hungry, but I still craved coffee. It was a strange desire to want something just because and not for nourishment or life support.

"Good morning, Sleeping Beauty," Katrina welcomed me.

"Good morning Super General," I replied, grabbing the mug Bob offered me. "What is all the commotion here?"

Death wasn't lying because the Loft was pretty busy. Eugene and Junior were by the computer area with Bartholomew working on something. Katrina and Bob were in the kitchen having breakfast, while Godmother, Ulises, Iason, and Constantine sat at the kitchen table.

"Work doesn't stop because of the holiday," Godmother told me.

"Are you leaving?" I asked her.

"The Order is in turmoil and our followers need guidance," Godmother explained. "We must cleanse and rebuild."

"That sounds serious," I replied.

"Eric has agreed to join the Order," Godmother announced in a casual tone. "We have meetings in all the major cities. We lost a lot of members, so it is time to hold them accountable."

"Translation: heads are going to roll," Constantine clarified.

"We will ensure this doesn't happen again," Godmother told him. "You still owe me a vacation. Once everything settles, I expect you in Salem."

"Yes, Godmother," I quickly agreed.

Godmother stood from her chair and made her way around the room blessing everyone. I was the last one. She kissed my forehead, then held me tight. I could feel her heartbeat and the smell of jasmine filled my soul.

"I love you, Godmother," I whispered to her.

"I love you, too, my sweet child." Tears rolled down her cheeks. "Please be careful. I know you are a Reaper now, but your enemies will be worse. Please take care of yourself."

"I will." I gave her another hug.

Godmother waved from the door before leaving. Ulises gave us a silent wave before following Godmother out the door.

"Should I be worried about those two?" I asked Iason, who adjusted his suit as he rose.

"Only if you don't get a wedding invitation," he told me.

"That serious?" Katrina whistled.

"I'm not sure if I'm ready for a step-daddy," I joked with her.

"You might be the flower girl, so be careful," Iason told me.

"Definitely not ready," I replied as he came closer.

"You still owe me lunch," said Iason. "I'm expecting you in San Diego for the birth, and don't be late."

"Is someone going to call me to let me know it's happening?" I asked just to be a pain because I knew he would.

"More than once if it's necessary." Iason kissed my cheek, and goosebumps spread all over my skin. "If you need to talk about the transition, call me."

"Thank you for everything," I told him softly. Iason had risked a lot for us, and I was grateful.

"Always." He headed towards the door. "I must go and supervise the love birds or your Godmother will never make her meetings."

"I'm not ready for that mental image," I told the group.

"I second that." Katrina put her plate in the sink and smiled at me. "Always a pleasure to battle with you but it's time for me to go."

"Thank you for everything," I told her.

"Stop it," Katrina ordered me. "Unlike your Godmother, I know you are going to be fine. Keep me posted. We are still on for skiing this winter, so don't flake out now that you're a Reaper."

Before I could whine about skiing, Katrina hugged me. She marched out the door without another word. Junior was next, but he looked ready to cry.

"Thank you for saving my family," he said.

"Thank Shorty because he gave me the idea," I replied. "They were moving the hostages underground. Edward and his vampires did the hard work."

"I almost killed you," Junior cried.

"You couldn't even if you wanted to," Constantine answered. "Reapers are immune to the horsemen's power.

The only thing you were going to do was tickle her. Stop beating yourself up."

"Now you tell me." Junior took a deep breath.

"Constantine is right, and nothing happened anyway," I told him.

"I still want to make it up to you," Junior stated, wiping his face.

"That is perfect," I said, looking at Constantine. "If you can handle this PR nightmare we are facing, we can call it even."

"That's it? A piece of cake," Junior announced. "We will have this fixed and covered by lunch."

With a new swagger in his step, Junior left the Loft with his phone in hand.

"His skills in manipulating the media are more terrifying than Famine's powers," Constantine told us, and I agreed with a nod.

"Enforcer, what are your plans?" I asked Eugene.

"I have no idea," he replied honestly. "We need to find a new Intern, so I will be helping with that. But can I still come over?"

"Eugene, of course you can." I rushed over and gave him a hug. "You are family."

"I know but everything has changed. You are a Reaper now," Eugene said. "You will be leaving, right?"

"You are?" Bob stopped cooking to look at me.

"How did you know?" I asked Eugene.

"Ninth told me Reapers don't have a continent. They just wander the earth doing Death's bidding." Eugene kicked the floor.

"Yes, Death gave me a mission," I told the group.

"You are leaving me?" Bartholomew left his computer area.

"We are leaving," I corrected Bartholomew. "You are coming with me."

"Both of you?" Bob's sea-green eyes sparkled with tears. "Who is going to manage North America? Is Haven over?"

"That would be up to you," I answered him.

"Me, why?" Bob asked, searching the room.

"Because I'm naming you the new North American Intern," I announced.

"What?" Bob put his hand over his heart.

"Please don't have a heart attack on your first day on the job," I told him.

"Isis, I can't," Bob whined.

"I couldn't think of anyone better," I said. "You are already trained, minus the third eye but Constantine can teach you that in a day. Besides, you are a better Intern than me. You have actually read the manual."

Everyone in the room burst into laugher.

"You have left big shoes to fill," Bob said, choking back tears. "I don't know if I can do this without you two."

"People, you are so dramatic," Constantine told us. "They are not moving out."

"We are not?" I asked, gasping.

"Girl, please," Constantine growled, the familiar sound making me giggle. "Do you honestly think we would send two newly-made Reapers out in the world for good? We trust you, just not that much."

"Thank God, I get to keep my room," Bartholomew told us.

"I'm glad your priorities are in order, Bartholomew," Constantine chastised him. "You will check in every night and come home a minimum of every two weeks. Is that clear?"

"Yes, Constantine," Bartholomew and I replied in unison.

"As for you, former Rookie and now Enforcer, we expect you here every Friday for our weekly meetings," Constantine announced to Eugene. "Is that clear?"

"Yes, Constantine," Eugene replied quickly.

"Good. Now that all that nonsense is fixed." Constantine hopped on the kitchen table and walked over to Bob. "This is the real question. Do you, Bob, accept the position of Intern?"

Bartholomew, Eugene, and I waited. Bob looked at each one of us before replying.

"It will be my honor," Bob announced.

The rest of us clapped.

"Isis, would you complete the ritual?" Constantine asked me.

"Ritual?" I replied with a question.

"Yes, silly girl." Constantine glared at me. "As the representative of Death on Earth, it is your responsibility to give Bob his gifts. Especially since this is your new recruitment process."

"You mean that kiss thing Death does is a ritual?" I asked Constantine, shaking my head.

"Would you prefer to cut your hands and share blood?" Constantine replied.

"Gross," I said quickly. "Kiss it is."

"Make sure to state your intentions as you release your powers," Constantine explained.

"Got it," I told him. "Bob, are you ready?"

"Yes." Bob lowered his head.

I held Bob's face with both hands and gave him a soft kiss on his forehead. I closed my eyes and pushed my powers into Bob.

From this moment, Bob, I declare you the new North American Intern. To ensure the safe passage of all the souls and the wellbeing of Haven.

I gave my powers a few more seconds to transfer before pulling away. As I removed my hands from his face, Bob looked dizzy. Eugene and I held him steady while he inhaled slowly.

"Get used to that because it happens all the time," I told Bob.

"You are glowing," Bob told me.

"That was fast," Constantine said.

"Eugene, do you mind taking Bob to bed?" I asked. "He will need to let things settle for a while now."

"His third eye already opened?" Eugene took a closer look at Bob, who was cross-eyed.

"It appears," I answered. "He is an overachiever. Get some rest, Bob. We will see you in two weeks."

"Okay," Bob replied, holding his head.

"See you next week, guys," Eugene said in a more cheerful tone.

"Stay out of trouble, Eugene," I told him as he waved from the door with Bob. "Constantine, shouldn't we stay here until he gets better?"

"Unlike most Interns, Bob has an entire Underground supporting him," Constantine answered. "A few days in bed will do him wonders. I'm sure Shorty can handle the clean-up process. You two need to hurry."

"Where are we heading?" Bartholomew asked.

"Spain," Constantine told us. "With all the Interns in recovery here, rumor has it that the country is in turmoil. I need you two to find out who instigated the situation. Death is convinced they are connected with the people who attacked us."

"I need to pack," Bartholomew told him.

"Your new gear and equipment are already waiting for you at the jet," Constantine interrupted him. "We need this under control as soon as possible, Reapers."

"What are the rules for this job?" Death's position always came with rules and guidance.

"Don't lose your head," Constantine replied with an evil grin.

"I like this job," Bartholomew told him.

"Take the Deathmobile. I will have Shorty pick it up later," Constantine told us. "Isis, I'm proud of you."

With those last words, Constantine marched back to the Command Station. Bartholomew grabbed my hand and pulled me toward the door.

"I love you, Constantine," I told my guardian.

"Ditto," Constantine whispered.

Bartholomew and I walked down the stairs hand in hand. Goodbyes were awful, but this was only a 'see you later.' I could handle that. Iason was wrong. I wouldn't lose everyone I loved. On my birthday for the Day of the Dead I would see them all again. I would escort my friends to their final destinations and guards their souls with my life. Being a Reaper had its perks.

"Are you ready for another adventure?" Bartholomew asked as we climbed in the Deathmobile.

"Adventure is the story of our lives," I answered him.

"When will we join the other Reapers?" Bartholomew buckled his seatbelt and waited.

"Hopefully, not for a long time." I pinched his cheeks and he relaxed. "Now to Spain. Hope you have been practicing your Spanish."

"Claro qué si," Bartholomew replied.

"Show off." I started the Mustang and took a deep breath.

This was not goodbye, only a short trip abroad. We would be home soon. Not to mention I had a date with a prince that I did not want to miss.

The End for now...

This was an absolutely wild and insane ride. If you are like me, and you need more of the Reapers' Crew, I have three fun novellas just for you.

- **The Origins of Constantine**- yes, that evil dictator has his own origin book, and it will take you deep into

Ancient Egypt.

- **From Eugene with Love**- because we all need more Eugene in our lives. Too bad the Pestilence crew is always up to no good.

- **Rise of the Reapers**- if you were curious how and why the Reapers were created, you need this one. We will go back in time to the fall of the Roman Empire.

If you are ready to start another fun adventure in the Reapers' Universe, then check out **The Hitman**. Our sexy-witch/cop Eric is given a new position - The Order's Assassin. You know Constantine can't be happy about this.

Acknowledgments

Dear Reader,

Let me confess, my friend, I laughed, cried, and was even numb by the end of this book. I still can't believe we finished this series. It has taken us years of hard work to reach this point. Thank you for trusting me with these characters and following us on this journey. It has been a non-stop adventure and I really hope that I made you proud. While Isis' story might be done, the excitement in the Reapers' Universe is only beginning. So, make sure to stay connected with me to keep up on all the adventures coming our way.

I want to take a moment to thank my tribe for believing in these characters and their journey. A huge thanks the amazing Mr. J. Patton Tidwell for being super-beta-reader. To Cassandra Fear and Michelle Hoffman for all their work editing Judgement. Thank you to my family, the Texarkana Community, and to all the dreamers that still believe dreams can come true. Above all, thank you to the Almighty for the gift of this story.

If you enjoy the story, please consider leaving a rating and possibly a short review. Your reviews help others find the books you love.

With love,
D. C.

About Author

D. C. Gomez was born in the Dominican Republic, but grew up in Salem, Massachusetts. She studied film and television at New York University. After college, she joined the US Army, and proudly served for four years.

Those experiences shaped her quirky, and sometimes morbid, sense of humor. D.C. has a love for those who served and the families that support them. She currently lives in the quaint city of Wake Village, Texas, with her furry roommate, Chincha.

Also By D. C. Gomez

In The Reapers' Universe- Urban Fantasy Books

The Intern Diaries Series

Death's Intern- Book 1

Plague Unleashed- Book 2

Forbidden War- Book 3

Unstoppable Famine- Book 4

Judgement Day- Book 5

The Origins of Constantine- Novella

From Eugene with Love- Novella

Rise of the Reapers- Novella

The Order's Assassin Series

The Hitman- Book 1

The Traitor (coming soon)

The Elisha & Elijah Chronicles (UF and Post-Apocalyptic)

Recruited- Book 1

Betrayed- Book 2 (coming soon)

Humorous Fiction

The Cat Lady Special

A Desperate Cat Lady (coming soon)

Young Adult

Another World

Children's Books

Charlie, What's Your Talent? – Book 1

Charlie, Dare to Dream – Book 2

Devotional Books

Dare to Believe

Dare to Forgive

Dare to Love